B's

P9-CQP-753

## John "Doc" and Lilah McCabe
Happily married for forty years and about to renew their wedding vows. They're itchin' for grandchildren—especially since they personally delivered *every* baby in Laramie, Texas!

## Jackson
Texas tall and fit—the doctor every mother orders for a son-in-law.

## Wade
Self-made millionaire oilman with the Midas touch in business—and in bed.

## Shane
The "baby" of the family and the wildest of the four McCabe boys—"It'll be a cold day in Hades before I ever settle down!"

## *Travis*
The oldest, most serious McCabe son is a single cattle rancher about to become an instant father of three....

Dear Reader,

As the hectic holiday season begins, take a moment to treat yourself to a fantastic love story from Harlequin American Romance. All four of our wonderful books this month are sure to please your every reading fancy.

Beloved author Cathy Gillen Thacker presents us with *A Cowboy Kind of Daddy*, the fourth and final title in her series THE McCABES OF TEXAS. Travis McCabe is the last eligible bachelor in the family and you know his matchmaking parents are not about to let him miss heading to the altar.

Also wrapping up this month is our special series DELIVERY ROOM DADS. Judy Christenberry's memorable *Baby 2000* has a truly heroic McIntyre brother caring for an expectant mother who just may have the first baby of the millennium.

Two holiday stories finish up the month with tales that will bring you lots of seasonal joy. Pamela Bauer pens a delightful small-town romance with *Saving Christmas*, and Jacqueline Diamond brings us an emotional story of unexpected reunions with *Mistletoe Daddy*.

Here's hoping your holiday season is filled with happiness, good health—and lots of romance!

Melissa Jeglinski
Associate Senior Editor

# A Cowboy Kind of Daddy

## CATHY GILLEN THACKER

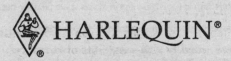

## HARLEQUIN®

TORONTO • NEW YORK • LONDON
AMSTERDAM • PARIS • SYDNEY • HAMBURG
STOCKHOLM • ATHENS • TOKYO • MILAN • MADRID
PRAGUE • WARSAW • BUDAPEST • AUCKLAND

ISBN 0-373-16801-2

A COWBOY KIND OF DADDY

# ABOUT THE AUTHOR

Cathy Gillen Thacker is a full-time wife/mother/author who began typing stories for her own amusement during "nap time" when her children were toddlers. Twenty years and more than fifty published novels later, Cathy is almost as well-known for her witty romantic comedies and warm, family stories as she is for her ability to get grass stains and red clay out of almost anything, her triple-layer brownies and her knack for knowing what her three grown and nearly grown children are up to almost before they do! Her books have made numerous appearances on bestseller lists and are now published in seventeen languages and thirty-five countries around the world.

## Books by Cathy Gillen Thacker

### HARLEQUIN AMERICAN ROMANCE

Dear Reader,

What an exciting year this is! Harlequin is celebrating its 50th year, and I am celebrating my 50th Harlequin romance novel with a brand-new series, THE McCABES OF TEXAS.

John and Lilah McCabe have four grown sons. All are strong, rugged, sexy men and successful in their own right. Life would be perfect, John and Lilah think, if only their four sons could find the right women to love and wed! But it isn't going to be easy....

The oldest McCabe, Travis, is a cattle rancher who wants to acquire the neighboring Triple Diamond Ranch and vastly increase his holdings. Second-born son, Wade, is a self-made millionaire/investor/oilman with the Midas touch. Jackson is a talented surgeon, who has vowed to get out of the shadow of his doctor-father and leave small-town life far behind him. Then there's Shane, the "baby," a rodeo cowboy with many a national championship under his belt.

As you might have guessed, I've fallen in love with all the citizens of Laramie, Texas, as well as the formidable McCabe sons and the feisty, spirited women who make their lives so much fun. I hope you enjoy reading this series as much as I've enjoyed writing it. And as always, I look forward to hearing from you—each and every one of you.

With warmest regards,

*Cathy Gillen Thacker*

# Chapter One

"Annie, you can't keep putting this off," Travis McCabe's deep voice rumbled over the phone lines.

*Want to bet?* Annie Pierce thought, giving her soon-to-be-famous Texas-style barbecue sauce another stir. "I know, Travis," Annie replied dutifully, reminding herself that Travis was not only her neighbor again, and the closest thing her late father had ever had to a son, but a person who had done her countless favors over the past two years. Favors she had, as yet, done nothing to repay.

"It's just I'm very busy today." Annie frowned at the four-year-old boys roughhousing in the middle of the kitchen floor. Identical triplets, they all had her red hair and freckles, fair skin and hazel-green eyes. They also had her fun-loving, feisty nature. Without, unfortunately, the wisdom and judgment her thirty-three years of experience brought.

Annie winced as her three sons rose in a tangle of arms, nearly knocking a half-dozen just-sterilized mason jars onto the kitchen floor. Annie dropped her spoon with a clatter and sprang into action to avert disaster, putting her slender body smack in the middle of them. Phone cradled between shoulder and ear, she used both hands to separate the wrestling trio.

"Tyler, Trevor, Teddy! You-all stop that right now!" Figuring this was no time to be talking to her know-it-all neighbor, Annie shouted into the phone, "I'll call you later, Travis!" Then she reached over their heads, jammed the phone back into the wall-base and, with a scolding look, put an end to the rough-housing once and for all. "Honestly," she said in her enough-is-enough tone. "Can't you boys behave for five minutes?" Completely exasperated, Annie stepped back to the stove and turned the heat from low to simmer.

"He started it!" Trevor elbowed Teddy.

"Did not!" Teddy pushed Tyler.

"Hey, watch it!" Tyler tried to shove Teddy and hit Trevor instead.

Immediately, they picked up the free-for-all where they'd left off. Once again, Annie vaulted forward and stepped in the middle of them. "Boys! I'm warning you!"

"It's not our fault, Momma. We just got too much energy," Trevor said.

Teddy, knowing a good excuse when he heard one, nodded vigorously. "Yeah, I 'spect that's just it, Momma. We probably need to be playing outside or something."

"Yeah, running around would make us tired. Then we would probably even take a nap!" Tyler enthused.

*That'll be the day,* Annie thought. In the fore-ground, the clothes dryer buzzed, signaling the clothes were dry. Annie looked longingly toward the laundry room. She really needed to get that. And it was a beautiful day. Only ninety degrees so far that morning. By afternoon, it'd be over a hundred. It would be too hot for the boys to be outside playing then. She'd have to keep them inside, in the air-conditioning. In that sense, summers in Texas were as bad as winters up north.

"You promise me you'll behave, and stay close to the house?" Annie said sternly. All three boys nodded. "No more wrestling. And no playing with the hose again. That was a *big* mess last night."

The trio took heed to her warning. "We'll be good," they promised in unison.

"Okay," Annie said, unable to completely curtail a sigh of relief. Her three precocious boys were a handful and always had been. "I'm going to hold you to that. Find your sneakers now."

"Awww, Mom."

"Do we hafta?"

"Yes." Annie regarded them sternly. "No shoes. No outside play. You know the rules."

While the boys scampered for their sneakers with the Velcro clasps, she headed for the laundry room, where a mountain of laundry awaited.

TRAVIS MCCABE DROVE slowly up the shady, tree-lined lane winding through the Triple Diamond cattle ranch Annie Pierce had inherited from her father. Rolling green pastures were interspersed with streams and enclosed with top-quality brown creosote fence. Thanks to the hard work of Travis's ranch hands, the property was still in top-notch shape and he wanted to keep it that way. Not an easy proposition now that Annie had moved back to the ranch with her three boys.

Travis frowned as he neared the house. It looked

as if the second-story doors of the brand-new barn were standing open. Even more unbelievably, he caught sight of two of Annie's triplets—impossible to tell which ones since they were all identical—leaning over the edge of the loft. The third was standing on the ground beneath them. Hands cupped around his mouth, he appeared to be shouting something to his brothers above. They grinned, waved, disappeared from view then popped back out again seconds later, hanging even more precariously over the edge.

He wasn't sure what they were up to, but it was obviously no good. Travis swore and cut the engine on his truck. Heart racing, he vaulted out and hurried toward them. He only hoped he could get there in time.

"LOSE SOMETHING?" Travis McCabe drawled.

"Travis!" Annie's breath caught at the sight of him standing in her back door. Some five years older than her, he was as handsome and commanding as ever in that uniquely Texas, cowboy way. Clad in jeans, chambray shirt, boots and Stetson, he had one triplet braced on each hip and another riding on his shoulders. All three of her boys looked chagrined, as well they should, Annie decided, considering the runny white and yellow goop smeared all over them and Travis's imposing, broad-shouldered six-plus frame, too.

Annie neared the four of them as Travis gently set down the boys, one at a time. Shaking her head at the sight of them, she wondered what in the world had happened. The boys had only been outside for about ten minutes. Travis wasn't supposed to be here at all. Though maybe it was good he'd happened along, considering what the triplets had been up to this time, she thought wearily. She peered at Travis's handsome face, taking in the nicely suntanned skin, blunt nose and sexy mouth—all of which seemed to be hopelessly smeared with something really yucky.

"Is that egg on your face?" Annie asked, lifting her eyebrows in astonishment and looking into his twinkling golden-brown eyes. "And...the boys?"

Travis swept off his hat, revealing cocoa-brown hair worn in a side part and cut in short tidy layers. He frowned at the messy goop staining the brim of his creased bone Stetson. "It's not marshmallow cream."

"How did you—" she started, confused. Then lightning hit. "Oh, no." Annie turned to the refrigerator, ducked her head inside, came back out again. Hands on her hips, she regarded the boys. "Not all two dozen!"

In unison, they shrugged their small shoulders aimlessly, and tucked their hands in the pockets of their shorts. "Well, we know eggs are baby chickens, 'cause we saw it on *Mr. Rogers,*" Tyler stated reasonably enough.

Trevor nodded enthusiastically. "The baby chickens popped out of the eggs. And we know birds fly."

"And so we had to see if the ones in the refrigerator could, too," Tyler explained.

Annie shut her eyes and took a deep, tranquilizing breath. Most of the time she was proud of how brilliantly inventive, creative and precocious her children were. But there were times when precocious times three twenty-four hours a day was too too much. Annie opened her eyes. "How exactly were you doing this?'' Annie demanded, almost afraid to hear the answer.

Suddenly, all three boys got busy looking at their toes.

Annie looked at Travis. He was so much taller than her boys. She couldn't believe he didn't know how to duck. The only explanation had to be a surprise attack. ''Were they in the trees?''

Holding her eyes deliberately, Travis drawled, ''Try the loft.''

The loft. *''The hayloft?''*

Travis spread his hands on either side of him. ''Is there any other?''

Annie's heart stopped at the thought of what could have happened had Travis not come along when he had. Feeling all the blood drain from her face, she pressed a hand to her chest and whispered a silent prayer of thanks. Thank heavens the boys were all right. Although not exactly unscathed, she decided as she dropped her hand and looked down at them once again.

''Uh-oh, guys, we're in trouble,'' Teddy said, correctly reading the expression on her face.

''You bet you are,'' Annie fumed as the barbecue sauce began to bubble over on the stove. She rushed to remove the heavy pot from the burner then swung back around to her boys. ''Time-out!''

''Awwwwwww, Mom!'' they said in unison.

''One more word—one more sigh—and it'll be the longest time-out you've ever had in your life,'' Annie said, even more sternly.

Immediately, the boys fell silent. One by one they climbed onto their chairs at the kitchen table and sat there glumly, their arms folded truculently in front of them.

Satisfied everything was under control, for the moment anyway, Annie turned to Travis, who was most in need of immediate attention. "I am sooooo sorry, Travis," she said, gesturing at his eggy state. She swept a hand from his head to his toes. "Your hat...your shirt...your face..."

Travis's eyes twinkled with amusement as, hat in hand, he said, "Got it all, didn't they?"

"Thank you for riding to my rescue yet again," she said, noticing his frank perusal of her. Feeling self-conscious in her skimpy white shorts, snug-fitting scoop-necked yellow T-shirt, and bare feet, Annie backed up until she touched the kitchen sink.

Travis gave her that slow, sexy smile, the one that had always turned her legs to jelly. He focused on her unmade-up face and loosely pinned-up hair. "You're welcome."

Looking away, Travis stared at all the jars on the table. "What's happening here?"

Aware her heart was pounding, Annie pulled a clean dishcloth from the drawer and dampened it beneath the water faucet. "I'm making the last of the barbecue sauce to take to the food exposition tomorrow."

Travis moved around beside her and leaned against the counter. "I didn't know you were involved in that."

Annie turned toward Travis, inhaling the brisk masculine fragrance of his cologne and the soapy-fresh scent of his hair and skin. She handed him the cloth so he could wipe the egg off his face. "I'm going to market my own sauce," Annie said, unable to completely keep the pride and ambition out of her voice.

To Annie's irritation, Travis looked surprised. "That sounds like a tough thing to do," he said, after a moment. He rubbed his face, getting about half the smeared egg in a single swipe.

Annie's slender shoulders stiffened. Travis's wasn't the first skepticism she had encountered, but for some reason she couldn't quite fathom, it rankled the most. "It's a long and complicated process, but I'm sure I'll get there eventually," she told him with determination.

He looked less sure. But to her relief said nothing further to discourage her.

Seeing a spot he had missed, she pointed to his cheek. He dabbed just below the spot. She pointed again. He scrubbed above it. Behind her, all three of her boys began to giggle quietly.

"You do it, Momma. He'll never get it!" Teddy said.

Figuring this probably could go on all day, Annie took the cloth from Travis and got the spot he'd missed, just above his cheekbone, being very careful not to actually touch him with anything but the cloth. Nevertheless, her breathing was as erratic as if she'd just run a race as she completed the task and stepped away from him. To her dismay, Travis looked equally distracted in a decidedly sensual way, too.

Which was impossible, Annie told herself sternly.

Travis had always been handsome. Rugged. Appealing. In that no-nonsense, take-charge, always-coming-to-the-aid-of-some-woman way of his. But she'd never been personally attracted to him. Never thought about him as anything but the cowboy next door.

If she was going all weak-kneed and silly on him now, it had to be...her nerves... The... Well, the something. Anything. But him.

"They got your car, too," Travis announced.

Annie dropped the dish towel in the sink. *"What?"*

Travis inclined his head in the direction of the mess. "Not to mention the sidewalk leading up to the house."

Annie shot another very disgruntled, disapproving look at the boys.

Not surprisingly, they remained impervious to all but the remaining dilemma of the "experiment" they had been conducting. "We wanted to scc if they would fly on the ground first, and when that didn't work we took them to the loft," Teddy said, scrunching up his forehead contemplatively.

"Hitting the car was an ax-cident," Tyler explained while Trevor nodded vigorously in his brothers' defense.

"We're sorry, Momma," Trevor continued sincerely. "We didn't mean to make a mess."

Annie never had been able to stay irritated with them for long. Especially once they recognized the error of their actions. "All right," she said wearily. "Go in and wash up and put on some clean clothes and then watch television, while Travis and I see to the mess outside," Annie said. "And no more trouble, boys," Annie scolded sincerely. "I mean it. Or you'll all be in time-outs for the rest of the morning. In separate rooms."

Nodding their agreement, the triplets leaped off their chairs and rushed to obey Annie's instructions.

Annie located and slipped on her sandals, while Travis waited—somewhat impatiently this time. Why, Annie couldn't begin to fathom.

THERE OUGHT TO BE A LAW against wearing shorts that short and a T-shirt that snug when a woman had a body like Annie's, Travis thought. And when had Annie Pierce turned into such a beautiful woman? She'd always been pretty. No doubt about that. Even as a kid in high school, when he'd first started working summers at her father's ranch, she'd been one of the prettiest girls around. Even if she hadn't seemed to recognize her own beauty. But now, at thirty-three...

Motherhood and approaching middle age were supposed to pack on the pounds and lessen a woman's appeal, but Annie had never looked better, nor more desirable. Her fair skin was sprinkled with freckles, and as smooth and flawless as ever. She'd grown her hair a little since the last time he'd seen her, but it was as thick and wavy and sexy as ever. She'd swept her bangs to the side and twisted up the rest of the thick red-gold waves in some sort of clip on the back of her head. It looked as if she had done it in a hurry because the ends were kind of tousled and messy in a really sexy but unplanned way and tendrils escaped to frame her face and the nape of her neck. She didn't seem to be wearing any makeup except maybe some sort of clear gloss on her lips, but she didn't really need it. Her oval face, slim straight nose, long-lashed eyes and full lips gave her a classic all-American-girl look that needed no artifice to make it appealing.

As for the rest of her, it was all Travis could do to suppress a groan as he watched her long slender legs eat up the ground as she led the way to her car. Was it his imagination or had her hips and breasts grown rounder and lusher, her waist more slender, since the birth of the triplets? As for the rest of her, had she always had that softly rounded bottom, and long lissome thighs? And what about her sexy knees, trim ankles and delicate feet? He'd never noticed. Maybe because he'd never really seen her in much of anything but jeans and a shirt or the occasional Sunday dress.

Might not have now, had he not just dropped in, without waiting for her to clear her busy schedule and invite him.

Annie shot him a look over her shoulder as she rounded the corner of the house. "Coming?" she demanded briskly.

*I wish.* "Right behind you," Travis said.

"I still can't believe they tried to make eggs fly," Annie fumed, shaking her head in exasperated rumination.

*Me, neither.* But then, what did he know about her little boys? Travis thought. Except they were cute as the dickens and smart and energetic as all get-out. Travis could only imagine the handful they'd be for Annie when they got older. Say, at seven or eleven or sixteen. Even now, it was clear they needed a strong male role model in their lives. Someone to help Annie ride herd on them. But Travis doubted there was any telling Annie Pierce that. Since her divorce a year or so after the triplets' birth, she'd been as independent as the day was long.

Heat baked down from the sun overhead. The sky was deep blue, with nary a cloud overhead. And it was awfully quiet inside. Travis inclined his head toward the rambling one-story ranch house with the white stucco exterior and red tile roof. "You sure they're going to be okay in there?" Travis asked as Annie waded through the red and white flowers she'd planted her first day back, two weeks ago.

"Yes. They're always good for a while after they do something they know is really bad," Annie murmured, reaching for the garden hose.

Travis tore his eyes from the delectable curve of her bottom beneath the hem of her shorts. "Let's wash off your car first," Travis said gruffly, ordering himself to get his mind out of the bedroom. "Before it literally fries the finish on your car in this heat," Travis continued as Annie switched on the water.

Annie turned, smiling, and handed Travis the garden hose. She went back to get the garbage pail and, returning, began picking up the eggshells that littered the ground.

"Are incidents like this par for the course?" he asked her.

Annie grimaced as she picked up a particularly gooey shell. "Let's just say they have a lot of bright ideas. And the older they get the more bright ideas they have. Especially at this ranch, which is a whole new playground for them."

Travis thought about all the things the boys could get into, out in the country. Watching him, Annie paused, clearly reading the concern he was trying not to show. "I can handle them, Travis," she said. "This morning is just a bad morning. I'm sure they'll be good the rest of the day."

Travis nodded, and finished hosing off her car, began spraying the sidewalk. "That's good, Annie," he said sternly. "Because, like I told you earlier," *and every day since you've been back,* "we need to talk."

Annie's lower lip shot out truculently. "And I told you. I'm busy today."

Travis knew from the look in her eyes she'd prefer to put off a discussion indefinitely, but that was no longer an option. And shouldn't have been thus far, either. "It won't take long." Deciding a different tack was called for to ensure her cooperation, he said easily, "I've got the papers in my truck. We'll just go over the facts and figures and be done."

Annie looked at him, a mix of temper and exasperation simmering in her pretty green eyes. "I'm not getting rid of you until I hear you out, am I?"

Travis shut off the hose and returned it to its spool. "No, Annie, you're not."

Annie sighed and sent him a censuring glare. "All right. But you'll have to go over things while I'm transferring the barbecue sauce to the jars."

Travis grabbed the briefcase from his truck. Head held high, she led the way back inside.

To Travis's amazement, all three boys were still in the living room, as directed, sprawled out on the floor in front of the television. They were watching Mr. Rogers, who was touring a post office, and showing them how letters were sorted after they were mailed.

*"Mr. Rogers,"* Annie whispered, a delicate hand to her mouth. "Very educational show. And very calming."

Travis could see that. He and Annie retired to the kitchen where instead of sitting down, she immediately set about washing her hands and going back to the stove. Figuring enough was enough, Travis set his briefcase down and blocked her way.

"Annie, just ten minutes. That's all I'm asking here," Travis said. It was all he'd been asking for the entire past two weeks.

"I can listen to you and fill these jars at the same time, Travis."

Travis pressed his lips together in frustration. "But you can't look at the numbers on the page and do that all at the same time." Determined to have his way on this whether she liked it or not, Travis curved his hands around her slender shoulders and guided her to the kitchen table, into a chair. "I've been keeping the ranch books for you, just as you asked."

Annie settled her bottom comfortably in the seat of the chair. "I know, Trav, and I appreciate that." Already bored with the discussion, she turned her attention to the large country kitchen with the plentiful white cabinets, gleaming wood floor and mint-green walls.

Joe, her dad, had kept the kitchen sparsely outfitted, with nary a blender or bread machine to be found. Since Annie had come back, she had added all manner of appliances, gadgets and potted plants. There were fragrant spices growing on the windowsill above the kitchen sink, leafy green plants on top of the refrigerator. Despite his mission, Travis found himself admiring the changes. Not to mention all the colorful artwork—and alphabet magnets—decorating the refrigerator.

"I also sold the last of your cattle as soon as they were ready to go to market," Travis continued, getting out the papers and spreading them in front of her.

"I need some iced tea. How about you?" Before Travis could stop her, she was up and out of the chair, and bounding over to the cabinet. She plucked two glasses from the shelf and carried them to the ice dispenser on the fridge door. She shot him a look over her shoulders as ice plunked down loudly into the glasses. "What about the excess grain?" Annie opened the refrigerator, brought out a glass pitcher and filled both glasses nearly to the brim with iced tea.

Travis forced himself to think about grain instead of the way her T-shirt hugged her breasts. "I bought it from you, at the same price you paid for it."

Annie set the glass of tea down in front of him. "Then I'm done ranching this land," she said with relief.

Travis frowned as she went back to the refrigerator and, moving like a dream, returned with a lemon, a knife, a bowl of sugar and two long-handled spoons.

Travis cleared his throat. "It's not that simple, Annie. Raising cattle brought in the income you needed to pay the mortgage on the land and the house and your taxes. Without it, you're in the red."

Annie shrugged, clearly not the least bit upset. She sliced off lemon for both of them, dropped a section into each of their glasses, then sat back down in her chair. "I've got money saved." She stretched her long bare legs out in front of her.

Travis released a short, exasperated breath and tried not to notice how close her slim, sexy legs were to his. With effort, he clamped down on his erotic thoughts. He didn't need to be thinking about how soft her legs looked, or how bare they were, or wondering how they would feel wrapped around him. Annie was his neighbor, for pity's sake, the mother of those three boys. He had a responsibility here. That responsibility did not include mentally making love to her. No matter how sexy or grown-up or all-fired womanly she had become.

He regarded her seriously. "You've already run through half the cash your father left you."

Annie nodded vigorously. "Which is exactly why I've got to sell this barbecue sauce," she retorted defiantly, lifting her chin. "I need to bring in money to stay here. That will allow me to do so."

Travis sighed. Joe Pierce had built up quite a spread. It nearly rivaled Travis's own. "You'd have to sell a lot of barbecue sauce to be able to afford this ranch," he pointed out calmly.

"Exactly," Annie replied, as confident in herself and her own abilities as he was worried about her financial stability. Not to mention the secret deathbed promise he had made to her dad to work behind the scenes to protect Joe's only daughter and her three sons. "And that's why I'm using the rest of what my dad left me to convert the barn into a commercial kitchen," Annie explained practically as she sipped her tea. "I've already hired an architect and a contractor. That's why I've been too busy to meet with you the past two weeks."

It was all Travis could do not to groan and bury his head in his hands. "Tell me you didn't sign anything," he pleaded.

Annie lifted a discriminating eyebrow. "Not that it's any of your business, Travis, but of course I signed something. Otherwise I wouldn't be guaranteed the job would get done right away." She looked at him as if he were a complete idiot.

He looked at her in exactly the same way.

Knowing he would get nowhere if they started to

argue, he held on to his composure by a thread. "Annie—"

Hot, agitated color filling her pretty cheeks, she cut him off stiffly before he could continue. "I can see you don't approve."

Travis ignored the feelings of desire generated by her closeness. "It isn't a matter of me approving or disapproving," he began carefully, wishing he could do what he really felt like doing right now. Forget all this business and take her to bed.

"We agree there," she cut him off once again.

"It's a matter of practicality." Undeterred, Travis continued making his points, too.

Annie folded her arms in front of her and leaned toward him. Mindful of her boys in the next room, she kept her voice low. "Practicality requires I get a job, Travis," she told him fiercely, oblivious to how the way she was sitting shifted her T-shirt and lifted her breasts. Not to mention inundated him with the sexy fragrance of her perfume.

"Obviously, I can't go back to being a flight attendant and still be here to take care of my boys. I'm still getting child support from their dad, thank heavens, but that's it."

Travis tapped his pencil against the paper. "The two of you didn't have any assets?" With difficulty, he kept his gaze away from the gaping neckline of her scoop-necked T-shirt. He'd already had one glimpse of the soft, swelling curves of her breasts and the shadowy valley in between. He didn't need another.

"I used the proceeds from the sale of our home to live on the past year." Annie shrugged again and sat back. "Reece and I split the furnishings, but other than that, well, my ex likes to spend what he makes and he does that very well.''

So Joe, who had never liked or approved of Annie's husband, had said. Travis, having met the man only once, felt the same. Annie's ex was self-involved, successful and completely oblivious to the needs or wants of everyone else. Annie—and her three boys—had deserved better. Much better. ''No alimony?'' Travis said.

Annie's expression turned fiercely independent again. ''Didn't want it. Didn't need it.''

Travis begged to differ on the latter, given Annie's current state of financial affairs, but he couldn't say he blamed her for not taking the money. Better for her self-esteem to support herself by herself. But she needed to be practical, too. It was Travis's responsibility to help her do that. ''Starting your own business is one option,'' he said carefully.

Annie nodded and took a long thirsty drink of tea. ''I'm glad you understand that.''

''Running cattle on the ranch is another,'' Travis persisted just as stubbornly.

Annie glared at him until her freckles stood out in sharp relief against the milky-white skin of her face. ''I told you, Travis, I have no interest in running cattle.''

It was still the right decision, Travis thought. He just had to make her see that. He leaned forward and looked into her eyes reassuringly. ''I could run them for you for a cut of the profits.''

''No.'' Annie's full lower lip shot out petulantly.

Travis found his own patience waning, too. Joe had warned Travis his daughter was stubborn. Until now, Travis hadn't realized how stubborn. ''You haven't thought it out or looked at the numbers,'' he accused, pushing the papers at her and trying to make her look at the numbers once again.

Annie shoved the papers right back. "I don't need to think it out or look at the numbers." That said, she shot out of her chair.

Travis stood up. "Is that so?"

"What I need, Travis," Annie continued, squaring off with him, face-to-face, "is to take care of myself and my boys on my own. And that—" Annie aimed a trigger finger at his chest "—is precisely what I intend to do."

# Chapter Two

Annie released a long, irritated sigh. "Stop looking at me like that," she demanded.

"Like what?" Travis asked. He shifted so he stood with his feet braced slightly apart. He jammed his hands on his hips, narrowed his eyes and waited for her to reply.

Annie flushed self-consciously despite herself. "Like it's the worst idea you've ever heard." She pushed the words through tightly gritted teeth.

Travis favored her with a challenging half smile she found even more disturbing than his sudden interference and total attention. "Is that what you think I'm doing?"

In the past, Travis had always kept his opinions to himself, no matter what he might have thought about Annie's admittedly impulsive way of doing things. To find him butting into her life now was both irritating and perplexing. Was it possible? Annie wondered. Could he be trying to take her father's place? Was he trying to be the dominant male influence in her life? As if she needed one! Annie propped her hands on her hips. "What you're doing is exactly what my father used to do," she told him coolly.

"And that is…?" Travis edged closer with a few determined steps.

Annie's heart pounded at the implacable note she heard in his voice.

"Pretending to humor me while you're thinking how to get me to do what you want me to do."

He didn't deny it. Just continued to regard her with that faint smile and that steady, analyzing look.

"Only in this case, Travis—" Annie stabbed the air with her finger as her temper rose "—I am not going to do what you want me to do. Any more than I am going to do what my father always wanted me to do."

"And what's that?" Travis questioned dryly, moving even closer.

"Marry you. Join our names and our fortunes, such as they are, and our ranches. And live here happily ever after." Catching a whiff of the soap and cologne essence that was him, Annie stepped to the side and lounging against the edge of the counter she folded her arms militantly.

He flashed her a contemplative grin. "Your father never said anything about the two of us marrying."

"You're right." Annie flushed despite herself, her neck and shoulders drawn tight as a bow. "Daddy was way too subtle for that. Instead, he just told me over and over and over how wonderful you were: How straightforward and kind and good and decent and hardworking. Face it, Travis." Annie's chin lifted as she tried to imagine life with a next-door neighbor so opposed to letting her live her life, unhampered by his opinion and well-meant, but highly aggravating, interference. "You were the son my dad never had," she told him emotionally, "and nothing would have made him happier than for me to bring you into the family in a permanent way.''

"Only one problem with that, Annie," Travis told her dryly. "To get married, you'd have to have a date first. And a kiss or two or three. And we never dated. And we certainly never kissed."

Only because he'd never asked her out or put the moves on her. If he had...well, it bugged Annie to realize how quickly she would have accepted both his invitation and his advances. Even knowing it was what her father secretly wanted for her.

"Well, fortunately for both of us," Annie said, "we're not talking about marriage here."

"Right." Travis braced a hand on either side of her and leaned over her, every inch the hard, indomitable male. "We're talking about saving your ranch," he told her sternly, underscoring his low words with a sexy, determined look. "And the only way for you to do that is for you to start raising cattle again or bringing in a lot more money than you are. And until you get your barbecue-sauce business up and running..." His voice trailed off lazily. Having captured her attention, made his point, he straightened and backed away.

She could see he thought it was going to take her years to get her business off the ground. He was wrong about that, too. She gave him a tight officious smile—one that let him know she did have other options besides turning to him and his ranching expertise. She announced sweetly, "Well, then, you'll be happy to know it's happening tomorrow."

Travis blinked, obviously confused by both her unwavering attitude and bold statement. "What is?"

"I'm going to the food exposition at the exhibition

hall in Fort Worth. I'm coming back with a contract.''
*I* hope.

''And if you don't…?'' Travis picked up his glass
and chugged down the last of his iced tea in a single
gulp.

''I will,'' Annie stated flatly, telling herself it was
her tension causing her heart to pound and mouth to
go dry, and not his proximity.

Travis sighed and set down his empty glass with a
thud. His gaze trailed over her hair, face, lips with
disturbing thoroughness before returning to her eyes.
''Who's going to watch the boys while you do this?''
he demanded impatiently, looking as if he too was
nearing his absolute limit.

''I am,'' Annie said flatly.

He blinked. Once again, amazed.

''They'll be fine, Travis,'' Annie said. ''They're
used to going places with me. They'll enjoy sitting in
the booth, watching all the people that come up to try
the sauce.'' Besides, the triplets always attracted attention. And they thrived in the spotlight. She was
betting their presence would draw potential marketers
to the booth, entice them to try her sauce, and once
they had, well, the rest would be history.

Travis looked at her as if she had either lost her
mind or was a disaster waiting to happen.

''Do you at least have help?''

Annie hated to admit she hadn't gotten that far yet,
though there were several people she planned to ask
to accompany her. But she wouldn't admit that to Mr.
Know-It-All-Himself. She merely shrugged and said,
''I don't need any.''

He watched her slip on an apron and begin to trans-
fer barbecue sauce into jars. ''Well, you're getting

some." He went to the table and gathered up his papers.

Annie pivoted back to him. "What do you mean?" she asked, stunned by his audacity.

Travis slid the papers back into the briefcase. "What time does this exhibition start?"

"Tomorrow morning, 9:00 a.m." Though why that mattered to him, she didn't know.

"What time you planning to leave?" he asked, his eyes never leaving hers.

Travis lounged against the kitchen table, radiating all the pure male power and casual sexiness of a big-screen hero. All sorts of romantic thoughts and fantasies came to mind. Resolutely, Annie pushed them away. "I'm leaving at 5:00 a.m.," Annie retorted as heat began to center in her chest and move outward in mesmerizing waves. "What's it to you?"

He reached for his hat, settled it square on his head. "I'm going with you."

Annie tingled all over at the timbre of his voice. Unless she got hold of herself, who knew what might happen? "You can't."

He arched an eyebrow at that.

Annie squared her shoulders and told him smugly, "There's no room in my car." Not that he could fit his frame into her small sedan anyway, even without her, the three kids and their safety seats. Not to mention the several cases of barbecue sauce, posters, flyers, sample cups and napkins. "And we can't exactly take your pickup truck, either."

Unfortunately, neither objection fazed him in the least. Travis merely smiled in that infuriatingly confident, all-male way. He nodded at her reassuringly. "You leave that to me."

Pulse racing, Annie followed him to the door. She couldn't believe that Travis, who had always been so...standoffish with her, was suddenly behaving as if she was somehow *his* responsibility. "I'm serious, Travis," she warned him hotly.

He turned and gave her an affable smile. "So," he said softly, "am I."

"HE'S THE MOST MADDENING man I've ever met," Annie said, some eight hours later, as she and her good friend, Kelsey Lockhart, patiently pasted Annie's Barbecue Sauce labels to the mason jars she was taking with her to the food fair the next morning. Kelsey was just as mule-headed and impulsive as Annie. The pampered, spoiled ne'er-do-well daughter, and baby of the family, Kelsey had never stuck with anything more than a few months at a time, and that included her beaus. But she was also the life of the party, a lot of fun to be around. Always ready to help out a friend, she was also one of the best listeners around. Right now, Annie needed someone to listen to her.

"I agree." Kelsey folded flyers in half. "Travis has always been annoyingly sure of himself and what he wants to do."

Ain't that the truth, Annie thought emotionally.

"But he's also a darn good rancher," Kelsey continued, looking very much the tomboy in her jeans, boots and plain blue chambray shirt.

"Well, that goes without saying," Annie allowed reluctantly, getting up to get another stack of plain white labels. She peeked in at the boys, who were busy building block towers in the living room. Satisfied all was well, for the moment anyway, she returned to Kelsey's side. "He learned everything he knows about ranching from my dad. Well, that and the classes he took at Texas A&M."

"Speaking of ranching...do you think he'll give me a job on his ranch if I ask him?" Kelsey said.

Annie's forehead creased. "Do you have any experience as a cowgirl?"

"Just what I got growing up, helping my mom and dad."

"I don't know." Annie sighed. "I really can't predict what Travis will do. He can be really maddening that way. Just when you think you've got him all figured out, boom, he does something that surprises you."

"Like invite himself along on this business trip of yours."

Annie frowned as she stacked labeled jars of sauce in carrying crates. "I don't know where he got the idea he can come in here and boss me around."

"Did he say that's what he wants to do?" Kelsey asked. Finished folding flyers, she lent Annie a hand. "Start running things here?"

"He didn't have to." Squaring her shoulders, Annie brought another crate to the table.

"You just sensed it," Kelsey guessed.

"As a matter of fact, I did. And you know why?" Annie pushed the image of Travis, as he had looked that morning, from her mind. "Because he's exactly like my father in that respect. You'd think he was agreeing with you. He'd pretend to be agreeing with you. And then the next thing you knew, you'd somehow end up doing what he wanted you to do, not what you wanted to do, and you wouldn't even know how it happened."

Kelsey grinned, making no effort at all to hide her amusement. "What do you think Travis wants you to do?" she asked.

"That's just it." Annie shrugged as shivers of sensual awareness coasted down her spine. "I don't know. But I'd swear..."

"What?" Kelsey leaned forward eagerly.

"That he's already got some plan in mind." Annie turned her troubled gaze to Kelsey. "That he came over here today, ready to give me some pitch."

Kelsey nodded knowingly. "Only you cut him off at the pass."

"Sort of." Annie paused and bit her lip, for the first time dwelling on all Travis hadn't said. "I had a feeling it was going to be some sort of talk that ended with me going back to the city to live and him continuing to run the ranch in my absence. Or me continuing to live here and him calling all the shots anyway. And darn it all, Kelsey, Dad didn't leave the place to Travis, he left it to me!" Although the way Travis was acting you wouldn't think he knew that, Annie thought. He seemed to think the responsibility for keeping the Triple Diamond in good shape had been left solely to him.

Kelsey shrugged, obviously seeing no problem. "Then do what you want to do," she advised sagely as she and Annie crated the very last of the sauce.

Annie set her chin. "I intend to."

"And while you're doing it?" Kelsey smiled. "Put in a good word for me, too."

*Five a.m.*

ANNIE STARED at the extended-cab pickup truck sitting in the driveway. Once again, Travis McCabe had surprised her. She stepped out onto the porch, beside him, inhaling a whiff of his crisp masculine aftershave as she did. She tilted her head up to his. "That's your folks' truck, isn't it?" Which meant John and Lilah knew he was going with her and the boys today. Annie wondered what they would make of that, then promptly decided she didn't want to know. Odds were, they'd think it meant more than it did.

Travis nodded in answer to her question. "I borrowed it for today. We can sit in front, the kids can sit in the passenger seat behind us, and we'll put everything else in the back." Annie saw he had lined the metal bed with blankets to cushion the boxes. A tarp tied over the top would protect them. She had to admire him on that score. He certainly had come prepared. But then, she'd known he would. Travis McCabe was the kind of man who left nothing to chance.

"What's in the coolers?" Travis asked. Looking very handsome in a white shirt, tan suede sport coat and jeans, he hoisted the first of the coolers into the truck bed.

Annie tore her eyes away from the just-shampooed neatness of his hair. He'd shaved, too. In the porch light, she could see just how close. "Beef brisket and chicken for the sauce-tasting," Annie said, trying not to get too worked up about having him go along for the ride. He was just being gallant, in his usual, to-the-rescue way. No doubt he felt that because they were neighbors now, and he'd been good friends with her father, he owed her more than the usual kindliness. She'd disabuse him of that notion, of course, but it would take a while.

Briefly, Annie showed him everything she had lined up in the front hall. "I'm taking all of this, too," she said. With a sweep of her hand, she indicated the small sample-size paper cups, napkins, flyers and business cards, and several advertising posters she'd had made at the print shop in town. To his credit, Travis did not look at all daunted. Methodically, she and Travis carried it all out to the truck, packed it up tightly, then went back inside for the boys, who were waiting in the kitchen.

"Ready to go, guys?" Travis asked gently.

Annie's three sleepy children, wearing identical khaki blue shorts and striped T-shirts, nodded. Travis and Annie led them out to the truck, buckled them into their safety seats and climbed in front. By the time they'd hit the main highway ten minutes later, all three boys were fast asleep.

"Not used to getting up this early, are they?" Travis said.

"No." Annie grinned, pleased that they were still too tired to create a ruckus. "And I was counting on it."

Travis glanced over at her trim navy-blue pant suit and carefully coifed hair. "You shouldn't have tried to do this all by yourself."

Annie resisted the urge—just barely—to stick her tongue out at him. She didn't want to talk about how she needed protecting, at least in Travis's eyes. Her dad had never understood that she could take care of herself and her boys just fine without some man watching over her and holding her hand. Travis apparently didn't understand that, either. "So, how are things going over at your ranch?" Annie changed the subject smoothly.

Travis shot her an amused look. "Just fine," he said dryly. "Thanks."

Annie settled back in her seat and looked out the window at the peaceful Texas countryside. "How many hired hands do you have working for you now?" she asked as they passed his ranch, the Rocking M Cattle Ranch, and headed for the interstate highway that would take them to Fort Worth.

"A dozen."

Annie contemplated that. The most her dad had ever had working for him was three or four at a time. But then, he had less land and ran less cattle than Travis did these days. "That's a lot."

Travis nodded, ever the consummate businessman. "It takes a lot to take care of my herd."

Annie recalled her promise to Kelsey Lockhart to put in a good word for her. She shot Travis a sly glance. "Any women working for you?" Annie asked casually.

Travis's jaw set. "No."

"Any women *ever* work for you?"

Travis slanted her a curious glance. "No." This, less contentiously.

"Why not?" Annie asked, turning as far as her seat belt would allow.

"Because herding cattle is hard, physical work."

Annie did not like the hint of chauvinism in his low voice. "Women can do hard, physical work."

Travis paused, but to Annie's disappointment, did not argue the point. "I have a male-only bunkhouse," he said. "No way could I put a woman in there with them."

Annie supposed that was true. "A woman wouldn't have to live there, if she lived in the area," Annie pointed out calmly. "A woman could bunk in town, for instance," Annie continued lightly. "And drive out to the ranch to work. It wouldn't be a problem."

Travis shrugged. "It's just easier to have the hired hands working for me live on the property. Or, if they're married, very close by. Besides—" he shot her an even more interested glance "—I thought you didn't want to work a ranch."

Annie flushed beneath his quick but potent scrutiny. "I, uh, don't."

"Then?"

Annie shrugged. "I just think it's maybe time you considered hiring a woman or two, that's all."

Travis smirked. "Thank you for your advice."

But he clearly was not going to follow it, Annie thought. Well, she'd tell Kelsey she'd tried but it did not look likely Travis would hire her. "Anytime," she said, disappointed. She had hoped Travis would be more open-minded than that.

Maybe he still could be, Annie thought later, as the sun began to come up in the east. She drew a deep breath, and though she risked earning Travis's ire so early in the day, persisted anyway. "By the way, I was talking to Kelsey Lockhart yesterday."

Travis's forehead creased. "What's she into now? Every time I hear her name, it seems she's working in a different field."

Annie reached for the thermos of coffee she'd brought along and poured Travis a cup. "I'm glad you brought that up." Their fingers touched as Annie handed the travel cup to him. "Because she's ready to switch occupations again."

"To what?" Travis shook his head when Annie

held up packets of cream and sugar, indicating he'd rather have his black.

"Cowgirl."

The corners of Travis's mouth turned down in dismay. "Oh, no—"

"Now Travis—" Annie turned toward him.

Travis shot her a quelling glance. "Don't even start," he warned mildly.

Annie drew a breath, then, "You have the best-run cattle ranch around," she persuaded softly, keeping her voice low so as not to disturb the sleeping trio in the back seat. "Where better to learn the ranching business?" Annie poured herself a cup of coffee, too.

"*Anywhere* else."

Annie balanced the cup between her knees as she broke open a packet of cream and poured it in. "She really wants to learn."

"For five minutes." Travis shook his head in exasperation. "Then she'll be on to something else."

Annie opened a packet of sugar and stirred it in, too. "You aren't giving her a chance," she complained.

Travis shot a look at the coffee cup between her knees. "That's because I don't have time to play Kelsey's what-do-I-want-to-be-today game."

Annie held the stainless-steel travel cup to her lips, sipped her coffee delicately. It was hot, delicious, and just exactly what they needed to go with the breakfast pastry she had packed. "She's just having a little trouble finding herself, that's all." Annie put the cup back between her knees and brought out the foil-wrapped bear claws. She wrapped one in a napkin and, holding his coffee cup for him, handed that to Travis, too.

"Well, let her find herself on someone else's land." Travis grumbled, lifting the bear claw to his lips.

Annie sighed as silence fell between her and Travis once again. She could see this was going to take effort. But at least she'd laid the groundwork, she reassured herself sternly. Kelsey would appreciate that.

"I KNOW YOU'RE thinking it. You might as well say it," Annie told Travis grueling hours later as they began to pack up the jars of empty barbecue sauce while the boys played with their toy cars on one of the four rectangular tables that enclosed their display booth.

The booths on either side of them had long ago emptied out, both entrepreneurs going off with potential investors to talk. To her crushing disappointment, Annie had no such pressing appointments. "I had a chance here this morning and I blew it," she finished with a sigh.

Travis must have read the despair on her face. "What are you talking about? They loved your sauce."

"As well as the seventy-seven other new Texas-style barbecue sauces displayed here today." And Annie didn't disagree with that assessment. All seventy-eight of the barbecue sauces had been popular with the attending crowd. All seventy-eight booths had eventually run out of samples to give out. And that was no surprise, either, Annie had eventually concluded. After all, what was not to love about any of the new sauces? Take an exquisitely prepared tidbit of chicken or beef brisket and dip it into a rich zesty barbecue sauce. No Texan in their right mind ever turned away from that! Barbecue was a state delicacy! Beloved by one and all! It still didn't get her anywhere.

"You didn't expect there to be so many sauces here today," Travis guessed sympathetically. His golden-brown eyes softened compassionately as they searched her face.

Talk about understatement! "Or for them all to taste pretty much the same," Annie concurred. All had the tomato, brown sugar, vinegar and spice base that was traditional in Texas.

Travis reached over to help her lift a box of empty jars, his warm capable hands brushing hers. "You don't know that personally," he chided as he transferred the weight from her arms to his.

"You're right." Annie turned and began taking down the posters advertising Annie's Barbecue Sauce. "I didn't run around and taste all seventy-seven other sauces myself." There hadn't been time or opportunity for Annie or Travis to visit other booths. Silence fell as they loaded the long, wheeled pushcart the exhibition hall had provided to get wares from inside the hall to the parking lot outside. "But I did overhear at least a third of the people say that my barbecue sauce didn't really taste any different from anyone else's." And that was something, she ruefully admitted to herself, she hadn't expected, either.

"Their palates probably just aren't that discriminating," Travis soothed. "I'm sure any true barbecue-sauce lover could have told the difference."

"Maybe, maybe not, but that's not the point." Annie planted her feet firmly on the concrete floor, folded her arms beneath her breasts and looked up at

Travis contentiously. "The bottom line is I didn't *sell* a single jar of my sauce. I didn't attract a single grocer or specialty-store buyer. I didn't take any orders for my product." As many of her competitors had.

Something akin to respect glimmered in his eyes. Maybe because she was sounding more like a businessperson than a dreamer. "It was your first time out," Travis said, looking, not for the first time that day, precariously close to taking her in his arms and keeping her there until she felt better.

Annie turned away from him and added the last of her business cards, most of which unfortunately still remained, to the top of the boxes loaded on the cart. She didn't know why, exactly, but Travis's mixture of patience and kindness was beginning to irritate her a lot. "For someone who didn't think this was such a hot idea in the first place, you sure are being awfully sympathetic." Finished loading up her business, Annie knelt and began gathering up the boys' things, too.

Again, Travis lent a hand, his tall muscular body bumping into hers more often than not. "I saw how hard you worked, Annie," he said as his rock-hard thigh brushed hers. "I saw how much you put into it." His low voice indicated he respected that.

She turned to face him and tilted her head up to his. She could guess what he was going to say next. She also guessed she wasn't going to like it.

"But it's a competitive business," Travis stated gently.

One he seemed to think she should reconsider getting into, Annie noted unhappily. "Tell me about it," Annie grumbled, upset at herself for not having actually attended a food fair before participating in one herself. She had just blown several thousand dollars on an amateurish attempt at getting her product noticed. She couldn't afford to make expensive mistakes like this. It didn't, however, mean she had to give up. Especially when she knew, maybe better than most, that in the end persistence, when combined with hard work, always paid off.

"I learned a lot here today," Annie murmured thoughtfully.

"And the boys had fun," Travis added cheerfully.

Annie smiled as she looked over at her three sons. Identical in more than looks at the moment, they were sitting on chairs, one arm stretched out on the table in front of them, their heads resting on their arms. With a free hand, they each clutched a small matchbox-size toy car or truck, which they ran slowly across the table in front of them, making soft engine sounds as they did so. "Yeah, they did have fun," Annie noted happily, glad she'd brought them along. They'd also received tons of attention, as usual, and helped attract lots of people to her booth, exactly the way she thought they would. "They'll probably sleep the entire drive back to Laramie." And that was just fine. She'd have lots of time to think of how to do things better.

"HOW'D THE FOOD FAIR GO?" Lilah asked later that evening when Travis drove his parents extended-cab pickup truck back to their ranch, and went inside to thank them for the use of their vehicle for the day. Lilah was writing out place cards for their rehearsal dinner later in the week. John was seated at the computer desk in the kitchen, confirming all the details for their second honeymoon.

Briefly, Travis filled his parents in on what had happened. "She must have been so disappointed," Lilah said, shaking her head in commiseration.

Travis nodded. *And then some.* "I felt for her," Travis confessed.

His parents exchanged a look. Finally, John cleared his throat, looked over at his oldest son and said, "I know you made a promise to Annie's dad—"

"Yeah, well, Annie doesn't know it, and neither does anyone else," Travis cut in brusquely. *He'd meant to tell her. He would have. If he hadn't been so sure she'd take it the wrong way and then do the opposite of what her father had wanted.*

"She's going to find out sooner or later," Lilah predicted gently.

*Not if he could help it,* Travis thought. *If he had his way, he'd keep his deathbed promise to Joe Pierce and see Annie and her sons were taken care of, without her ever being the wiser.*

"We also know how you like to—how shall we put it?—rescue damsels in distress," John attempted a light tone despite the seriousness in his eyes.

"Now don't blame me for that," Travis said, helping himself to a generous slice of his mother's peach pie. "If anyone taught me how to help others, it's the two of you."

Lilah stood, went to the refrigerator and got out the vanilla ice cream. She shut the door with one hip, plucked an ice-cream scoop out of the utensil canister on the counter and added a dollop of ice cream to Travis's dessert dish.

"Helping people is fine," John said. "Your mother and I have made careers out of helping our friends and neighbors." Travis knew that was true. As the physician and nurse who had started Laramie Community Hospital and single-handedly brought quality health care to the community, they'd won the love and respect of everyone in Laramie.

"But there's a difference between helping someone and becoming emotionally involved with them," John warned.

Travis sighed. He had only to look at his parents' faces to know they weren't just talking about his one-time fiancée, Rayanne. It seemed every woman he'd ever dated had needed his help in some way. Unfortunately, when they no longer needed his help, he generally lost interest. Although, there had been times when it had happened the other way, and the woman had lost interest. And damningly, it hadn't mattered a bit to him, either. Unfortunately, he never seemed to know at the time he was helping a woman out that his attraction to her wasn't going to last. He was getting tired of confusing being needed with being loved. And vice versa. "I'm not interested in Annie," he stated bluntly, pushing the image of her from his mind.

She was a beautiful woman, no doubt about it. No man could resist a second or third look at her fiery red-gold hair, pretty face, mesmerizing hazel-green eyes and shapely body. That fact had been proven time and again at the food fair. But then, he already knew that. Since he'd spent time with her again, he couldn't seem to erase her image from his mind, or forget the unique, wildflowers and sunshine fragrance of her hair and skin.

"That's too bad," Lilah said. "Because you know that Alice—Annie's mom—always sort of hoped the two of you might one day become involved." Lilah shook her head reminiscingly. "Why, I remember when you two were children. I never saw two kids who spent so much time eyeing each other as the two of you."

Had Travis been the blushing type, he would have turned beet-red. Fortunately, he wasn't. Never had been, never would be. "Mom, that was years ago," he said, exasperated. "For all you know, I had a smudge of barbecue sauce on my cheek or she had a piece of corn bread in her hair, and that's all we were looking at."

Lilah grinned in a way that let Travis know the romanticizing hadn't been confined to Annie's mother. "I'll have you know you were both very tidy children," she said with a knowing wink.

Travis rolled his eyes at his mother's unabashed matchmaking. "There's nothing there, Mom. If I'm lucky, now that she's living next door to me, we'll be friends," he said sternly. "But that's all." Annie Pierce was far too stubborn and single-minded a woman for him. Guaranteed.

"WHATCHA DOIN'?" Teddy, Trevor and Tyler asked from the other side of the screen door early the next morning.

Travis straightened. "I was going to leave a note for your mom to call me later," he said.

All three sets of hazel eyes widened curiously. "Why?" Teddy asked.

"Because we still have some things to talk about," Travis said reluctantly. *Things I'd like to talk about in private.* He studied the boys, who were still in their pajamas, but also had the wide-awake look of three kids who had been up for hours. "Is she awake?"

Travis looked past them for any sign of Annie and saw, to his disappointment, none. She had been quiet and depressed when they'd said goodbye the previous night. He found himself just wanting to make sure she was all right.

"She always wakes up when we do," Trevor reported cheerfully.

That was good, Travis thought. He wouldn't want the Triple Threat running around unsupervised again. And there was no telling what they might get into if Annie were sleeping.

Silence fell between them.

Travis waited. The boys didn't ask him in. Nor did Annie appear. Finally, he asked, "Is she busy?"

All three boys nodded vigorously.

Again, nothing else was forthcoming. "You think I could talk to her a minute?" Travis asked expectantly.

The triplets looked at each other, trying to decide. "Yep. But you can't bother her," Tyler said solemnly. "And you can't be bad, neither, 'cause if you are, then you don't get to go see the horsies with us tonight after supper."

Trevor frowned. "He's not going to see the horsies! We are!"

Teddy scowled. "Well, you better not be bad anyway, 'cause we don't want to take any chances."

"I promise I'll behave," Travis said, glad to see Annie had things a little more under control this morning than she did two days ago, when he had first come to talk to her. "Where is your mommy, anyway?"

Tyler yawned. "In the kitchen."

"Making breakfast?" Travis asked.

"No. She said she's getting sauce this time, no matter what it takes," Tyler parroted.

Sauce as in barbecue sauce, or sauce as in getting sauced? Travis wondered uneasily. Somehow, he couldn't see Annie reaching for the bottle to fix her problems. But why she'd be messing with barbecue sauce so early this morning was beyond him. The food fair had been yesterday. She'd said she had none other scheduled, period.

Figuring he'd find out soon enough, Travis took off after the boys, who were already leading the way through the living room. His heartbeat accelerating in anticipation of seeing her, Travis rounded the corner to the kitchen and heard a Trisha Yearwood CD playing softly on the stereo. Deliciously tousled, deep in thought and completely oblivious to his presence, Annie was standing there in her pajamas, a bottle of fine whiskey in her hands. To his amazement, she'd uncapped it and was holding it gingerly beneath her pretty nose. Before he could get out a single word, she'd made a face, sniffed delicately, put it to her lips and started to take a sip.

That quickly, Travis had seen all he needed to see. Cursing himself for not having known just how desperate she was, how sad and upset, he rushed forward, grabbed Annie by the waist with one arm and the bottle of whiskey with his other hand.

Startled by his presence and upset by the intervention, she let out a small shriek. Scowled, and tried to wrest the bottle back out of his hands.

Not about to let that happen, especially with all three of her children looking on, Travis tightened his grip on her waist, tugging her closer yet. He lowered his voice to her ear. "Annie—for pity's sake—don't!"

# Chapter Three

"Just what do you think you're doing, cowboy?" Annie drawled, trying not to notice how good Travis looked and smelled this early in the morning. He was wearing a white cotton shirt and jeans that made the most of his tall, muscular frame. The straw cowboy hat drawn straight across his forehead gave him a sexy, don't-mess-with-me look.

"Saving you from making a big mistake, obviously," Travis said.

Annie's fingers tingled from the warmth and strength of his even while her stubborn determination to complete her mission—without his interference, no matter how well intentioned—grew. "Listen up, cowboy," Annie said in her best imitation of kick-butt John Wayne. "This is my kitchen." She tilted her head back and glared up at him, all too aware of the strong, protective arm he had encircled around her waist. "If I want to sample my dad's whiskey and make sure it's still good, then that's exactly what I'm going to do." Determinedly, she put her other hand on top of his and tried to get back the whiskey—to no avail. He held on to the bottle every bit as tightly as she did.

"I know you've got problems," Travis said sternly, a hint of the sympathy he felt for her in his eyes.

Annie rolled her eyes and blew out an exasperated breath. "You do."

"But sampling every bit of liquor you have in the house—" Travis inclined his head at the nearly two dozen other liquor bottles she had lined up on a counter still littered with the remains of breakfast "—is no way to solve them."

Annie did her best to curtail a furious smirk. Boy, was he on the wrong track here! "You think I've been sampling all of these?"

Travis shrugged his broad shoulders indolently. "The caps are all off," he volleyed back bluntly.

"Then I must really be able to hold my liquor," Annie said, looking over the array of liquor from her dad's cabinet, most of which went back at least ten years, and could be traced to either a gift or party. "'Cause I count—whoa—at least twenty bottles here." There was everything from scotch and bourbon to coffee-flavored vodka and amaretto.

"Exactly the point, Annie." Travis inclined his head at the three boys who were lined up against the kitchen wall, clearly enthralled. Travis's voice dropped a compelling notch as he leaned forward and whispered in her ear, his warm minty breath ghosting over her face. "What kind of example are you setting for your boys here?"

"A good one, I hope!" Annie retorted, still struggling to get control of the bottle in his hand. "I want them to know I am not giving up despite yesterday's debacle."

Abruptly, Travis went very still. Annie's shoulder

was pressed against his chest and she could feel his heart thundering powerfully.

"What are you talking about?" he demanded, eyes darkening all the more.

"What do you think?" Annie shoved at his chest with her free arm and finally stepped away. Still holding on to the whiskey bottle with one hand, she whirled to face him, using every ounce of dignity she possessed. "I'm getting ready to start coming up with another barbecue-sauce recipe. One that will be totally unique."

Travis began to relax. His eyes still holding hers, he loosened his grip on, and then finally let go of, the whiskey bottle. "And you're putting whiskey in it," he deduced slowly and calmly.

Annie squared her slender shoulders defiantly. "Maybe a drop or two. I don't know yet. I'm thinking about adding a lot of things," she admitted reluctantly as she took another self-conscious step back away from him. "And if you would look around, you would know that," she finished as she inclined her head in the direction of the counter. Behind the liquor were bottles and jars of all kinds of Cajun seasonings that her dad had favored, plus a big basket of ripe tomatoes, twelve different kinds of vinegar, plus peppers, and onions, and Tabasco. "I've been raiding the cupboards and racking my brain since 5:00 a.m."

"Yeah," Tyler piped up helpfully. "Mommy says she's going to make the bestest barbecue sauce there ever was, and she doesn't care how long it takes to get sauce."

"Oh." Travis grinned, looking slightly embarrassed, and stepped back.

"Now, if you don't mind—" Annie lifted the whiskey bottle to her lips. Unable to help herself, she wrinkled her nose at the sweetly medicinal aroma, and hesitated all the more.

"Do you even know what it's supposed to taste like?" Travis asked with a frown, still watching her closely.

Wondering how he could have known about her embarrassing lack of drinking expertise, Annie flushed warmly. "Well. No," she admitted reluctantly. "But—"

"Here. If anyone is going to do this—" Giving her no more chance to dillydally, Travis took the bottle from her purposefully.

Admitting to herself she really didn't want to be sampling whiskey this early in the morning anyway, Annie planted her hands on her pajama-clad hips and scowled at him. "You're telling me this is a man's job?"

"You're telling me it's not?" Travis plucked a clean coffee cup from the mug tree on the counter and poured a half teaspoon or so in the bottom of it.

Annie tensed as she watched him take a decisive sip, swirl it around in his mouth and then drink it down. "Well?" she demanded curiously.

He shrugged, looking as relaxed and easygoing as ever. "It's fine."

Annie breathed a sigh of relief, glad she had another flavoring to play around with. "Good, then."

Travis looked over his shoulder at the rapt trio behind them.

Still want to go and see the horses?" he asked.

They all nodded vigorously. "Well, I'll take you, but you have to go get dressed and make your beds first. Deal?'' He held up a hand. They all high-fived him, then ran off.

Aware what a ludicrous sight she must make in her flannel pajamas, her hair twisted on top of her head, Annie planted her bare feet firmly on the wooden floor beneath her and propped both hands on her hips. Thanking heaven she'd at least washed her face and brushed her teeth as she did upon rising every morning, she regarded Travis pointedly. ''You know, it's customary to ask the mom's permission before you offer to take her sons somewhere, never mind tell them what to do.''

Travis's glance drifted leisurely over her in a decidedly sensual appraisal, lingering on the vee of her pajama top, before returning to her face. ''I wanted a few minutes alone with you,'' he told her quietly.

Wishing belatedly that she had a robe on, to protect her from his sensual appraisal, Annie flushed self-consciously. ''That doesn't—''

''Sit down, Annie.'' Travis smiled and protectively curved a strong arm around her shoulder. He lowered his voice to a hushed but seductive whisper that did nothing to lessen the impact of his warm, sexy touch. ''Knowing the Triple Threat, we don't have long.'' His eyes twinkled. ''I came over to talk to you about your land.''

Annie blinked in confusion even as she let him push her into a chair. ''What about it?'' she asked over the tumultuous rhythm of her heartbeat.

''I want to buy the ranch from you.''

Annie stared at him in silence. Her nerves were jangling and her throat was so tight she could barely swallow. She supposed she should have seen this coming—after all, weren't all the ranchers in the area interested in acquiring her property—hopefully, for a song? But like a fool, she hadn't seen it coming, hadn't even guessed that might be the root of Travis's interest in her and the boys and their welfare. Obviously, he had wanted the inside track, and she had given it to him.

"To expand your ranch?" she supposed, not sure why it should hurt to learn his wanting the land was at the root of Travis's helpfulness. She just knew it did.

Travis nodded, eyes serious. "You're sitting on nearly ten thousand acres of prime grazing land, Annie, with a stream running through it," he told her quietly. "And I'll give you fair market price. If you invested the proceeds wisely, you could live off the interest and never have to work again a day in your life if you didn't want to. You and the boys would be secure." He touched her arm reassuringly.

Shoulders stiff, Annie shrank from his touch. Despite her efforts to the contrary, she was unable to quell the emotions riding roughshod inside her. "And suppose I wanted to work?" Her chin jutted out stubbornly as she challenged him with both voice and manner. "What then?"

Travis's expression was as impassive as his eyes. "You could do that, too," he returned with a tranquility that grated on her nerves even more than his calculated, but oh so chivalrous, proposition. He leaned toward her earnestly. "The point is, you wouldn't have to come up with a barbecue sauce or anything else to sell. You wouldn't have to worry about coming up with the money every year to pay the taxes. Or do as you have been and dig into your savings or sell off part of the assets—up to now, cattle—a little at a time to pay the taxes every year, Annie. Your future, and the boys', would be set." Travis paused as he searched her face, behaving like the protector he so clearly thought he was. "It's what your father would have wanted," Travis told her sternly. "You know it. And I know it."

Annie couldn't deny her father had talked to her a bit about selling the land before he died. She'd humored him—he'd been so sick it would have been unthinkable to do otherwise—but she hadn't ever really considered it. The Triple Diamond Ranch was where she'd spent her entire childhood. All the memories of her mother and father were here. Now that she was divorced, she wanted her sons to grow up here, too. She hoped being here would, in some way, counter the neglect they endured from their father and give them the same sort of emotional security she had enjoyed as a kid, the feeling she could do anything, if only she set her mind to it. But clearly, she noted with dismay, Travis McCabe did not see it this way. He saw it only in terms of the red and black numbers in a ledger.

Tension shimmering through her, Annie stood and began to pace, her bare feet moving soundlessly on the smooth wooden floor in her kitchen. She stared out at the backyard, at the wooden swing set her father had erected for her when she was a kid. "You think I don't care about this place?" she asked.

Travis crossed to her side in two long steps. He lounged beside her, hips braced against the counter. "I know you have sentimental feelings." He continued to search her face.

Annie felt the heat of her indignation climb from her chest, up into her neck. "I grew up here, Travis."

She curled her hands over the rim of the double-basined stainless-steel sink. "I spent my whole childhood in this house, on this land." Grimacing, Annie put the stopper in the right hand side of the sink. She squirted in dishwashing soap with a vengeance, and turned on the hot water. She watched the bubbles rise right along with the water. "Every memory I have of my mother before she died when I was nine happened right here," Annie said, more emotionally than she would have liked. "Many of the memories in this very kitchen." When the water was three-quarters of the way to the top, Annie turned off the faucet. She began collecting breakfast bowls and glasses and slipped them into the sudsy water.

"I know that," Travis replied gently. He handed her a couple of bowls, too. "But you need to be reasonable. This place is too much for you alone. And without substantial income, you can't afford the upkeep on it."

"Which is exactly why I am working so hard to perfect my barbecue sauce," Annie said, shooting Travis a resentful look as she began to scrub the dishes with a dishcloth. "I know I've got a good start here. A good basic sauce. It just needs that something extra that will set it apart from all the rest. Once I have that, plus a new name for it and a new marketing approach, I'll be in business."

Travis sighed and began to look impatient. "Annie, this is lunacy." He clamped his lips together as if he was not going to continue, then did anyway. "I was there yesterday. I saw how difficult, if not damn near impossible, this is going to be for you or anyone else, for that matter, to pull off."

Annie nodded grimly. Now they were getting

somewhere. "I had a feeling you felt that way but were too polite to say it." She washed a dish so vigorously water sloshed over the rim of the sink and onto the floor. Swearing, Annie rinsed the dish, put it in the drainer, then knelt down to wipe up the mess.

Travis grabbed a paper towel and knelt with her. His large hand fought for space alongside her smaller one. "I can't let you throw away everything your father struggled his whole life to build."

Nose to nose with him, Annie glared at him. "It's not your decision to make," Annie repeated through her teeth.

Travis slid a hand beneath her elbow and helped her up. "Dammit, Annie—"

"Dammit, what?" Annie echoed sarcastically.

"I promised I wouldn't—" Looking as if he'd said too much, Travis stopped abruptly. Firmly shut his lips.

"What?" Annie angled her head up at him and searched his eyes. "What did you promise?" She didn't know whether it was the anger, or the proximity to him, or the fact that he had just had a damn good view of her breasts, but her pulse was suddenly racing to beat the band.

Travis grimaced all the more. A muscle worked in his cheek. And, for a second anyway, he couldn't quite look her in the eye. Swallowing hard, he turned back to her. "I promised myself I'd look after you," he said in a quiet, restrained voice. His golden-brown eyes gentling, he continued, "I owe your dad a lot."

Annie nodded, not about to dispute that. She knew her dad had done a lot for Travis. Not just teaching him everything he knew about how to run and build a ranch from the ground up, but also treating him like a very good friend, even a son. Annie shook her head and went back to washing dishes. "That may be, Travis, but I am also sure my father did not intend for me to be another in a long line of ladies you rescued."

"What do you know about that?" he demanded gruffly, abruptly looking as irked as Annie felt.

Annie slanted him a provoking grin. "The same thing every woman in Laramie knows," she told him with quiet sarcasm. "That after Rayanne's death, you dedicated yourself to rescuing the entire female population of Laramie County. Some lady needs you, you're there, pronto." To the point, Annie had begun to get annoyed just hearing about it. Why, she didn't know. It wasn't as if Travis McCabe meant anything to her, then or now. "But I don't need a knight in shining armor helping me out, Travis," Annie finished sternly.

"How about a cowboy with a pickup truck, a ranch and a horse?" Travis countered in a low, sexy voice that sent shivers of awareness shimmering over her skin.

"This is not funny," Annie retorted right back, fresh color coming into her cheeks despite herself. She swung around to square off with him and found he had leaned down and toward her at the same time. Her face was suddenly, dismayingly, close to his. So close, in fact, that it would have taken very little effort for them to kiss.

Annie jerked in a quick revealing breath. Swallowed around the unprecedented desire forming inside her. "You've got to mind your own—"

"Hey, Mom! Travis!" Tyler, Teddy and Trevor raced into the kitchen in mismatched shorts and

T-shirts, and skidded to a halt just short of Travis and
Annie. They had also scrubbed their faces, made a
stab at combing their red hair and brushed their
teeth—easy to see by the toothpaste stains on their
shirts. "We're ready!"

"IT'S REALLY NICE OF YOU to go along with us, too,"
Travis said, fifteen minutes later, after Annie had
showered and dressed.

Annie looked around the kitchen. All three of her
boys were sitting patiently at the table, waiting on her,
while Travis finished up the rest of the breakfast
dishes.

"Didn't really have much choice, did I?" Annie
muttered cantankerously, still a little irritated by the
way he had invited the boys first, then checked with
her after their hopes had already been raised. She was
also irked to find he had interest, not just in her and
the boys, but in her ranch.

"The boys and I will follow you in my car," Annie
said, determined to retain at least that much control
over the morning's events.

Travis frowned at his pickup truck, clearly wishing
he had room to drive them all over. But there was no
way they could fit Annie, Travis and three safety seats
with three boys all on one bench seat. Three would
have been possible, but not five.

As soon as they were all safely buckled into their
respective vehicles, Travis led the way over to the
Rocking M cattle ranch. He parked in front of the
ranch house, and indicated for Annie to do the same.
The rambling, two-story log cabin with a long, wrap-
around front porch was no bachelor pad, but a place
meant for a big family, much like Lilah and John's.

Annie and Travis helped the boys out. Tyler looked up at the big trees shading all sides of Travis's house. "Hey, Travis, how come you don't have apples on your trees?" he asked.

Travis smiled and patted Tyler affectionately on the head. "Because those aren't apple trees, pardner. They're live oaks."

Trevor fit one of his hands in Travis's larger one, then chimed in, "We've got apples on our trees out back. They're green."

Teddy wrapped his arms around one of Travis's legs. He craned his head way back, to look up at him. "Yeah, Mom says when they're red we can eat them."

Tyler latched on to Travis's arm. "We never ate apples off a tree before," he reported energetically, still making his way, along with Travis, his two brothers and Annie, to the adjacent stables.

Trevor asked. "Do you have peaches?"

"No." Travis smiled, guiding all three boys with the expertise of a longtime dad instead of a childless neighbor. "I don't have any peach trees, either."

"Well, we got peach trees now, too, and a couple pear trees," Teddy said, kicking up the dirt with the toe of his boot. "Only there's no fruit on 'em."

"We had a bad frost earlier in the spring that killed all the buds and ruined the fruit," Annie explained to one and all. She wanted the boys to know why there was fruit on some of their trees, and not others.

"Will we have peaches and pears next year?" Trevor asked Annie, coming over to fit his hand in hers.

"Maybe." Annie squeezed Trevor's hand warmly, wishing the five of them didn't look, and act, so much like a family at the moment. "If the weather cooperates," Annie continued after a moment. "It's hard to tell."

"But we don't got horses," Tyler said, letting go of Travis's arm and tucking his hand into Travis's larger one. He looked up at Travis with a combination of affection and hero worship. "So I'm glad you do." Tyler smiled from ear to ear.

"Me, too," Travis said, smiling back.

No sooner had they walked into the stables, and begun making their way down the row of beautiful horses, than one of Travis's hired hands appeared. Annie recognized him as Brady Anderson. Good-looking in a rakish, devil-may-care way, he had only been in Laramie a year or so, yet had already established himself as one of the best cowboys around. No one knew much about where he'd come from. If Brady had his way, Annie guessed, no one ever would.

"Ma'am." Brady lifted his hat and nodded at Annie.

Annie smiled and nodded back. She knew some, but not all, of Travis's ranch hands.

Brady turned to Travis. "There's a gal here to see you. She's been waiting around for nearly an hour for you to come back." Brady lifted his eyebrow in an inquiring manner. "Says her name is Kelsey Lockhart."

WITH THINLY VEILED impatience and as much politeness as he could muster, Travis left Annie and the boys in the stable and stepped just outside with Brady Anderson. Keeping his guests in view, he listened to Kelsey make her speech about why he should hire her. Then did his best to let her down gently. "I've no doubt you are a hard worker, Kelsey," he said, noting her trim, fit appearance and no-nonsense ranching clothes. To her credit, the youngest of the four Lockhart sisters looked ready to work, and work hard. But that, Travis reminded himself practically, wasn't really the point. "And I recall what a talented rancher your father was," he acknowledged with an encouraging nod. "So you're right, ranching may well be in your blood. But I don't hire on women as ranch hands here."

"Well, now, that's not exactly true, is it?" Brady Anderson interrupted. "Seems when I started here, little over a year ago, there was a gal here punching cows by the name of Calamity Sue—"

Travis shot Brady a look. "She was a champion rodeo gal in her own right, and she was only here for a couple of days during that one branding season when she was trying to save enough money to go back on the professional circuit." Which she had done, lickety-split. "She didn't really work here, not in any permanent way. It was more like she was just helping out. And that only happened because I was so shorthanded that year."

"Still," Kelsey took the opening provided her by Brady Anderson, "if you gave one woman a shot— even temporarily, Travis, you should give me one, too."

Like heck he should, Travis thought. He smiled at Kelsey, prepared to be just as stubborn as she was. "Nope, not today, Kelsey. Nice try, though."

Kelsey swept her Stetson off her head, slammed it against her thigh and glared at Travis resentfully. "I was really hoping you'd be more open-minded."

Travis shrugged. He'd never been a chauvinist. He didn't think he was one now, either. "If I was short-handed, I might've given you a chance," Travis said. "But I'm not. Now, if you'll excuse me, Kelsey, I've got to finish showing Tyler, Teddy and Trevor the horses."

"I think you're making a mistake, not giving her a chance," Annie said as they walked out to the corral to commune with the horses there. She frowned as Travis handed out carrots to the boys. "Brady Anderson would have hired her."

Irritation creased his suntanned features. "Brady Anderson is sweet on her," he volleyed right back. "Or hadn't you noticed?"

Annie had noticed. The only problem was Kelsey wasn't paying any attention.

With Travis's help, the boys each got to feed a horse a carrot. They petted the horses a final time then headed back to the car.

To Annie's dismay, Travis insisted on helping them into their safety seats, then followed her back to her ranch, and once again helped her unload the boys from the car.

"Maybe next time you boys come over, you can go riding. Of course to do that, you're gonna need to be outfitted proper," Travis said as they headed for the front porch. He paused at the foot of the steps and propped one boot on the bottom step. Leaning down so he was at eye level with her sons, he braced his forearm on his thigh and asked, "You boys got hats and boots and jeans?" he asked while a silently swearing Annie watched.

Tyler, Teddy and Trevor mimicked Travis's actions, propping one sneaker-clad foot on the bottom step, too. "Our boots are too small," Trevor reported.

"And so are our jeans." Tyler tried to prop his arm like Travis's and couldn't quite get it.

"But we got real cowboy hats," Teddy said, mimicking Travis's manly stance as best he could. "Just like yours."

Annie frowned at Travis. Once again he had brought up something she would just as soon he not bring up. Realizing it, chagrin appeared briefly in his eyes. "Well, maybe I can take you over to the Western-wear store and get you dressed up right," he promised, apparently determined to get in her good graces again.

"Really, Travis, that isn't necessary," Annie said with a smile that she did not begin to really feel.

At the veiled meaning beneath her words, Travis merely quirked his eyebrow and continued to regard her steadily. When was Annie going to realize he was there to help her? he wondered, upset. "It's no problem," he retorted easily.

"Maybe not for you," Annie interjected just as firmly. She knew Travis could afford to spend whatever he wanted. He was that successful. But Annie didn't want her boys depending on someone who might not be there in the same attentive way tomorrow. They'd already been abandoned twice in their young lives, first by their father who apparently could care less about them, and then via death, their grandfather. Annie didn't want them suffering any more loss. And with Travis interested mainly in acquiring her ranch and moving her and the boys out of here, once and for all, she couldn't, to her growing disappointment, see the two of them had any future as friends.

"Besides, they've got a birthday coming up this week," Travis continued genially, "don't they?"

Annie flushed uncomfortably, surprised Travis had remembered, when thus far their own father hadn't.

Travis straightened. Immediately, all three boys did the same. Travis squinted down at them thoughtfully and stroked his jaw with the flat of his hand. "How old are you boys going to be again? Fourteen?"

They erupted in giggles, just as Travis wanted. "Five!" they corrected in chorus.

Travis nodded thoughtfully. "Five is a good age."

Teddy squinted up at him. "How old are you, Travis?"

One corner of Travis's lips slanted up in a sexy grin. Crinkles appeared at the corners of his eyes. "Thirty-eight."

Tyler was so excited by the revelation he promptly revealed, "Our mommy's thirty-three."

And a mighty fine-looking thirty-three, Travis thought, glancing over at Annie.

He doubted she knew what she had done to him, in her pajamas, and was still doing to him, in her khaki walking shorts and sleeveless knit shirt.

He tore his eyes from her trim figure, pushing the image of soft alabaster skin from his mind. He didn't need to know how Annie looked undressed. When just the sight of her fully clothed was enough to send blood rushing to his groin. And keep it there.

"Let me know when they can go," he told Annie casually, more than willing to take the boys off her hands every now and again if it would give her a break. After all, that was why he'd injected himself into her life—to honor his deathbed promise to her father and make sure she and the boys were all right. "I'll take them over to the Western-wear store myself." He regarded her steadily, not the least bit shy about admitting, "It's the least I can do, given all your dad did for me over the years."

Annie nodded and, to Travis's relief, did not dispute that her father had taught Travis everything he knew about cattle ranching. Gently, she touched all three boys on the shoulder, immediately and effectively garnering their attention. "Okay, boys, run on inside," she told them sweetly. "It's time for our puzzle contest and lunch."

Travis waited until they had dashed off, whooping and hollering all the while. He turned to her quizzically, prodded, "Puzzle contest?"

Annie nodded. Planting her feet squarely in the grass beneath the steps leading up to the front porch, she said, "They put together puzzles while I fix their lunch. It keeps them busy and where I can see them, and calms them down prior to eating."

Travis nodded his approval. "Good idea."

"One of many that I've had."

Travis caught the sarcasm in her words. He studied the new color that had swept into her fair, freckled cheeks. "Now, what bee has gotten under your bonnet?"

Annie's lower lip shot out petulantly. "To be precise—you!"

"Why?" Travis tried, without success, not to notice how soft and kissable and bare that lower lip of hers was. Reluctantly, he tore his gaze from her mouth and shifted it back to her sparkling hazel-green eyes. "What have I done?" he demanded, incensed.

Annie came forward until they were standing toe to toe, and nose to nose. "Has anyone ever told you that you are too much of a take-charge kind of guy?" She pushed the words through clenched teeth.

Travis grinned ruefully. "I think you just did," he drawled, aware this was the first time he had ever really seen her angry. And that she looked pretty as all get-out when she was angry.

"I want to solve my own problems, Travis." Annie planted both hands on her hips and continued to regard him feistily. "I've had enough men trying to run my life as it is." She blew out a long, exasperated breath.

Travis lifted a curious eyebrow. "Those men being...?"

"My father, who thought I couldn't make a single decision on my own." Annie brushed her bangs out of her face with the heel of her hand. "And my ex-husband who thought his skill as a management consultant carried over into our home life as well."

*Now they were getting somewhere.* Travis regarded her knowingly. "You're still mad at me for offering to buy your ranch," he guessed.

"Not to mention not supporting my decision to try to market my own barbecue sauce!" Annie retorted vehemently.

Exasperated, Travis rubbed at the tense muscles in the back of his neck. "I have your best interests at heart," he said.

Annie continued to glare at him as even more color swept into her cheeks. "I don't need you having my own best interests at heart." She jabbed her index finger lightly against his sternum. "The only thing I need you to do is stop interfering in my life,'' she fumed.

Travis grinned, aware that never in his life had he wanted to haul a woman into his arms more than at that very moment. Unable to completely repress a mischievous grin, he prodded in a low Texas drawl, ''Is that what you call what I've been doing?''

Annie nodded and dropped her jabbing index finger from his chest. ''As a matter of fact, yes.''

*So be it.* ''I'm still buying the boys Western wear for their birthday,'' Travis announced.

''Fine.'' Annie lifted her shoulders in a charmingly indifferent shrug. ''Buy the boys whatever you like,'' she dared, her hazel eyes sparkling with temper. ''I'm sure they'll love it. But as for the rest, Travis,'' she warned soft and low, in a voice that set his pulse racing, ''I want you to mind your own business!''

Travis gave Annie a look that swept her from head to toe and felt a wave of sheer emotion unlike anything he had ever felt before. Sensing she was about to run, he wrapped his arms around her and tugged her close. ''You are my business, Annie.''

''Since when?'' Annie responded indignantly, splaying her hands across his chest.

''Since right now,'' he said gruffly. And then he did what he'd been wanting to do all day. He lowered his head and kissed her.

## Chapter Four

Annie had known Travis wanted to kiss her. She had seen the desire in his eyes numerous times in the past few days. She just hadn't thought he would. But now that his lips were on hers, tenderly coaxing, recklessly taking, she realized something else. She wanted him, too. And that lent a dangerous edge to an already reckless moment. She wreathed her arms around his neck and melted against him, kissing him back every bit as passionately as he was kissing her. Until their bodies melded in an instant of boneless pleasure and nothing mattered but the need flowing between them.

Travis kissed her as if he meant to have her and make her his. And Annie felt his intent in the fierce sensuality of the kiss. Just as she felt her own need to be needed, wanted, loved again. Not halfheartedly, as she had been before. But like this—wholly and completely. Stunned by the chemistry surging between them, the yearning, a tremor of unwanted desire spiraled through Annie with treacherous speed, melting her insides, weakening her knees. Completely caught up in the moment and his unabashed conquest of her, she made a soft, helpless sound in the back of her throat, and then all was lost in the shattering sensuality of his embrace. Annie moaned again, loving the warm, hard, wonderfully male feel of him, and that was when it happened, a door slammed. Three sets of sneakers thudded across the front porch.

Realizing—too late—they'd just been busted, Annie grimaced and pushed away from Travis. Reluctantly, he let her go. Not nearly as mindful of their audience as she.

"Did you see that?" Tyler demanded excitedly, elbowing both his brothers.

"Yeah!" Trevor's jaw gaped as he elbowed his brothers right back. "Momma was kissing Travis!" he said, completely amazed.

"No," Teddy echoed, blinking furiously. "Travis was kissing Momma!"

Travis grinned, looking abruptly—smugly—pleased, having obviously figured out by her sons' reactions—and Annie's—that this was something that hadn't happened before, at least with her three sons bearing witness. "You're both right," he drawled.

Meanwhile, a furious Annie was still trembling from his heated kisses. "Another reason why we can't continue this," she told him beneath her breath.

"Or another reason why we should," Travis said just as quietly as he turned to face her. Annie looked in his eyes. She knew this wasn't the last time he would ever kiss her, even as Travis wrapped both arms around her waist and gathered her close. To her growing dismay, Annie's heart beat in urgent rhythm with his.

"Boys, get the puzzles," she ordered, resisting the urge to kick Travis in the shin. Before they ended up kissing again.

All three boys continued to watch them, raptly fascinated. "We already did," Trevor said, his eyes widening.

Annie smiled brightly, deciding she would kick Travis in the shin as soon as her boys were not around to see. "Go ahead and start them then," Annie encouraged, as if she wasn't already trembling with anticipation of another wickedly sensual kiss. "I'll be right there."

The boys still didn't move. Reluctantly, Annie tore her eyes from Travis and gave them a look.

"We want to see if you're going to kiss again," Teddy reported.

"Yeah, we never saw Momma do that 'afore," Tyler confirmed. "Not even with our daddy."

Trevor nodded. "It was just like on TV."

"Was it?" Travis grinned, the warmth of his body, where it pressed against hers, giving new heat to hers. He rubbed his thumb across Annie's lower lip, sensually tracing its shape. He winked at her. "Maybe we should try it again, just to see."

Annie trembled in a way that let him know just how sensitive she was to his touch. "No," she said just as stubbornly. "We shouldn't."

"It's not gonna happen again?" The boys looked disappointed in a way that let Travis know this was more excitement than they'd had in a while. Or should have again, Annie thought.

"No. We're not going to kiss again," Annie said firmly.

"Sure?" Travis murmured, looking more enamored of her than ever. "I kind of liked it myself."

At his gentle teasing, the boys grinned all the more.

Annie motioned her sons back in the house. "Boys, scoot. I mean it. I'll be right there."

"Okay." They sighed in unison, clearly disappointed that the unprecedentedly romantic show wasn't going to continue right away. "'Cause if you're not, we're coming back out to get you," they warned.

Travis waited until they had disappeared before he spoke again. "Quite a few chaperons you've got there."

Her own temper soaring, Annie shoved away from him. No matter how good his kisses had felt, or how right it had felt to be in his arms, she could not afford to be distracted this way. Glad she had come to her senses at long last, she tossed her hair feistily. "A good thing, too, given your behavior this morning, Travis McCabe." She scowled.

Travis grinned and playfully tugged on a lock of her red-gold hair. "Keep looking at me like that, Annie, and I'm liable to kiss you again," he teased, clearly determined to get a rise out of her, and succeeding.

*In your dreams, cowboy.* "Like I said, it's not going to happen." She was not going to kiss him again! Or let him kiss her! Not while he still wanted to buy her ranch and make it his! Annie pointed a lecturing finger his way. "Furthermore, in the future, I want you to mind your business while I mind mine." Travis's mouth opened. Before he could get a word in edgewise, she cut him off. "And don't tell me I'm your business, because I'm not!" Not waiting for his reply, Annie fled.

"WHAT'S WRONG, Momma?" Tyler asked what felt like a lifetime, but was in reality only half a day, later.

"It's the sauce." Annie frowned, unable to help

feeling at least a tiny bit dejected. She had been working on it all afternoon, to no avail.

"Don't you like it?" Teddy asked, his small freckled nose wrinkled in concern.

Annie shook her head and stared at the labeled dollops of sauce spread over her kitchen table and countertop. Her plan to put Travis out of her thoughts—through hard work on product development—was not working any better than her efforts to perfect her sauce. "I keep trying to make my barbecue sauce special and it's not working," Annie confided the root of her concern to her sons. She'd added everything she could think of, to the basic sauce. And to her mounting disappointment, all she'd done was make a perfectly good, if somewhat basic, sauce weird and unpalatable.

Trevor sighed, clearly bored, and tired of waiting for the results Annie wanted so badly. "Can we go outside and play on the swing set while you keep working then?" he asked on behalf of himself and his two brothers.

Annie didn't know what they could do outside they hadn't already done in abundance. They'd already been in and out a good five times over the course of the long afternoon. Swinging, sliding, playing ball, moving sand in their dump trucks, and catching bugs. "You promise me you'll stay in the backyard, where I can see you from the window?" Annie ascertained, wanting no repeat of the eggs-flying-from-the-hayloft incident.

The three boys nodded. "Okay," Annie said. "But if you get too hot, come back inside."

"It's shady out back, Momma," Tyler said, already putting on his shoes.

"Yeah, 'member?" Trevor closed the Velcro flaps on his sneakers hurriedly. "There are lotsa trees."

"Fruit trees," Teddy added, scrambling to catch up.

"Yes, I remember." Annie smiled. Grinning, her boys slammed out the back door, and Annie went back to her experimenting. As if on cue, some fifteen minutes later, the boys slammed back in, hot and sweaty. They paused long enough to get big drinks of water, then went into the living room to play with the car and truck village they had built in between jaunts outside.

The next time Annie looked up, it was almost six o'clock. Surprised the boys had allowed her to lose track of time like that—usually they started clamoring for their supper around five in the evening— she went into the living room. And was promptly aghast at what she saw.

ALL THREE BOYS were curled up on the floor in the fetal position. All three looked close to tears.

"My tummy hurts, Mommy," Tyler said.

"So does mine," Trevor added miserably.

Teddy nodded gravely. "Mine, too."

"Hurts where?" Annie said, noticing the boys were pale and sweaty despite the pleasantly cool air-conditioned interior of the house. Tyler pointed to the center of his tummy. Trevor pointed to the right side of him. Teddy pointed to his left side.

Aware this looked like the kind of medical emergency slash calamity every mother dreaded, Annie's heart began to pound. She knelt beside her sons and did her best to stay calm. Panicking would not help any of them. "Did you boys get into anything you're not supposed to?'' she asked gently, trying her best not to let on how alarmed she was.

''No, Momma,'' Tyler, Teddy and Trevor replied in unison. None of them met her eyes. A bad sign.

''Boys, if you ate something,'' Annie persisted even more kindly and patiently, ''you've got to tell me.'' Although what that could possibly be Annie didn't know, as the boys continued to deny, by their silence, having gotten into any poisons.

All chemicals and cleaners were under lock and key. The same went for medicines. Annie had taken child-proofing her house in the city very seriously. And she had done the same for her father's ranch house and barn before ever moving back here with the boys.

Nevertheless, Annie did a quick sweep of the house and barn. Everything was as it was supposed to be. There was no way the boys could have gotten in the combination locks. Was it possible the boys had contracted some weird sort of illness? she wondered frantically. Possibly at Travis McCabe's ranch that very morning?

Teddy moaned. Trevor and Tyler joined in. All three were doubled over in pain.

''We're going to the doctor,'' Annie said.

For once, there were no complaints. Another sign of how much trouble the boys were in, Annie noted worriedly.

''Call Travis!'' Tyler insisted weakly.

''Yeah, we need him.'' Sweating profusely, Teddy nodded.

''Maybe he can make us feel better.'' Tears of dismay poured from Trevor's eyes.

''Where's the phone book?'' Annie asked, rifling

through everything she could think of in an effort to find Travis's number, to no avail. She couldn't find her phone book anywhere and she didn't have Travis's number memorized, either.

"Call the operator, Momma," Trevor suggested between moans of pain.

"Good idea." Annie punched zero. When the operator came on, she asked to be connected to Travis McCabe. Seconds later, his voice rumbled over the phone lines. "Travis McCabe here—"

Annie had never been so glad to hear anyone's voice in her life. "Travis, it's Annie," she said urgently.

"What's wrong?" he demanded, instantly alert.

"The boys are sick or something. I've got to get them to the emergency room."

"I'll be right there."

Travis pulled into the driveway three minutes later, not in his pickup truck, but in a dusty red sport-utility vehicle that seated at least nine. "Where'd you get this?" Annie asked as he vaulted out of the driver's seat and she hurriedly ushered him inside.

"Borrowed it from one of my men." His expression one of tenderness and concern, Travis knelt over the boys, who were still curled up on the living-room floor.

"Travis, I don' feel so good," Teddy whimpered.

"Me, neither," Tyler moaned.

"My tummy aches," Trevor sobbed softly. "Can you make it better?"

Travis scooped up Tyler and Teddy while Annie picked up Trevor and cradled him in her arms. "My brother Jackson can," Travis told the three boys confidently. "He's a doctor and so is his wife, Lacey. They're going to meet us at the emergency room."

Tyler curled into Travis's strong shoulder. "Like on TV?"

Teddy curled up on his other. "Like the place where we were borned?"

"Yes, like that," Annie said as together, she and Travis carried the boys out to the truck. "You called ahead?" she asked, as they gently laid the boys down on the two rear seats.

Travis nodded. "On my cell phone while I was driving over here. I've got all my brothers and my folks on speed-dial."

Travis and Annie spent the rest of the drive into town comforting the boys. As promised, Jackson and Lacey and several nurses met them at the emergency-room entrance of Laramie Community Hospital.

"Do you think this could be appendicitis?" Annie asked Jackson and Lacey as the boys were wheeled into an examining room.

"If it is, it would certainly be one for the record books," Jackson McCabe said as the nurses lined up the three gurneys side by side. "Even if they are identical triplets."

"But we won't know until we examine them," Lacey McCabe said with a reassuring smile, already unlooping the stethoscope from around her neck.

Travis and Annie stayed with the boys while they were undressed and put in cartoon-character hospital gowns. Jackson and Lacey examined them and asked the same questions Annie had asked. To everyone's frustration, nothing conclusive turned up. Jackson and Lacey exchanged looks. Lacey lifted an eyebrow. Jackson nodded. Lacey left briefly then returned with three E.R. teddy bears, one for each of the boys. "Mind if we talk to the guys alone for a few minutes?" Jackson asked Annie. "I've got a brand-new stethoscope I'd like to show off. I can teach them how to listen to their tummies."

Annie was desperate enough to try anything the two doctors and nurses thought would work. "Sure, if you think it will help," Annie said with a shrug.

"We do." Lacey smiled while Travis and Annie went out into the waiting room.

"They're going to figure this out," Travis reassured her as Annie paced back and forth.

Annie felt herself tearing up as she wrung her hands in front of her. A knot of fear settled in the region around her heart and wouldn't go away. "I don't know what I'd do if anything ever happened to them," she whispered in a choked voice.

Travis wrapped his arms around her and held her close. His strong, male presence was like a port in the storm. "Nothing is going to happen," he told her firmly, despite the fact he looked every bit as worried about her sons as she was. He rubbed his hand reassuringly over her back. "We got them here. They're safe. We've got the best docs in Texas looking after them." He paused again, his expression determined. "They're going to figure this out."

Annie wished she was as sure of that as Travis. In any case, it was good to know she could count on him. Being a single parent of three rowdy boys was hard enough under normal circumstances. Being a single parent in a medical or any other type of emergency was darn near unbearable. "Thank you for coming as quickly as you did and helping me get them here," Annie told him in a low voice that shook with nerves.

Travis nodded seriously. "I was glad to help. Besides, you would've done the same for me."

Annie nodded. That she would have. Whatever else was going on in the relationship, they were still neighbors, and still, despite the passionate kisses and his desire to buy her ranch, apparently on their way to being friends after all.

Jackson and Lacey came out beaming. "Mystery solved!" Jackson told them both happily.

Beside him, his wife, Lacey, grinned triumphantly, too. Her relief was evident as she explained, "The Triple Threat have a green apple tummyache. They're getting some antacids now and an antispasmodic that will probably make them sleepy, but come tomorrow morning, they'll be good as new."

Annie clapped a hand to her forehead. "I should have known," she murmured, embarrassed she hadn't seen this one coming. The clues of incessant curiosity and impending mischief had been there. She just hadn't picked up on them. With a rueful shake of her head, she told the group, "They've been doing nothing but talking about the green apples on the trees out back. They were so excited. They couldn't wait to eat them."

"Yeah." Lacey smiled with all the gentle patience and compassion of a top-notch pediatrician. "They told us. They just didn't want you to know. They were afraid they'd get in trouble."

Annie sighed. She was definitely going to have to keep a better eye on them, Intuit and anticipate more. "Can I see them now?" she asked.

"Sure. Go on in." Lacey smiled again.

Jackson nodded at their three charts. "We'll get the paperwork ready for their release."

When Annie and Travis went in, all three boys were sitting on their gurneys. Dressed again, cradling their brand-new hospital-issue teddy bears in their arms, they looked properly sheepish by all the fuss and commotion they had caused.

"We're sorry, Momma," Trevor said.

Teddy nodded. "We knowed we weren't s'posed to eat the apples till they were red."

"Then why did you?" Annie asked gently, wondering if she would ever truly know in advance how her three boys' minds worked.

Tyler explained the rationale behind their actions. "Because we ate green apples 'afore and we liked 'em. Lots."

*Aha,* Annie thought. *Now they were getting somewhere.* "But those were a different kind of apple, honey. Those were Golden Delicious. Those are supposed to be eaten green. These aren't."

"Yeah." Tyler sighed. "Dr. Jackson and Dr. Lacey explained that to us."

Teddy looked worried as he asked, apparently for all three, "Are we in trouble?"

Annie paused. She didn't want to let them off the hook entirely, lest they try something as foolish, and potentially dangerous, again. But she didn't want to go overboard, either. Especially after what they had been through that evening. Her expression stern, she released a long, slow breath. "I think your tummy-ache has been punishment enough," she said finally, making meaningful eye contact with each one of her boys. "Just promise me you won't do it again," she said softly and seriously. "No more picking fruit off the tree and eating it until I am out there to help you get it, and bring it in and wash it. Understood?''

Teddy, Trevor and Tyler nodded vigorously, their intent not to disobey that dictum again obvious.

''Good.'' Annie hugged them by turn, letting them know all was forgiven.

''I'm glad you're okay, guys,'' Travis said, hugging each child, too.

The boys nodded. ''Us, too,'' they said, and hugged Travis and Annie back as warmly and appreciatively as any two parents on earth.

IT WAS ALMOST NINE O'CLOCK by the time they arrived back at Annie's ranch. ''What do you think? Should we try and wake them or put them straight to bed?'' Travis asked with a nod at the sleeping trio in the back.

''I vote for straight to bed,'' Annie said, figuring that as exhausted as they were, the boys would sleep straight through until morning. As expected, they were sleeping so deeply they barely woke as Travis and Annie carried them into the house and tucked them into their beds.

Exhausted, Annie retreated to the kitchen, and felt immediately overwhelmed. Her culinary workshop was just as she had left it. Filled with dirty dishes and littered with the remains of her barbecue sauce in all of its many variations. Looking at the enormous mess, it was all Annie could do not to groan out loud. It would take her several hours, minimum, to clean this up, when all she wanted to do was grab a bite to eat, climb into bed and pull the covers over her head.

''Did you have any supper?'' Travis asked with a sympathetic glance at her face.

Annie shook her head wearily. She didn't know why—she wasn't usually the helpless, dependent type—but she wanted to put herself in his arms and just stay there until she felt better, more energized and reassured, too. "Never got around to it," she said softly. She looked deep in his eyes, wondering how much she had really put him out this evening. He had acted as if charging to her rescue this evening was nothing. She knew better. He had dropped everything to come and help her. Gone way beyond simple neighborliness in his efforts to comfort her and the boys and provide a shoulder for her to cry on. He had acted as if he wanted to be the man in her life. The man the boys turned to, too. "What about you?" A weary smile tugged at the corners of her lips. Amazing how right he looked standing in her kitchen that time of night. Amazing that after the evening they'd had he could still have the good-humored patience of a saint.

Travis hooked his thumbs in the belt loops on either side of his jeans. "I usually don't eat until eight or nine in the evening," he said, and the way he looked at her indicated he was clearly angling for an invitation to stay.

Annie was tempted to ask him. And she knew she'd be wise not to ask him. They had completely different life-styles. His time was his own. He called all his own shots. Her life was dictated by a million things, all of them having to do with three redheaded little boys, and her need to find a way to support them, fulfill herself and still have plenty of time to spend with them, as they were going to be this age only once. She didn't want it to pass her by before she had truly enjoyed and savored every minute of their growing up.

Annie lounged against the counter. But she wished just once she'd had time to put on some makeup or tamed her wavy hair in something more done than a loose, tousled upsweep. Why, she wasn't quite sure. She had given up on having a romantic life of any kind soon after the Triple Threat was born.

Not sure where to start—cleanup or food preparation—Annie looked at the nearly empty pan of barbecue sauce sitting on the back of the stove. To her disappointment, there wasn't even enough left of the basic mild variety to flavor a single piece of chicken or beef. She wouldn't have minded having some barbecued something for dinner.

Travis turned, so they were facing the same direction, and lounged against the counter beside her. His arm and shoulder nudged hers companionably as he settled in, crossing his long legs at the ankle. Inclining his head over at her, he asked, "Did you make any headway today with your sauce?"

Once again, Annie was surprised at the tenderness and compassion in his eyes. "No. I feel like I'm close, but—" Annie shrugged, and flushed, a little embarrassed at having to go back to the drawing-board stage after all her big talk.

Travis, to his credit, did not seem to think less of her because of it. "Not there yet," he guessed gently.

Knowing the dishes wouldn't get done on their own, Annie picked up a handful of saucers and spoons and carried them to the sink. She began to rinse and stack them one at a time. "I feel like I'm close."

Travis shrugged his broad shoulders. "Then you probably are."

Annie watched the broad muscles strain against his white cotton shirt and remembered without wanting to how it felt to be enveloped in their seductive warmth. "Thanks for saying it." Even if she shouldn't be allowing him to protect her, or look after her, in any way.

"I mean it." Travis gathered up saucers that were scattered around the kitchen and carried them to the sink, too. Evidently realizing she could use some encouragement, he winked at her. "I have a feeling you accomplish pretty much whatever you set your mind to, don't you?"

Annie flushed, with pride this time. "Usually," she allowed, her fingers brushing his as she accepted the new stack of barbecue-sauce-stained dishes.

"Then you'll get there," Travis soothed.

Annie swung toward him, not afraid to call him on his abrupt change of attitude, and find out what was behind it. Not lust, she hoped. She didn't want Travis or any other man saying what he thought she wanted to hear just to get into her bed. Or had he changed his tune to get her to sell her land? Her chin took on a challenging tilt. "That's not exactly the tune you were singing this morning."

The corners of his mouth quirked up sexily at her prodding. "Let's just say I've had time to reflect."

That could be good, and that could be bad. Annie studied him warily. "And what have your reflections taught you?" she asked just as wryly.

Travis moved. An instant later, her back was to the counter. He was standing directly in front of her, his hands braced firmly on either side of her. "That some things are worth waiting for."

Annie had only to listen to his tone, and see his face, to know he wasn't talking about barbecue sauce any longer. And she would have known it even if he hadn't caged her body with the stronger, taller, warmer length of his. Her breath caught in her throat, her heart beat wildly in her chest and her head tipped back all the more. "Travis—"

A knowing smile curved his lips. He leaned down and dropped kisses along her temple. "Let me get close to you, Annie," he whispered, burying his face in her hair.

Aware she was already weakening, and he hadn't even kissed her—really kissed her—yet, Annie splayed her hands across his chest. Hitched in a quick, bolstering breath. "I don't think that's wise." She nearly moaned as his lips found her again, blazing a fiery path across her forehead to the underside of her ear.

"Why not?" he coaxed, working his way down the slope of her neck.

Annie arched against him. Her fingers curled into his shirt, even as she struggled against the sensations coursing throughout her body. She closed her eyes, thinking maybe if she didn't see him it wouldn't feel so erotic, so right, being here with him this way. "Because I can't have an affair," she whispered, inhaling another quick, jerky breath.

Travis drew back slightly and simply waited until she opened her eyes. "Is that what you think I'm interested in?" he demanded, hurt warring with the passion in his eyes.

A shudder ran through her as she clung to him.

"I'm certainly not in the market for a one-night stand, *or* marriage," Annie said. And when it came to sleeping with someone, there were three options. Marriage, an affair or a one-night stand.

"Is *that* what you think I'm interested in?" His eyes widened in surprise. "A one-time thing or marriage?"

"You know what I mean." Annie felt herself blush.

Travis paused, his lower half resting against hers. And although he was no longer kissing her, she could feel the depth of his arousal, the depth of his need. And she wanted him, too. She wanted to let go of her caution, and just feel. Just need. Just take each moment as it came in a way she never had been able to before. And probably never would again.

"I'm not sure I understand," Travis said slowly, tracing the arch of her eyebrow with gentle strokes of his thumb.

Annie sighed heavily as she searched his eyes. "I mean, there's a reason they've never seen me kissing anyone. I can't get involved impetuously," she told him sadly, seriously. "I have the boys to consider. And I don't want them hurt." Even if it meant she had to walk away from the only joy not connected to her sons that she had known in a very very long time.

TRAVIS STUDIED Annie's upturned face. Despite the tumultuous events of the evening, she was as lovely as ever. He studied the more than usually disheveled upsweep, the flushed color in her pretty cheeks and the cautious sparkle in her hazel eyes. "I would never do anything to hurt them," he said, carefully underscoring every word.

Annie bit into her soft, bare lower lip. "I know you wouldn't mean to," she allowed, dropping her eyes.

Travis slid a hand beneath her chin and lifted her gaze back to his. "Not even accidentally, Annie," he said firmly.

A pulse throbbed in Annie's neck as she regarded him in silence, clearly wanting to trust him, but not quite able to. Probably because of what her louse of an ex-husband, Reece, had put her through.

"I care about them, Annie," Travis told her gruffly, wishing he could take her to bed and make love to her until all the sadness and uncertainty in her eyes went away. "And I care about you, Annie." A hell of a lot more than he should. Or had ever realized. Until her dad had died and he'd begun to get to know her, a little at a time. But that promise he had made to Joe—the promise he had sworn Annie would never know anything about—also worked to keep them apart.

"Of course you care about me." Annie's shoulders stiffened. Her back ramrod straight, she moved away from him. "We've known each other for years."

"Have we?" Travis challenged as Annie went to work on the stove with a sponge and a bottle of spray cleaner.

She shot him a glance.

Assured of her attention, he stood beside her and continued, "Do I really know you?" He peered at her closely. "I don't think you know me."

Annie wrinkled her nose in aggravation. "Of course we do!" She scrubbed the stove with a vengeance as she reminded him, "You worked for my dad summers while I was in high school and you were in college."

That was true, Travis thought as he watched her go to town on a particularly stubborn stain. "We didn't spend any time together." Travis tore his eyes from the faint jiggling motions of her breasts beneath her cotton shirt. This was no time to be thinking how well she filled out her clothes these days, he reminded himself sternly. Picking up a stack of dishes, he slid them into the sink with the expertise of a man who had long done dishes for himself. "We said hello, goodbye, that was it. In fact, back then—" Travis rolled up his sleeves and made short work of washing the saucers "—I had the distinct impression what you did know of me you didn't like at all."

Annie let out a beleaguered sigh and turned away from the now-gleaming stove top. "That's because I was jealous." She grabbed a clean dish towel out of the drawer.

"Why?" Travis slanted her a curious glance. This, he hadn't expected.

Annie's pouty lower lip curled ruefully as she began to dry the dishes he'd cleaned. "Because my dad used to look at you the way I wanted him to look at me." She shook her head unhappily, remembering. "Because he treated you with admiration and respect."

Travis studied the unhappiness in her eyes. And once more found himself wishing he could simply kiss all her past sadness away. "He loved you, Annie," Travis told her gently. "You were the most precious thing in the world to him."

Annie's eyes lit up even as she continued to regard him warily. "I know that," she replied softly. "But he didn't respect me, Travis. He didn't think I could take care of myself or the boys or this ranch, and because of that he worried about me constantly.''

Guilt washed through Travis, followed swiftly by regret. When he had promised Joe he'd work behind the scenes to protect Joe's only daughter and her three sons, Travis had never figured on getting close to Annie. Never mind wanting to confide in her. He had figured, just as Joe had, that Annie would resent any attempts to protect her. And promised silence. And Travis was the kind of man who never broke his promises, no matter how inconvenient they later became.

Travis looked at Annie sternly. "He wanted you to be happy."

Annie rolled her eyes. "And he wanted me to have someone to take care of me, because he didn't think I could take care of myself," she continued in a low, resentment-filled tone that only served to make Travis feel all the more guilty and devious.

Travis was silent. "So your dad was old-fashioned, Annie," he said eventually, reminding himself he was only doing what Joe had deemed needed to be done. "There are worse things."

Annie arched her delicate eyebrow in pointed disagreement. "Not to a girl who's fifteen or sixteen," she said.

Travis guessed that was so. He recalled all too well how independent-minded he had been in his teens. Still was. "You proved yourself when you began working as a flight attendant," he told her confidently. "You've been all over the world."

Annie nodded, grudgingly allowing that was so. "And now I want to be here where I grew up," she said stubbornly. "I want the boys to be here, too."

There went his plans to buy her ranch. At least anytime soon.

Another silence fell between them, shorter this time. "Then this is where you should be," Travis said finally, telling himself his sudden interest in Annie had nothing to do with his interest in the property she had inherited from her dad, or the way her three boys needed a dad and she needed a husband, or even the desire that hit him full-bore whenever he was near her these days. He was not indulging in his Sir Galahad routine again. He was merely fulfilling his deathbed promise to her dad. Which was yet another reason why he shouldn't haul her into his arms and kiss her soundly again, no matter how much his libido was urging him on.

"Thank you for realizing that," Annie said politely.

Travis grinned and with effort reminded himself to be the gentleman Lilah and John had raised him to be. "It takes me a while, but eventually I catch on," he drawled.

Another silence fell between them, happier this time, and fraught with new tension. Because now Annie was looking at him as though she wanted to kiss him again, too. "I guess I better go."

Annie nodded and reluctantly put her dish towel aside. "You probably better."

Travis picked up his hat and headed for the door. He'd barely reached the door when he began to reconsider his decision not to kiss her. After all, what could one little kiss hurt? He bargained silently. Everyone needed a kiss every now and then. "You'll call me if there are any problems?" he asked, studying her upturned face.

"You can count on it," Annie said.

"And Annie…?" Wanting to have both hands free, Travis settled his hat squarely on his head.

She paused just in front of the door and turned slowly, her delicate red-gold eyebrows arched in surprise. She looked as though she had been a million miles away. "Hmm?" she asked, a gentle, absentminded smile on her lips.

"One more thing." Giving her no chance to think, no chance to protest, Travis clamped both hands around her waist and brought her against him, length to length. Annie was still gasping with a mixture of shock and surprise when his lips landed firmly on hers. Her lips parted. His tongue swept inside, drawing in the taste of her, the softness. Her arms curled around his shoulders and she sagged against him in equal parts surrender and wonder. And Travis knew, if he didn't call a halt now, he would never get out of there. Not tonight. Maybe not ever. His need to be close to her was so potent as to be magical. But it wouldn't be right for her boys to find him in Annie's bed. Which meant, he thought as he reluctantly let the kiss come to an end, he had no choice but to tell her good-night and let the unexpectedly eventful evening come to an end.

Annie blinked and caught her breath as he released her. "What was that for?" she gasped.

He touched the end of her nose playfully. "I think you know."

Annie followed him through the front door, then halfway down the walk. "I meant what I said, Travis," she warned.

Travis slowed his steps to an amble as the warmth

of the Texas night surrounded them. "I know you did."

Annie matched her steps to his. "I'm not getting involved with anyone," she insisted stubbornly.

Travis grinned, his eyes sparkling mischievously in the spreading yellow glow of the porch light. Truth was, he didn't want her getting involved with anyone else. "You don't have to," he said. *Maybe this wasn't exactly what Joe'd had in mind for his daughter. It didn't mean it was wrong. It couldn't be. Not when it felt so right.*

"And why is that?" Annie demanded, her low voice quavering emotionally.

The edges of his lips curved up smugly. Travis tipped his hat at her, aware he felt happier and more content than he had in a long time. After just a couple of kisses and two days of spending time with her, and her boys. He winked. "'Cause you already are."

ANNIE WAITED until Travis left, and then she did what she always did when distressed. She picked up the telephone and called a friend. "The man is impossible!" Annie fumed to her good friend Kelsey Lockhart as she stirred a pan of split-pea soup that, along with a garden salad, was going to comprise her dinner.

Maybe not so impossible," Kelsey allowed.

Annie tensed as the soup began to bubble. "What do you mean?"

"Travis called me back and offered me a job on his ranch."

Annie blinked in amazement. "When?"

"Early this afternoon," Kelsey crowed, pleased. "I start tomorrow."

Annie shook her head. Every time she started to get Travis figured out, he turned right around and did something that amazed her. "You're kidding."

"Nope. Whatever you said to him must have hit home, because he said he owed it to me, one would-be rancher to another, to give me a chance."

"Would-be..." Annie echoed, even more amazed. "Kelsey—"

"Yes, I'm thinking about buying the ranch my sisters and I grew up on and making it a showplace once again."

Having struggled to operate one from afar the last two years, Annie knew running a ranch was no small undertaking. She didn't want Kelsey, who was known to be one of the most fickle women ever to reside in Laramie, Texas, to lose her shirt. Not to mention what little she and each of her sisters had inherited from their folks. "Do you have that kind of money?" Annie ladled soup into a bowl and carried it to the table.

"Not alone. I'm looking for a partner. Someone who knows the ranching business inside and out and wants to own his own ranch, too," Kelsey said.

Annie shook her head in amazement. "That is news."

"Yes, well, don't tell anyone," Kelsey warned. "I have to break it to my sisters and I have a feeling they are not going to approve."

Knowing Meg, who was responsible to a fault, Dani, who refused to romanticize anything, and Jenna, who'd struggled for years trying to get her own business off the ground, to little result, Annie could imagine that was so.

"So back to Travis," Kelsey continued as Annie

dug into her soup. "Do you really think he's got a hankering for you?"

Annie let the thick creamy soup melt on her tongue. "He's certainly acting that way," she said after a moment.

Kelsey chuckled appreciatively. "Now for the fifty-thousand-dollar question," she teased.

Annie rolled her eyes, prodding right back, "And that would be...?"

"Do you have a hankering for him?"

"HEY, MOMMA! Whatcha doin'?"

Annie looked up from the telephone instruction manual she'd been poring over for the past half hour to see all three of her boys peering at her over the edge of the kitchen counter. She didn't know why they had to make these things so difficult. "I'm programming the speed-dial on our telephone," she said absently, continuing her chore.

While the boys watched in rapt attention, she punched in a series of numbers. "How come?" Tyler asked.

Annie smiled as the function she had punched in at last appeared to work just as it was supposed to. "So I don't have to hunt for phone numbers in an emergency."

The way they were looking at her, it was clear they didn't understand.

Annie punched in a second series of numbers. "If I want to call the fire department, I punch number two. If I want to call the sheriff's department, I punch number three. If I want to call Dr. Lacey, your new pediatrician's office, I punch in number four."

She continued down the list, programming the numbers in, in the order she had decided upon.

"So who's number 1?" Teddy asked, balancing on one foot.

Annie had been afraid they would ask that. And yet they probably needed to know that, too, in case of an emergency involving her. "Our closest neighbor," she said, telling herself, and them, with a look that it was really no big deal.

"Is that Travis?" Teddy piped up.

Remembering the way he had kissed her the night before as he got ready to leave, remembering the way he had unabashedly staked his claim on her, Annie fought a blush. "Yes. Number one on speed-dial is Travis," she told the boys matter-of-factly.

But it didn't mean anything, Annie told herself firmly. She just wanted to know she could call his ranch if anything came up and she needed immediate assistance. It would take up to thirty minutes for fire or police or ambulance to respond. The green-apple incident the previous day had convinced her she needed a faster response time in an emergency, particularly a medical emergency, hence the speed-dial.

The rumbling sound of a car engine outside had the boys running for the front windows. "Hey, Mom, someone's here!" Trevor reported excitedly.

"Yeah, and they got a big green Jeep!" Teddy said.

"It looks brand-new!" Tyler announced.

Annie frowned. She didn't know anyone with a big green truck, never mind a brand-new one. She put the phone back in the cradle and headed to the front porch where the boys were standing. There was a big green truck all right. New enough to still have the sticker on the window.

Travis climbed out of the driver's seat. He waved at Annie and the boys and then swaggered in their direction. "Just stopped by to see how the boys were feeling this morning." He shot all three of her triplets a gentle, concerned look, then knelt down to face them at eye level. "Your tummies okay?" he asked tenderly.

"Yeah." Teddy hugged Travis. "We're all better." Trevor hugged him, too.

"But we had to have cream of wheat for breakfast." Tyler threw his arms around Travis's neck, as well.

Finished, they all gathered around him, as eagerly as if they were greeting their daddy at the end of a long day. "Dr. Lacey said we gotta have a bland diet for a day," Teddy said.

"Yeah, I remember." Travis grinned. He patted them all on the shoulder, then straightened slowly, looked over at Annie. "How's your mommy this morning?"

"Mommy is fine," Annie said tartly, knowing the real reason he had come over—besides to check on the boys—was probably to put the moves on her. Worse, she'd been secretly waiting for him to do just that, even though she knew it wasn't wise.

"Momma's been busy," Tyler said, grabbing Travis around the waist and capturing his attention once again.

"She's been speed-diving our phone," Trevor added as informatively as ever.

"Dialing. Speed-dialing," Annie corrected, blushing as Travis tipped back his hat and looked over at her. She wished he would stop looking at her that way, as if she were a sumptuous dessert he was dying to try out.

"And guess what, Travis?" Teddy finished, jerking on his sleeve. "You're number one!"

## Chapter Five

"Is that so?" Travis asked.

"Yep, you're number one on speed-dial." Tyler nodded. "Momma just showed us."

"Because you're our closest neighbor," Annie explained, giving him a look that urged him not to read anything special into that.

Travis's smile widened, letting her know he was reading something special into it anyway.

"What brings you over so early?" Annie persisted, doing her best not to be affected by his handsome, virile presence.

Travis shrugged, his tall broad frame blocking out a big square of summer sunlight. "I just got a new Suburban. I thought the boys might like to go for a ride in it."

Annie looked at the nine-passenger sport-utility vehicle in her driveway. She twisted her lips together in a perplexed frown and tried not to look as impressed as she was. "That's awfully big for a single guy, isn't it?"

"I'm not always going to be single, Annie," Travis said as if there could be no doubt about what was in either of their futures. "In fact, the more I think about it—'' he leaned toward her familiarly ''—the more I think my mom and dad are right. It is time I settled down with a family of my own.''

Annie crossed her arms and looked at him with amused patience. ''Jumping the gun a bit, aren't you?'' she teased. ''Usually you need a wife first, then children.''

Travis smiled and continued to look at her steadily. ''Unless they're a package deal. Kind of like you and the boys,'' he said.

At the implication, Annie's heart skipped a beat.

Tyler plucked at Travis's sleeve. ''Can we go for a ride right now, Travis?''

''Sure.'' Travis looked only vaguely distracted by the interruption. He turned to Annie slyly, in a way that let her know that had been his plan all along. ''If your mom says it's okay.''

Now that her boys had seen Travis's new sport-utility vehicle, she knew there would be no rest for her until they had actually ridden in it as well. Figuring it was better to just do it, then field questions about his new SUV all day, Annie allowed, ''Well, I was going to go to the grocery. It seems we're out of eggs.''

''Isn't that a coincidence,'' Travis said, arching his eyebrows playfully. ''I'm out of eggs, too. Why don't we go together?'' The group walked into the kitchen. Making himself at home, Travis went over to pour himself a cup of coffee. ''We can try out the cargo area of my truck, see how many bags of groceries we can actually fit in. That is,'' he paused, coffee mug halfway to his mouth, ''if you don't mind doing an errand or two of mine while we're in town first.''

The boys, who had been following Travis's every

move with idolizing gazes, looked at Annie hopefully. "Please?" Tyler, Teddy and Trevor clasped their hands in front of them.

Annie rolled her eyes and shot Travis a beleaguered look. "All right. Get your shoes," she said.

As the boys ran off to obey, Annie looked at Travis. "The trip will tire them out."

Travis nodded. "When is nap time?"

Annie rolled her eyes. Boy, this man had a lot to learn when it came to her boys. "You just wish they took naps," she said, inhaling a whiff of his brisk, masculine cologne as she passed.

His dark eyebrows drew together in perplexed fashion. "They don't?"

Annie shook her head in regret. "Not for a year now," she told him. "Like the Energizer bunny, they go all day."

Travis's eyes lit up. The familiarity and ease between them deepened. He put his hand over hers. "Then I admire you even more."

Annie had the strong suspicion he wanted to do more than just hold her hand for a minute. He wanted to take her in his arms and kiss her. Not about to let him, she extricated her palm from the warmth of his and gracefully edged away. "For what?" she asked.

He set his mug down on the counter and closed the distance between them yet again. Letting her know he intended to do much more than just become comfortable in her house. "For being able to keep up with them," he said softly.

The question was, could she keep up with Travis? He seemed several steps ahead of her already. Acting as if they were already some sort of team. Buying a car more suited for her and her boys than his bachelor life-style.

"We're ready!" the Triple Threat shouted, barreling back in the kitchen in a tangle of arms and legs. Travis grinned at the commotion, and after making sure everyone, including Annie, was correctly outfitted for their adventure, led the way outside.

It took five minutes to get all the safety seats transferred to Travis's new Suburban, another five to get the boys buckled in right. Feeling more like the mom—and wife—in their makeshift "family" than she ever had in her marriage, Annie climbed into the passenger side. Travis waited to help her with her door before circling around to the driver's side.

The nine-passenger jeep had beige leather bucket seats in front, and two bench seats behind that. It was luxurious inside and out, with everything from state-of-the-art climate control to a deluxe stereo system. "You didn't tell me you were buying this," Annie said, settling in comfortably. How long had he been wanting a family, anyway?

Travis shrugged. "Just decided this morning," he said.

Annie's eyes widened. She knew you could walk in and buy a car in under an hour now and drive the new one right off the lot. She had, in fact, done it the last time she had purchased a car. She just hadn't expected Travis to make such a major change on the spur of the moment. He seemed much more organized, much more of a planner, than that.

"I didn't want to be caught without a vehicle big enough to transport you and the boys again," Travis explained when Annie continued to stare at him in stunned amazement.

"You're presuming I'm going to need you like that again—" Annie said, making no effort to hide her exasperation as Travis switched the radio from the twenty-four-hour ranch report to a popular country-and-western music station.

"I know you will," he said with a mesmerizing, yet oddly paternal, smile. "And if you think about it, so will you."

Precisely what Annie feared. Travis would be so easy to depend on. She could get used to this without even half trying. To him dropping in, helping himself to her coffee, helping her with the boys, as well as a kiss or two or three every now and then. And then what? What would happen if he did this for a while, and she began to depend on him, and then later he went his separate way? Decided, just as her ex-husband had, that she and the boys were too much for any one man to handle? Or married someone else and had children of his own? What then?

"Where are we going?" Annie asked, pushing away the unsettling thoughts. She wasn't going to let herself depend on Travis as anything but a neighboring rancher, and that was that.

"The first stop is the Western-wear store. I want to get the boys' sizes."

Annie couldn't deny she'd rather he give them something practical for their birthday later in the week. "Does this mean you're coming to their party?" She had sent out invitations to all the Mc-Cabes the previous week, as well as the Lockharts, and all her old friends who were still living in the area.

"Wouldn't miss it for the world," Travis grinned, his hands capably circling the wheel as he guided them toward town. "I'll stay around to help you clean up, too."

"That isn't necessary," Annie said firmly.

"You say that now. But when the party's over, and you finally get the tykes into bed, I'll wager you'll be singing a different tune."

Travis parked in front of the Western-wear store. Annie and the boys piled out. The owner had been expecting them and Travis had all three boys measured in no time. Their favorite colors were also noted. Then they got back in the Suburban. "Where next?" Annie said as she laid her head against the leather headrest.

"The Laramie Nursery School." Travis shot her a companionable glance. "Wouldn't you know it, they just happen to have three openings in the five-year-old class for the summer, and since these guys are going to be five the day after tomorrow, they're eligible."

Annie straightened, angrily aware that the triplets had just heard every word. "Travis—"

Keeping his eyes on the street, Travis placed his index finger against her lips. "Don't say a word, Annie, until you've taken the tour. Then we'll talk."

Travis parked in front of a white brick building with a shady fenced-in play yard. He ushered Annie and the boys in. The director took them back and showed Annie and the boys around the spacious classroom. One wall was covered with paper, and the kids were drawing their own murals. Others were playing cars and trucks, or house, or building creations with wooden blocks. All fifteen looked happy, busy, content. Annie liked the teacher of the five-year-old class, too.

"We have a morning and afternoon session," Miss Merryweather told Annie and the boys. Perky and personable, she seemed to have excellent control of the entire class, as well as the goodwill and affection of all her students.

"As I explained to Travis," Miss Merryweather continued, "the afternoon session is full, but we do have space available for all three boys for the morning. Class starts at eight and ends at noon. Meantime, if you'd like to let the boys play with the others for a few minutes, and see how they like it, while you go over the required paperwork and fee schedule—"

Knowing how much they'd missed their old play groups in Dallas, Annie consented. But as she studied the tuition and multiplied it times three, she also knew she couldn't afford it. Once again, Travis seemed to read her mind. He covered her hand with his. "I'll loan you the money for their tuition, Annie."

She shook her head vigorously. She didn't like being beholden to anyone. "I can't let you do that."

"You'll pay me back when you get your barbecue-sauce recipe perfected."

He suddenly sounded so sure of her success. Annie hadn't realized it until this moment, but she needed someone else to be confident in her, too. "You really think I can do it?" She studied his face.

"When you have the time and opportunity to work on it uninterrupted?" Travis nodded. "Sure."

Annie didn't deny she could get her business off the ground faster if she had time to concentrate on it. Nor could she deny how happy her three boys had looked to be around other children, either. Perhaps this was the best way after all. She certainly couldn't risk any more "green-apple" incidents, due to a lack of attention on her part. "I'm paying you back, Travis," she promised, deciding it would be both foolish and shortsighted of her to pass up his offer of assistance, especially when it would benefit them all in the long run.

Travis squeezed her hand, the warmth and reassurance of his touch a balm to her senses. "I'm sure you will."

Their last stop was the grocery store. While Annie concentrated on buying what she needed for more sauce and more experimentation, Travis pushed his own shopping cart and took charge of the boys. They were delighted to be able to "help Travis" with his grocery shopping.

Annie was less pleased when she saw what was in his basket. String cheese, milk, juice, their favorite kind of peanut butter, jelly, cereal, ice cream and cookies. Absent were meat and potatoes and anything and everything else she would've expected to see in a bachelor's shopping cart. "Who was selecting the groceries here, Travis, you or my boys?"

Travis shrugged his broad shoulders amiably. "They've got to have stuff they like to eat over at my house, too," he told her guilelessly, while Tyler, Teddy and Trevor cheered him on. "When they come to visit."

"Yeah, Travis says we're welcome anytime," Trevor said.

"Oh, he does, does he?" Annie said.

All three boys nodded vigorously.

Annie pushed her cart to the checkout line. She looked at Travis, knowing she was going to have to set some boundaries, and this apparently was going to be the place. "You and I," she told him softly but sternly, "are going to have to have a talk."

"YOU CAN'T KEEP doing this," Annie said as Travis helped her put her groceries away while the boys went out to play on the big wooden swing set out back.

"Doing what?" Travis lifted a bushel of juicy red tomatoes onto her kitchen table.

Annie lifted a mesh bag of sweet yellow onions onto the counter. She turned to face him as Travis unpacked fresh jalapeño, red and green peppers. "Being so helpful."

Travis shrugged, the muscles of his powerful shoulders straining against the soft blue chambray fabric of his shirt. He narrowed his gaze at her playfully. "I thought that was what neighbors were for, particularly neighbors who are number one on a lady's speed-dial."

Too late, Annie realized she shouldn't have let the boys see her doing that. She swallowed around the growing knot of emotion in her throat.

"I'm serious, Travis." She didn't want him playing husband to her or daddy to her boys, no matter how good or right it felt.

"So am I," Travis replied softly. Their eyes met and everything around them seemed to fade. "I'm here to help you, Annie," he told her quietly. "Any way. Anytime."

"Thanks," Annie said, aware her insides were warm and liquid, as if he had just thoroughly made love to her. She scowled at him. "But I think you've done enough for now." He had only been in her life in a significant way for a couple of days, and in that time he had made her achingly aware of how alone and lonely she had been since her husband had left her and her father had died. And much as she wanted to, she couldn't go back and undo the hurt that had been done.

"I could take the boys to school tomorrow," Travis offered.

Annie shook her head, aware she had already weathered more disappointment in one lifetime than she had ever wanted to endure. "I'll handle it."

He reached out and smoothed a strand of her hair. "Then let me pick them up afterward."

Aware it was all she could do not to lean into his touch and glide into his arms, tilt her face up for yet another stolen kiss, Annie shook her head. "I'll handle that, too," she said firmly, feeling a touch of panic. Travis had a way of making her forget all about her previous decision not to bring another man into her life in any intimate way until her boys were grown, if then.

"Goodbye, Travis." Deciding their lives were already far too intimately intertwined as it was, Annie smiled and, ignoring his look of disappointment, showed him the door. "Thank you and goodbye."

"It was so much fun, Momma," Trevor said as they arrived home the next day at lunchtime. "We got to do the mural and play toys and everything."

Telling herself she was not the least bit disappointed that Travis had not telephoned or stopped by once since the previous morning, Annie ushered the boys inside the Triple Diamond ranch house. "I'm glad you had a good time." She hung their pictures on the refrigerator, much as her own mother had done long ago, and then brought out the lunch of fruit, sandwiches and chocolate milk she had made for the boys.

"And we get to go back tomorrow, too," Tyler added as he settled down enthusiastically in front of his plate.

Teddy nodded. "Yeah, and then we can play with the other kids."

"That's great, guys." Annie smiled at her sons. She had expected them to be exhausted. No such luck. After their first day at school, they were more excited than ever. Annie was rarin' to go, too. In fact, she couldn't wait to get started on her barbecue sauce right after lunch. That morning, she had narrowed down the list of ingredients that enhanced her basic barbecue sauce to ten. She hoped to come up with a combination of those ten ingredients that would give her sauce a unique flavor.

Fortunately, the triplets had already thought up a way to entertain themselves for the afternoon while Annie worked in the kitchen. "We want to play school. Can we, Momma?" Trevor asked. "Can we bring our cars and trucks and blocks in the living room and pretend that's our class at the nursery school?"

"That sounds like a great idea," Annie said.

"Can we bring our coloring books and crayons out, too?" Tyler wanted to know.

Annie nodded. "Yes, just remember to put your crayons back in the box when you're through with them, okay? We don't want them to get stepped on and broken."

As soon as she had the boys situated, Annie went back into the kitchen. She started by adding a touch of vanilla and a touch of mesquite flavoring to the basic sauce. The flavor was unique all right, but not quite what she was looking for. She then tried onion and paprika. Apple cider and cinnamon. Bourbon and onion. Bourbon and mesquite and onion. Red wine and vanilla.

On and on she went, documenting each combination, putting the possibles in the refrigerator to chill, discarding the truly awful ones altogether. Every fifteen or twenty minutes she looked into the living room to admire whatever the boys were building, or they would come into the kitchen for a drink or snack. Before she knew it, it was almost five o'clock. The boys were clamoring for supper. Annie had fifteen combinations that worked pretty well. And a kitchen that was a royal mess.

"Guys, I have to clean up before I can start anything else," Annie said, pushing her hair off her forehead. "Can you give me a half an hour or so?"

Tyler, Teddy and Trevor nodded. "We're making you a surprise anyway with our school stuff," Tyler said.

"Yeah, we'll call you when we're ready to show you," Teddy added.

"No peeking till we're done," Trevor admonished.

Figuring they were creating the usual surprise play village made of building blocks, and cars, and miniature play-set people, Annie promised not to interrupt. While she washed the dishes and cleaned up, and yearned for another surprise interruption from Travis, she could hear the boys giggling and whispering excitedly. Thankful she still had some roast chicken and mashed potatoes left over from the night before, she slid the casserole into the oven to heat, sliced up some fresh fruit and heated green beans on top of the stove. By the time she'd set the table, poured the milk and dished up their plates, the boys were finished, too. "Come see what we did for you first, Momma," they said, beaming from ear to ear.

Proud at the way they had behaved themselves all afternoon, Annie let them lead her down the hall, and into the living room. Annie blinked. Stared. Let out a long, tremulous sigh. Looking at what they'd done—"just for her!"—she didn't know whether to laugh or cry.

IT WAS A LITTLE AFTER NINE when the phone rang. Thinking it might be Annie—missing him as much as he missed her and wanting to tell him how the triplets' first day of nursery school had gone—Travis put down the book he'd been reading and picked up the receiver. His pulse picking up in anticipation of hearing her low, sexy voice, Travis smiled and said, "McCabe here."

"Travis?" A child's voice demanded agitatedly. "Is that you?"

Travis frowned. "It's me, all right. Who is this?"

Shuffling sounds and a lot of whispering and what sounded like crying and sniffling dominated the other end of the line. "It's us, Travis!"

Travis put down his book with a thud. "Us as in Teddy, Tyler or Trevor?" he asked, wondering what kind of trouble the Triple Threat had gotten themselves into that Annie did not know about.

"It's all of us. And you gotta come quick!"

"Why? What's happened? Where's your mom?" he asked anxiously, already on his feet and hunting for his keys.

"She's in the bathroom!" Teddy spoke a little louder.

"She won't come out!" Tyler added from the background.

"She's been in there a long time. We think maybe she's stuck!" Teddy said.

"Stuck?" he repeated, confused. What could Annie possibly get stuck in, in her bathroom?

"Yeah. We heard her crying," what sounded like Tyler continued.

"And then she stopped!" Tyler said even more anxiously.

"We think maybe she broke her vanilla thing," Teddy added worriedly.

"She cried before when she broke her vanilla thing," Tyler interjected.

Travis grabbed his hat. He had no idea what they were talking about. He only knew Annie might be hurt, stuck or in some way in need of his assistance. And that thought alone was more than he could bear. "What vanilla thing?" he demanded.

"You know!" Tyler retorted impatiently.

No, Travis didn't. That was the problem. And right now he didn't know if he should call the fire department or the life squad. Or simply go over and check things out first. "Did you try to get into the bathroom?" he demanded, his frustration with the situation mounting. Clearly, Annie needed help with those boys even if she couldn't or wouldn't yet admit it.

"We can't go in there. We'll get in trouble," Tyler predicted.

"Yeah, we're s'posed to be in bed," Trevor said for his brothers.

"But somebody's gotta help her and that's why we speed-dialed you."

"Is she still crying?"

"Yeah. We hear-ed her a minute ago. She was crying real hard."

Which meant whatever had happened, she was still alive. If nursing a broken bone. Deciding it would be better if he went over and investigated first—he didn't want the boys seeing anything that would be traumatic for them—Travis said sternly, "Listen to me, I'll be right there, but when I get there, you boys are gonna have to let me in. Now go to the living room and sit down and wait for me so you can open the door. Okay?"

"Okay."

To Travis's relief, the boys were waiting for him when he arrived. Although it had been only two or three minutes since they had stopped talking on the phone, they were not only worried sick and in a total panic, they were crying hysterically, too. "You gotta get her out, Travis. You gotta get her out," Trevor wailed, waving both his little arms.

Teddy nodded and tugged on Travis's shirtsleeve urgently. "She's been in there a long time!"

"Yeah," Tyler added worriedly, jumping up and down on both feet. "She's never in there that long!"

Not sure what he'd find—had Annie slipped in the shower or tub—maybe hit her head, broken an ankle—Travis directed the boys to sit down and wait for him on the sofa. His heart racing, he grabbed the portable phone and, able to hear bathwater running on the second floor, headed straight for Annie's bedroom.

ANNIE KNEW she'd been in here a long time. Almost half an hour. But as she added more hot water to the cooling water in the tub, she knew she deserved a good long soak after the evening she had. Not that the calamity was over yet, she admitted wearily, taking a long sip of tea. The fact of the matter was, she'd be days getting that off the—

"What the—" she said as heavy footsteps sounded in the bedroom. Before she could so much as draw another breath, the bathroom door swung open without warning and Travis came charging through, a ranch-size first-aid kit in one hand, telephone in the other.

"Travis!" Annie shot bolt upright, nearly dropping her delicate china teacup in the process. "What in heaven's name are you doing here?" she demanded.

"Annie!" His alarmed glance skimmed her face before turning to the bubbles streaming off her breasts. He blinked. Blinked again and shook his head as if he'd just seen the most amazing thing in his life. "You're all right!"

"Of course I'm all right!" Annie fumed, abruptly aware she was naked as could be except for the cover of water and bubbles. Blushing furiously, she sank until her chin touched the top of the bubbles again. While Travis took in the dimmed lights, the soft music playing on the stereo, the vanilla-scented candles, the cup of soothing chamomile tea at her elbow.

"Why on earth would you think I wouldn't be?" Annie demanded of him, enraged.

"The boys—I—just a minute." Travis swept from the room as urgently as he'd come in.

Annie took advantage of his absence long enough to stand and, still streaming water everywhere, step out of the tub and wrap her soft pink terry-cloth robe around her. She was just bending over to shut off the hot water, when Travis came storming back in, her three pajama-clad boys in tow. She could tell by their faces they had all been crying and had in fact worked themselves up into quite a state of hysteria. She shook her head at them, almost afraid to ask, and even more afraid to hear the answer. "What is going on here?" Annie demanded. When they didn't answer right away—merely exchanged guilty looks—she continued sternly, "Did you boys call Travis?"

Reluctantly, all three nodded. "We thought you was sick or somethin'," Tyler said.

Trevor shrugged. "You never stay in the bathroom that long!"

Not when they were awake, she sure didn't. And for good reason, Annie thought. "I was taking a bubble bath," she exclaimed. "I thought you were asleep."

Abruptly, all three lower lips began to tremble. "We can't sleep."

"We're still sorry."

"We didn't mean to hurt the wall."

Travis lifted an eyebrow in Annie's direction. Annie glanced at him and felt all the more exhausted. Days like this...no, make that weeks like this...she wished she had a husband to share all this with. "It's a long story," she said wearily, running a hand through her hair once again. She turned back to the boys and knelt down so she was at eye level with them, "Guys, I told you. I'm not mad at you. I know you-all thought you were doing a good thing."

More sniffles all around. "But instead we made a mess," Tyler said, rubbing his eyes.

"Yes, you did. But you're not going to do it again, so it's fine." Annie reassured all three boys in turn. "We'll fix the wall."

The boys turned to Travis. "We wanted to do it, but Momma won't let us help."

Annie patted them all on the shoulder once again. "It's too complicated, honey."

Travis looked at Annie. "Maybe I can help," he said.

Normally, Annie would have refused. But tonight she was so exhausted, so discouraged, so completely wrung-out emotionally, she couldn't. She needed help and by golly, she was going to accept it. "How are you at reading bedtime stories and putting children to sleep—for real, this time?" she asked.

Travis shrugged and smiled. He spread his hands wide. "I'll give it a try."

IT TOOK AN HOUR and four complete readings of *The Velveteen Rabbit,* as well as a cowboy tale or two thrown in for good measure, but finally all three of Annie's sons fell sound asleep. For real, this time. Relief flowing through him, Travis walked downstairs to the living room.

This time the lights were on.

Annie was in her flannel pajamas and a robe. She had another cup of tea beside her and a yellow note-pad on her lap. Despite the long soak, she looked harried and exhausted. In need of both adult company and a friend. "Not as easy as it looks, is it?" she said, looking grateful for his efforts nonetheless.

Travis sat down on the sofa beside her. "I never thought it was," he said gently. "But then I grew up the oldest of four boys, so I know how rowdy and mischievous little boys can be.''

Annie sighed and looked at her previously beautiful living-room wall. ''Only this time they weren't being mischievous,'' she said.

Travis nodded in mute commiseration and followed her gaze to the gigantic crayoned mess. ''I know. They told me. They were just trying to make you a beautiful mural on the wall, just like at nursery school.''

''Only they didn't understand they were drawing on paper at school, drywall here.''

''And this paint in here isn't washable, I gather,'' Travis said dryly.

''Nope. Not at all.'' Annie pointed to the scribbled mural on the far wall. ''Which means I'm going to have to repaint.'' Annie yawned and propped her elbow on the back of the sofa, her head on her upturned hand. ''I was thinking a pale yellow. Something light and soothing. And hardy enough to stand up to anything that might accidentally get spilled or scribbled on.''

''Sounds good.'' Travis paused, knowing this had to be said. ''You know,'' he began with chagrin as he lifted his eyes to hers and rubbed his jaw with the flat of his palm, ''the reason I burst in on you like that—''

''You wanted to see me naked?'' Annie interrupted, tongue in cheek.

''Still do, as a matter of fact,'' Travis quipped, glad she was able to see the humor in such an embarrassing situation for them both. Not that he didn't want to see her naked. He did. But at the right time. In the right place. For the right reason. "But no," he continued gently. "That's not it."

Annie inclined her head ruefully and refused to look away. "A shame," she drawled.

"I know, isn't it?" Travis grinned. He covered her hand with his. "I thought you'd fallen and hit your head or broken an ankle—"

"And needed rescuing," Annie surmised.

And kissing. And holding. And loving, Travis thought. Sensing now was not the time to put the moves on her, not with any guarantee he'd get out of here without making love to her, he stood. Aware of the growing tightness at the front of his jeans, he shifted his weight and did his best to push the image of her, bubbles streaming down her taut, glistening body, from his mind. "Anyway, I'm glad you're okay," he said, and headed for the door.

"Travis?" Annie's voice stopped him.

He turned, his hand on the knob.

Annie smiled. "The look on your face when you burst in and saw me... It was kind of funny, too."

Travis chuckled, glad she hadn't been able to read his mind. "I bet."

"Thanks for caring enough to come investigate."

He nodded, for once feeling only slightly guilty about the promise he had made to her dad. "Anytime."

## Chapter Six

"We figured if we can't rustle up any grandchildren of our own, we'd just borrow some," John and Lilah McCabe told Annie early the next morning when they stopped by just after breakfast, along with their son Travis. The two elder McCabes were dressed for a day off, in casual slacks and loose cotton shirts. "So if it's okay with you and the boys," John continued with a jovial wink, "we'd like to pick up the boys at nursery school at noon and take them out to our ranch for a picnic lunch."

Lilah's bright blue eyes gleamed as she read Annie's mind. "Lacey and Jackson are going to be there, too, so we'll have four adults to three kids—"

An excellent ratio, Annie thought, particularly since all four adults had medical backgrounds. Aware there was one member of the sales team who had been largely silent thus far, Annie chanced a look at Travis. She knew the hours ranchers kept. He had probably been up half the night. Yet he looked freshly showered and shaved in a cream-colored chambray shirt, jeans, a straw cowboy hat held against his thigh.

She knew he had engineered all this. The thought that he cared enough to look after her made her feel safer and more relaxed. As though maybe she didn't have to handle absolutely everything alone anymore. And after striving to be so independent for so long, the change was nice.

"Sorry, guys, you're going to be outnumbered," Travis teased as he shot an affectionate look at Annie's three boys. Who, as it happened, were busy doing some calculations of their own as they ate their breakfast cereal.

"And if they bring their suits, they can go swimming this afternoon in our pool," Lilah continued her sales pitch as she sat down at the table with the boys and stirred cream and sugar into her coffee. "Then maybe you and Travis can both join us—and Wade and Josie and Shane and Greta—for dinner this evening."

The boys looked at Annie eagerly, clearly hoping she would say yes. She knew they hadn't been out nearly enough since they'd been back in Laramie. They loved to go to new places and meet people. And she needed a break from mothering; it was very kind of John and Lilah to give it to her. "That sounds lovely." Annie smiled her gratitude, then turned to her sons. "Boys, do you want to go?"

Tyler, Teddy and Trevor nodded enthusiastically. "We like to go swimming," Teddy told Lilah.

"We know how to swim, too," Tyler added seriously, taking a gulp of juice.

Trevor wiped his mouth with the back of his hand and chimed in, "But Mom makes us wear our safety vests and sunscreen anyway."

"But we know how to swim. 'Cause we took lessons."

"Only there's no pool here at Grandpa's," Teddy

sighed loudly, "'cept the baby pool Mom fills with the hose, and that's no fun."

"Boys, I don't think John and Lilah need to know all that much," Annie said, embarrassed at the depth of information they were revealing, as usual. Not to mention the "mural" they'd crayoned across an entire living-room wall.

"Nonsense." John sat down next to Lilah. Extending a hand, he high-fived all three of her boys. "We love hearing them talk. And we'll love having them visit."

Annie knew that was the case. John McCabe was not only a family physician, he was a family man.

"You and Travis will come, too?" John continued. "Say around six or so?"

Annie nodded, happy that John and Lilah had been gracious enough not to say anything about the living-room wall. If she didn't have so much to do, she'd paint it herself that morning. Certainly, she needed to find a way to get it painted before the boys' birthday party later in the week. "Can I bring anything?" Annie asked.

"Can't say I'd mind having some of that barbecue sauce of yours we've been hearing so much about." John winked.

Lilah nodded. "It'd go great with the chicken I'm going to toss on the grill."

"Done," Annie said. "Although, just so you know—" She shot Travis a glance, not sure whether to be pleased or embarrassed that he had been bragging about her efforts so energetically "—I'm still perfecting it."

"Travis said you'd been working on it diligently,"

Lilah added, sounding impressed by Annie's ambition.

Annie nodded as she shifted her glance to Travis once again. He was still lounging in the doorway, making himself at home in her sunny kitchen. She felt a thrill of excitement mixed with a tingle of alarm. He was just her friend and neighbor, a former protegé of her father's. Yet it felt so intimate having him here, so right. And that feeling increased as his glance slid approvingly over her short-sleeved red camp shirt, trim khaki shorts and sandals. He even seemed to like the red bandanna she had tied around her hair. His gaze touched her lips, lingered briefly, before returning to her eyes, "I'm headed into town now. So if you want, I could drop the boys at nursery school for you," he offered casually.

"Yeah, Mom, we want to ride in his new truck again," the boys said.

"Okay. But first we have to round up all your swim gear and give it to the McCabes, okay?"

"And we'll need a note from you, letting the school know that we'll be taking the boys at noon," Lilah said.

It took ten minutes to gather up everything the triplets needed. Another five to say goodbye to John and Lilah and get the kids buckled into Travis's brandnew Suburban. Annie waved goodbye to them, then went back into the house. Deciding to get started right away, she had another big batch of sauce simmering on the stove when the doorbell rang again forty minutes later. To her surprise, Travis was standing on the other side of the screen door. He had a paint sample card in his hand. "This the sunshine-yellow you had in mind?'' he asked her, pointing to a sample by that very name.

Annie studied the pale-yellow shade. ''It's exactly what I had in mind,'' Annie marveled.

''Good.'' Travis grinned. '''Cause I've got four buckets of it, mixed and ready to apply. Along with rollers, drop cloths and a paint pan. And this stuff is guaranteed kid-proof, by the way. Crayon, chocolate, ketchup, even ballpoint pen and marker is guaranteed to wash right off or your money back.''

Annie blinked. Travis McCabe didn't look like her fairy godmother, but he was certainly acting like one. ''Thanks.''

He dipped his head in acknowledgment, all the while holding her eyes. ''Glad to help.''

Annie lifted her chin. ''What do I owe you?'' She didn't mind him helping her out or vice versa, but if they were going to be neighbors, she wanted to keep things square.

Travis shrugged his broad shoulders. ''Lunch.'' He favored her with a sexy smile that did funny things to her insides. ''I figure I'll be about halfway done by then. Maybe a little more.''

Annie's eyes widened at the notion of spending the entire morning with him underfoot. ''You're going to paint this morning?'' she echoed in astonishment.

''Or however long it takes,'' Travis retorted casually. He swaggered back to the Suburban, all lazy confident male, and lifted the tailgate. Muscles flexing, he began unloading supplies onto her front porch, lifting the heavy gallons of paint as easily as if they were feathers. ''I figure the sooner your walls get back to normal, the sooner you'll feel better.''

Annie couldn't deny *that* was true. Especially with

the boys' birthday party coming up in a few days. She'd be embarrassed for their guests to see the living-room wall looking as if it had been scribbled to death. Yet she didn't have time to paint the entire room. And get ready for the party, too, and take care of the boys, and perfect and market her barbecue sauce. Hence, every time she looked at the "mural" her boys had done for her, she felt overwhelmed. As if there wasn't enough of her to go around. Never mind get everything done that needed to be done. She propped her hands on her hips. Not sure where this was leading, or where Travis expected it to lead. To her bed, maybe? Pushing the unexpectedly erotic thought away, she queried dryly, "Don't you have a ranch to run or something?"

Travis grinned. "And plenty of hands to help me do that." Silence fell between them. He looked at her gently. Protectively. "I want to be here for you, Annie, whenever—however—you need me."

The unsettling feeling in her tummy increased. "Because of my dad, or because you want my land?" Annie guessed.

Travis looked at her steadily. "Because of you."

ANNIE SPENT the rest of the morning alternately trying to add the pièce de résistance to her barbecue sauce and trying to reassure herself that Travis's earlier announcement had not been a declaration of intent. So what if he had kissed her and she had kissed him back. So what if there was an attraction simmering between them and he had looked at her as if he wanted to get her into bed. So what if he genuinely seemed to care about her boys and was darn good with them, and for them, to boot. None of that necessarily had to mean anything, did it? You could kiss someone a couple of times, even call on them in an emergency or two, and accept a favor or two, without falling into bed with them, couldn't you?

The bottom line was she liked having him around. So had her dad. And so did her boys. If he wanted her and the boys to temporarily give up their hard won independence and lean on him from time to time, and they wanted him to feel he could count on them right back, simply as one neighbor to another, that was all for the good.

She just had to stop making more of this than there was.

They were being neighbors. Friends. Maybe even good friends.

Despite the fact he still wanted to buy her land. And she still didn't want to sell.

Nevertheless, Annie couldn't help peeking into the living room from time to time, just to see how he was doing. Couldn't help admiring the rippling muscles in his shoulders, arms and back. The controlled precision of his fingertips. And the boundless energy with which he used both. Later, as the day warmed up, and he had to open the windows in the living room for ventilation, he took off his shirt, draped it over the back of a chair. When Annie caught sight of his buff chest and powerful build, she couldn't help taking a second, third, and even fourth look.

Abruptly, Travis swung around to face her. "Want something?"

Annie nodded and did her best to act immune to his bare chest. Even though her fingers itched to explore the velvety mat of cocoa-brown hair and suntanned skin and her mouth was bone dry. "I, um, need you for something,'' Annie managed to say finally.

Travis grinned as if he knew darn well the reason behind her sudden discomfort. He rubbed his hands on a rag. "Now those are words I thought I'd have to wait a lifetime to hear,'' he teased.

Flushing self-consciously, Annie rolled her eyes. Ignoring the jump of her nerves, she pivoted on her heel, taking in the scent of his soap and sweat mingled with his cologne. "Oh, hush, and come in here.''

"Yes, ma'am.'' Travis snatched up his shirt, shrugged it on and followed obediently. He was still doing up buttons as he entered Annie's kitchen.

The kitchen was filled with sunshine and pungent, wonderful smells. It was also, Annie had to admit, an unqualified disaster zone. Little saucers of barbecue sauce were everywhere. The counters were filled with every "secret ingredient'' possible, pulled from her pantry. Plus the cubes of homemade bread, diced chicken and beef brisket that were going to serve as part of his lunch and her experiment.

"Okay, sit down here.'' Annie pulled out a chair, and curling a hand around the swell of his biceps, wordlessly guided him into it. "I'm going to blindfold you in a minute.''

He shifted so he could look at her, his rock-hard thigh rubbing up against her knee. His eyebrows lifted. Interest simmered in his golden-brown eyes. "Getting a little kinky on me?''

Annie gave him a flirtatious look and did her best to ignore how good it felt, having him here with her all morning, both of them working separately, yet so near. She could too easily get used to this. "You wish I were getting a little kinky on you,'' she returned dryly. Sobering, she shot him a glance. "I just want to know if this sauce is as good as I think it is." She needed an honest opinion and she was sure Travis would give her that.

He angled his head to look at her, as if she was being silly to even ask. "I'm sure it is," he said.

"Don't spare my feelings, Travis," Annie warned as she bustled about the kitchen. All too aware of the heated glance he sifted over her from head to toe every time she turned her back, and sometimes even when she didn't, she said sternly, "I want the absolute unvarnished truth. To make sure I get it—" Annie whirled and gave him a flirtatious look "—I've put some not-in-a-million years flavors in there, too."

Travis shook his head in amusement. Paint flecks dusted the layers of his rumpled hair. "That's my Annie," he drawled, looking all the more mesmerized by what she had planned for them.

Trying not to thrill at the possessiveness in his voice, Annie spooned up a little sauce, dipped a morsel of roast chicken in it. Using her fingertips, she fit it between his lips. Waited with bated breath for his response.

"Mmm," Travis said finally, his sigh of satisfaction as soft as the sunshine pouring in through the kitchen windows.

Annie leaned against the table, her bare thigh treacherously close to his arm. "You like it?"

Travis groaned again, this time making no effort to contain his pleasure. "Yes. Very much."

Annie wasn't surprised. That particular sauce variation was sensational, if she did say so herself. Her confidence building, Annie grinned. She dipped another piece of chicken in yet another sauce, held it to his lips. Trying not to think about how those same lips felt moving over hers, or how much she wished he would kiss her again, she watched carefully as he devoured the second sample, too.

Travis frowned. "I don't like this as much."

"Good." Her chin tilted. "You're not supposed to." Expression serious, she fixed a third sample for him to try.

"Oh, yeah." Travis sighed, his expression one of pure ecstasy. "I like this one, too."

"Which one do you like better? The first or the third?" Annie asked.

Travis considered her for a moment, then leaned closer, bringing the tantalizing fragrance of his cologne with him. "I don't know," he said finally, shooting her another appreciative glance. He shrugged his broad shoulders. "They were both so good."

Being careful not to get too close, lest she lose her focus, Annie fit a fourth sample between his lips. "Try this."

"Nope," Travis said immediately. His lips curled in distaste. "Too vinegary."

Annie grinned, pleased her assessment was directly in line with his. "You and I are of one mind, Travis."

Travis waggled his eyebrows at her and teased in a soft low voice that sent thrills coursing over her body, "I always knew we would be."

Annie's eyes drifted to the playful curl of his mouth, the seductive glint in his eyes, then immediately moved away. She couldn't afford to get distracted, she thought as she briskly squared her shoulders and turned away. Not today, when she had her very own barbecue sauce to perfect....

The next ten minutes were filled with other sauces, other trials. To Annie's surprise, Travis was much more patient with the taste-testing process than she would have expected him to be. Maybe because he seemed to really be enjoying the various flavors, not to mention the feel of Annie's delicate fingers against his lips.

The problem was, she was enjoying the process of tempting him, and testing him, too. Maybe too much, Annie scolded herself sternly. Fortunately, they were nearly finished with the sampling. "Time for the blindfold," Annie said finally. She removed the red bandanna from her hair and tied it across his eyes.

Marveling that a take-charge cowboy like Travis would allow himself to be so vulnerable to her, Annie said, "Okay, I'm going to give you four in a row and I want you to tell me which is the best." She touched his broad shoulder reassuringly. "Ready?"

Travis shrugged. His slow smile could have inspired a thousand love songs. "As I'll ever be."

The next few minutes seemed to take forever as Travis sampled and gave opinions while she scribbled down the results. To Annie's delight, his tastes were as definite and fine-tuned as her own. And he didn't confuse any one variation with another once—even blindfolded. "All four are exceptional, Annie, but I'd have to say the third one is the best," Travis noted eventually.

That was what Annie thought, too, but she had to be sure. Her pulse racing, she said, "Are you ready to try the same thing again?"

"Sure," Travis said, not appearing to mind the blindfold in the least.

Not that it was going to be easy pretending this

was not a big deal, Annie thought. She was nearly going out of her mind, wanting to kiss him again, every time she fit her fingers against his soft, sexy lips.

"Well, what do you think this time?" Annie asked with a pounding heart and swiftly building libido after he'd gone through all four samples again.

His lips curved with self-assurance as he reported smugly, "The fourth this time."

*Right again.* "One last time?" Annie asked triumphantly.

"For you, Annie, anything."

"Well?" she demanded the second he'd finished.

"No doubt about it." He let out a low, admiring sigh. "The first."

Annie's triumphant laughter filled the room as she whipped off his blindfold. "Well, you and I are of one mind, at least," she told him happily. "I think I've found my secret sauce. I just need to try it out a little more, do some more taste tests, maybe with a group of people this time."

Travis really didn't think that was necessary, except to build Annie's confidence in her product. Building on her basic recipe, she had concocted a phenomenal sauce. But that was no surprise. Annie was one phenomenal woman. "What's in it anyway?" He pushed the chair back and vaulted lazily to his feet, hoping that would ease the building pressure at the front of his jeans. There wasn't much hope in ridding himself of the need to kiss her—and soon. That need was escalating with every excitement-filled second that passed.

The flush of victory pinkening her cheeks, Annie plucked the brown sugar and vanilla from the counter and headed for the pantry. She tossed her head and sent him a look. "I'm not telling."

Travis caught the drift of her perfume as she passed by him again. "C'mon." When her back was to him, he let his gaze rove the length of her long, sexy legs and bare feet. Her khaki shorts and camp shirt clung to her supple curves. What wasn't revealed, Travis could imagine just fine. "After all that tasting I just did, I deserve to know," he continued teasing her. When Annie raised her hands above her head to put the Tabasco sauce and vinegar in the spice cupboard, he caught a glimpse of her trim midriff. It looked every bit as sexy and silky as the rest of her.

"Nope." Annie shot him a playful glance over her shoulder that raised his pulse—and the stakes—another notch. "I'm still not telling and that's final." She plucked up a mesh bag of onions and another of garlic, and headed back to the pantry.

Travis fell in step behind her, appreciating the subtle sway of her hips. They'd been working all morning. It was time for a break. Past time. "Oh, I think you'll tell me," he said.

Annie tossed the onions into a vegetable bin, the garlic in another, then swung around to face him in a drift of flowery perfume. Her hazel-green eyes sparkled like Christmas lights and she looked so pretty standing there, her red-gold hair spilling down around her shoulders, he could hardly believe he'd let an entire morning go by without taking her in his arms.

"And why is that?" Annie prodded, backing up subtly and putting as much space as she could between them in the tiny space.

"Because if you don't," he promised softly, deciding there'd been too much space between them already. He took her gently by the arms and guided her back against the wall. "I'll have to kiss it out of you."

The sparkle in her eyes grew even brighter. Her freckles stood out against the creamy glow of her skin. She shook off his light restraining grip. "You wouldn't," she retorted flippantly, the pink in her cheeks growing even pinker. Her breath took on a quick, excited meter.

"Watch me." Deciding to go for broke, and do what he'd been wanting to do all morning, Travis braced a hand on either side of her.

She tilted her head up, the upward curve of her lips and the tilt of her head daring him to take this mischief even one step further. Still looking at him askance, she continued to breathe as if she'd just participated in a ten-kilometer run, and taunted cheekily, "I *still* won't tell."

Travis decided he liked the excited glitter in her eyes. He also liked the way her chest was rising and falling with each ragged intake of breath. "We'll see about that," he promised. Grabbing her around the middle, he pulled her against him. He fastened his lips on hers. And once he felt her surrender, felt the softness of her body against his, there was no stopping with just one kiss. He stroked, he teased, he caressed, until she surged against him, threading her hands through his hair. Until she was kissing him back passionately, wildly, wantonly.

Tormented beyond his wildest dreams, he drew back, cursing his own restraint. "Give up?"

Her breath coming hard and fast in her chest, she stood on tiptoe and nipped his bottom lip. "No," she retorted, just as stubbornly. Both hands flattened against his chest, she regarded him with a sultry look. Her eyebrows lifted contentiously as she demanded, "You?"

Travis shook his head slowly, already lowering his head and claiming her lips once again. "Not a chance," he growled.

As his lips fastened over hers, Annie moaned. She knew he had never expected her to meet him toe to toe when he had challenged her to a kiss. The truth was, she hadn't either. There was no room in her life for a man. She had complications galore already. But the instant his lips had touched hers, every bit of her resistance had fled. She could tell herself she didn't need Travis in her life, but she did. She could tell herself she didn't need to feel like a woman, but she did. She could tell herself she didn't need to be taken, made his, but she did. She'd been alone for so long. Without pleasure, without intimacy. To have Travis know her, to have him be able to make her head whirl and spin was an incredible, unexpected gift. She tilted her head back, stroking his tongue with hers. With unrestrained passion, she strained against him. Loving his warmth and his strength. And the feelings he engendered.

His lips left hers, dropping kisses at her temple, along the curve of her cheekbone, the delicate shell of her ear, the pulsing hollows of her throat. Their eyes met and the air between them reverberated with excitement and escalating desire. Annie had never felt anything like this in her life. "If I didn't know better, I'd think that you'd been wanting to do this all morning," Travis said.

Annie struggled to control her suddenly shallow breathing. I *have.* The only way she would survive this was by making light. Cheeks pinkening, she volleyed right back in the same devil-may-care tone, "You should never have taken off your shirt." Try as she might to forget it, she still had an image in her mind of him painting away bare-chested, the muscles of his broad shoulders, strong chest and long, sinewy arms flexing and glistening in the morning sun. And even though he had a shirt on again now, she still had an image in her mind of golden skin and a mat of thick, velvety cocoa-brown hair arrowing down into the waistband of his jeans.

Travis rubbed his thumb across her lower lip, absorbing the dewy moisture from their kiss. "Like that, do you?"

He had a beautiful body. What she'd seen of it thus far, anyway. She'd be foolish to try to deny it'd had an impact on her. Annie tilted her chin up and regarded him defiantly. Knowing she was honest to a fault, knowing that wasn't about to change, she said, "I'm uncomfortable admitting it, but yeah, I did like seeing you that way." It had brought a whole new—undeniably sexy—dimension to her view of the rancher next door. A whole new dimension to her view of herself.

He looked her in the eye, his expression suddenly, unbearably tender. His voice gentling, he lifted her hand and pressed his lips against the palm. "You should never be embarrassed about wanting to be close to someone, Annie."

"Is that what we're doing here?" Annie drew a galvanizing breath as shimmers of awareness swept through her. "Getting close?"

His eyes dancing with mischief, he backed her

against the wall again, braced his arms on either side of her. "You tell me."

Her heart fluttered once, in anticipation, then her lips were once again inundated with a kiss that was warm and sweet and soft. Held against him that way, it was impossible for her not to respond. She groaned low in her throat. Her arms swept around his back, and her hips tilted against him until she was vividly aware just how much he wanted her. Deep inside her, an exquisite empty ache throbbed, begging her to throw common sense to the wind, go with her feelings and make love to him. Here. Now. Before either of them could come to their senses.

As if reading her mind, he swept her up in his arms, carried her through the half-painted living room and into her bedroom. He set her on her feet, next to the bed. A tender smile on his face, he put both his hands on her shoulders. "If you want to opt out of this, Annie," he told her solemnly, a gentleman to the end, "now's the time."

In answer, she caught his head and brought it swiftly down to hers. She didn't know what the future held. Wasn't sure at that moment in time that she wanted to know. She only knew she hadn't made love in forever, hadn't wanted a man in forever. Now that she did, she didn't want to let the moment go.

Refusing this once to shy away from what her brain was urging her to do, Annie kept right on kissing him. Long and hard and deep. Slow and sweet. Until her heartbeat hammered in her throat and her breath sounded in her ears and she was so aroused she could hardly think. Her breasts molded against the hardness of his chest, and his hands swept up and down her back, tracing the shape of her, bringing her ever closer. She never thought she could feel so reckless and wanton. She just wished it were dark. Though the drapes were drawn, there was enough sunlight filtering through to illuminate everything. Including the battle scars of her pregnancy, tiny white stretch marks running up her sides.

"Maybe we should get under the covers," she urged, suddenly feeling a little nervous, and a lot shy. It had been a long time for her. A very long time. What if he found her lacking? She didn't want to disappoint. And common sense told her it was a lot easier not to disappoint in the dark. Why, oh why, had she let them start this in the middle of the day? she wondered anxiously.

A sexy smile tugged at the corners of Travis's lips. As in sync with her feelings as ever, he guessed at the reason for her sudden skittishness. "Shy?"

He clearly wasn't, Annie noted, zeroing in on the quiet amusement in his eyes. "And a little self-conscious," Annie admitted, her heart racing, her palms damp at the thought of what lay ahead. Was it going to be as wonderful and exciting as she hoped it would be?

"Well, you shouldn't be." Travis's gaze darkened appreciatively. He buried first his hands, then his face, in her hair. "You're beautiful, Annie." His breath was warm and coaxing against her skin. "And you don't need a mirror—or me—to tell you that."

Annie's heart skipped another beat. Having seen how he looked at her, having felt how much he desired her, she had expected things to proceed at a fast and furious rate, so she didn't have to think, didn't have time to wonder or worry. Not surprisingly, Travis appeared to want to savor everything as he discovered the woman she'd become. Wondering if there was anything he didn't plan to do to her before all was said and done, Annie shivered as his warm palms slid back up to her shoulders, down her spine. She had no doubt he'd pleasure her. But to risk more than just sex...to risk falling in love with him, and not being loved in return.... Was this what she wanted after all? She'd thought they could separate sex and love. Make it all about the physical and only that and then walk away. But now, looking into his eyes... seeing the tenderness there, the understanding... Suddenly, an uncomplicated tryst with no strings and no expectations didn't seem all that likely. "Travis—"

The look in his eyes invited her to run wild with him. His fingertips slid beneath her blouse, caressed the skin at her waist with infinite patience, inched upward. "Let me see you, Annie. Let me see all of you. I promise you," he told her hoarsely, looking at her in a way that made her feel wanted and beautiful in a way she'd never been. His voice dropped to a ragged whisper. "Neither of us will be disappointed."

Travis captured her lips, his kiss as demanding as it was tender. Her head swam with the scent and taste of him. Shudders swept through her body as he laid claim to her mouth with a predatory possessiveness— stroking, probing—until she wanted him more than she'd ever wanted anything in her life. In no particular hurry, he opened her blouse, pushed it off her shoulders, dropped it onto the floor. He sighed with sheer masculine pleasure as his glance roved her breasts. "Just as I thought. Beautiful. And soft as silk," he murmured as he smoothed the creamy flesh spilling from the lace cups with the pads of his thumbs. Her nipples beaded and ached even before he opened the clasp and slipped that garment off, too.

With the same single-minded attention he applied to everything else, Travis sat on the edge of the bed and tugged her down onto his lap, so she was sitting with her knees between his spread thighs. She felt his arousal pressing against her hip. Wanting to touch him, see him, too, she reached for his belt buckle and the fastening of his jeans.

He took her hand and lifted it to his shoulder. "We'll get there," he murmured huskily as he cupped the underside of one breast and lifted it toward his mouth. "Right now I want to taste you."

His lips fastened on her breasts, suckling gently. The friction of his lips and tongue was almost more than Annie could bear. Her back arched. Her thighs fell even farther apart. His free hand slid between them, stroking the tender insides from knee to pelvis and back again. Feeling herself beginning to slide inexorably toward the edge, and he hadn't even touched her there yet, Annie twisted away from him and vaulted off his lap. She was teetering on the edge of blissful oblivion. And she wanted him to catch up. "I'm way ahead of you," she gasped.

He laughed softly and caught her around the waist. Tugging her close, he unfastened her shorts. "Don't be so sure about that, Annie—it's been a long time— too long—for me, too." He pushed her shorts down, then with her wearing only her bikini panties, he pulled her back down, so her bottom was once again resting against his blue-jean-clad thigh.

Annie sighed as his glance fell to the pale lines zizagging along her hipbones, up her sides. "Stretch marks," she sighed, sorry he had seen them. "When you give birth to triplets, you can't avoid them."

His fingertips traced the slender indentations. "I love them, too."

Looking into his eyes, she could see he really did. "Now, where were we?" He grinned.

Annie barely had time to suck in a breath before he bent his head. Worshiping her other breast with the same loving attention as the first, he slid his fingers beneath the elastic of her panties. Touched and traced the dampness that flowed. As he caressed the satiny petals, finding the tenderest part of her, Annie quivered with unimaginable pleasure and nearly shot off his lap. Travis released a sound that was part chuckle, part moan, and one hundred percent male triumph.

Holding her fast with one strong arm laced around her waist, Travis stroked upward, in. His fingertips made lazy circles. Straight lines. Moved out. In. And out again. Over and over until Annie was writhing on his lap, mindless with desire. Her heart swelling with joy, with the tenderness she had found, Annie cried out. He kissed her temples, then her cheeks, framed her face between his hands. "Now?"

Annie nodded, never more sure of anything in her life. "Now."

Travis tugged off her panties and laid her gently on the bed. His eyes never leaving hers, he stripped off his clothes. She could see and feel how much he wanted her in the hard, throbbing length of him, the bunched muscles, the scorching heat of his skin. She could see how much he cared by the gentle determination—the restraint—in his gaze.

She trembled as he stretched out over top of her.

Wanting, needing more, she wrapped her arms and legs around him, and lifted her hips to his. He penetrated her slowly, cupping her bottom with both hands, lifting her, and filling her with the hot velvety length of him. And then they were one. Kissing hotly, rapaciously. Moving toward a single goal, seeking release, sweeping past barriers, climbing ever higher. Unable to help herself, unable to hold back a second longer, Annie arched against him, tears sliding out of the corners of her eyes. "Don't cry, Annie," he whispered, even as she moaned and shook and fell apart in his arms. "Don't cry."

"I can't help it," she whispered back, tears continuing to slip down her face as she looked deep into his eyes. She kissed him again, a kiss brimming with emotion and a hunger she hadn't known she possessed. "You make me feel so beautiful, Travis. So wanted." And she needed him more than she had needed anything in a very long time.

"That's because you are beautiful," Travis whispered harshly, trailing kisses down her neck. "And you are wanted." And suddenly it was his turn to come, her turn to give. She wanted him to want her as he'd never wanted anyone else. Blood rushed hot and needy through her veins. Moaning against his mouth, her tongue twining with his, she arched and plunged, the insides of her thighs rubbing the outsides of his. Bucking slowly at first, then writhing, demanding, doing what it took to make him, too, relinquish control, join her at the edge of ecstasy and beyond.

They clung to each other until the intensity passed. No sooner had they caught their breath than Travis cupped her chin in his hand and lifted her face to his.

Gently, he searched her face. "I want to make love to you again," he told her huskily.

Looking into his eyes, Annie believed it. This was not going to be a one-time-only love affair. And yet, given the demands of her life—the commitments, the responsibilities, the pressures, not to mention the time and energy it took to raise three little boys—was it possible they would have anything more than this one day? And if that were the case— "Travis..." Annie sighed. Knowing, like it or not, they had to be practical.

He bent and kissed her again, thoroughly, deeply. "Let me, Annie," he murmured, already taking her lips in a long, thorough kiss. Not about to take no for an answer. Not now or ever again. "Just let me."

"WE'VE GOT TO TALK about this," Travis told Annie as he put on his shorts and jeans.

Annie slipped on her panties and fumbled with the clasp on her bra. "I don't see why."

Travis stepped behind her and did it for her. "You haven't looked me in the eye since we left the bed." He watched as Annie flushed and snatched up her shirt. Sank onto the edge of the bed. "How's that for a reason?"

"I don't do this, Travis." Annie's hands trembled as she shoved her arms through the sleeves of her blouse. "I don't have affairs."

Travis had known that. It was what had made it so special. "Neither do I," he said quietly, retrieving his paint-spattered work shirt.

Annie hopped around, putting on her shorts. Misunderstanding what he meant, she whirled to face him. "Okay, so maybe making love twice in one afternoon doesn't constitute an affair—"

Travis pushed to his feet, not above using his superior size to inject some control in the situation. "It does in my book."

Annie regarded him in stony silence. "You're not saying—?"

Travis closed the distance between them. "Yes, Annie, I am. I don't make love to a woman like it's no big deal. When I do, it's for one reason. And one reason only. To claim her as mine."

The corners of her mouth trembled. Annie lifted her chin, clearly struggling for an air of cool challenge. "Is that what you think just happened?"

Reminded just how stubborn, single-minded and independent Annie could be, Travis shrugged. "What would you call it?"

That was just it, Annie didn't know. Was she in love with Travis? She couldn't be. He was her friend, her neighbor, her childhood rival for her father's affection. She couldn't afford to ruin things between them with any messy emotional involvement that ended as badly as her marriage had. She twisted her hands in front of her. "I'd call it inevitable."

Travis did his best to swallow his disappointment. "Because you hadn't been with anyone for a while?" he guessed.

The flush in Annie's cheeks deepened. "How did you—"

"Because I know you," Travis said gently, aware of an exultant sensation he had not felt in a long time. "And I know how much something like this means. Even—" he arched his eyebrow deliberately "—when you pretend it doesn't."

Annie's lower lip thrust out truculently. "I get lonely, Travis."

Loneliness was not what that had been about. Travis knew it, and he was betting, deep down, so did she. He shrugged. "So? I get lonely, too, sometimes. I'd wager everyone does."

Annie picked up her sandals. Leaning against the bureau, she put one on, then the other. "I get—"

"Horny?" Travis said for her, amused at her continued attempts to downplay what had just happened between them.

Annie glared at him. "That's *not* the word I would have chosen."

Travis nodded smugly as he continued buttoning his shirt. "Exactly my point."

Annie straightened, propped her hands on her hips and blew out an exasperated breath. "I don't—"

Travis closed the distance between them. He put his hands on her shoulders, holding her in front of him when she would have run. Again. "Lovemaking is connected with emotion for you, Annie, the same as for me."

Annie blinked in confusion and went very still. "I thought with men—"

"It was all physical and only physical?" Travis guessed at what she'd been about to say. He shook his head in admonishment. "Don't let anyone sell you that bill of goods, because it's just not true."

Annie sighed, returned to the bed and sat down on the edge of it. "Maybe you should tell that to my ex-husband," she said wearily.

"Why?" Travis sat down next to her. He reached for his boots. Slipped them on. "What did he do?

Cheat on you after the triplets were born or something?''

Annie grimaced. ''Before, actually, while I was pregnant and, as he so kindly put it, undesirable.'' Looking restless again, she vaulted to her feet.

Travis stood, too. ''He told you that at the time?'' he asked, stunned.

''Later,'' Annie delineated grimly. She reached for the sheet and began making the bed. ''When the triplets were six months old, we still hadn't made love again yet, and he got caught with his girlfriend.''

Travis walked around to the other side of the bed and lent a hand, studying her indignant expression all the while. ''You had no idea?''

Annie reached for the blanket, and then the bedspread. ''I knew he was unhappy. He hadn't really wanted a baby, and then to have triplets—well. Plus, my father was ill and it just seemed everything was going wrong at once.'' She sighed heavily.

Following her lead, Travis folded the bedspread down and placed the pillow on the edge of the seam. ''I'm sorry, Annie.''

''I know.'' Annie blew out a steadying breath. She smoothed the bedspread over the pillow, tucking it neatly over the pillow. ''So am I.'' She lifted her head and looked him straight in the eye as Travis again mimicked her actions and did the same. ''It's never any fun when a marriage that never should have been undertaken in the first place ends,'' she told him wearily.

Travis circled around the end of the bed. He wrapped a comforting arm around her slender shoulders. ''But just because your ex was a real SOB doesn't mean all men are.''

Annie leaned against him, the contentiousness she'd exhibited earlier drained out of her. "I know that, Travis," she told him wearily, resting her head on his shoulder.

"And yet...?" Travis probed, sensing there was more.

Annie turned to face him. "I don't want to read too much into this."

She wanted, Travis thought, to safeguard herself from hurt by not allowing herself to get involved with anyone again. He understood that. He'd done it for years. He also knew, from experience, it didn't work. Avoiding emotional entanglements only made you lonelier and more unhappy in the end.

"Suppose I do?" Travis challenged as he held her close. Cupping her chin, he lifted her face to his. "I want you, Annie." He scored his thumb across her lip. Seeing the disbelief in her hazel eyes, he continued softly, "I wanted you yesterday and today. I'll want you tomorrow." He pressed a silencing kiss to her lips before she could interrupt. "It doesn't matter what you say or do—that's never going to change."

*I WANT YOU, ANNIE. I wanted you yesterday and today. I'll want you tomorrow.* Try as she might, Annie couldn't get Travis's words out of her head. They were there through the cleanup of the kitchen, through the shower she took later when Travis retired to his ranch to do the same. Through the drive to John and Lilah McCabe's ranch, through the swim session, even during dinner, and the barbecue sauce–tasting that went on before, during and after the meal. And she was still thinking about his promise to her as they got ready to end the evening.

"Your sauce is a hit. And you're still a thousand miles away," Travis whispered in her ear as the boys reluctantly began the slow process of gathering up their things.

Annie bent to pick up a damp beach towel, still draped over a pool chair. *That's because I want you, too, and wanting you that way scares me. I don't want to be hurt again.* She shrugged, and knowing she'd be lost if she looked at Travis too closely, avoided his eyes. "It's been an eventful day."

"I'll say." Grabbing her by the waist, Travis tugged Annie behind Lilah's rose arbor, out of sight.

In an agony of anticipation, Annie watched his head lower. "Travis—"

"One kiss, Annie," he murmured, his low voice radiating with passion. He closed his arms around her determinedly and fit her against him. "That's all I'm asking."

The next thing she knew, his lips were on hers, and the towel she had in her hands was sliding to the ground. Realizing what she'd known all along—that it was as pointless to fight this as it was to fight him—Annie wreathed her arms about his neck and kissed him back. Thoroughly. And completely. And that was when they heard it—the riotous sounds of giggling times three.

"Oooooh," Tyler, Teddy and Trevor said in unison, "yuck!"

## Chapter Seven

"Kissing! Can you believe it?" Teddy asked.

Trevor shook his head in mute exasperation. He tossed the toy sailboat in his hand from one palm to the other. "There they go again," he said solemnly as Annie and Travis reluctantly, but quickly, moved apart.

"Doing what?" Jackson McCabe asked curiously as he sauntered around the rose arbor to see what all the commotion was about. Jackson looked at Annie and Travis, who were both standing there as innocent as could be.

"Mommy and Travis are kissing!" Tyler made a face. Annie blushed, and Travis ducked his head, despite themselves. They were busted now, Annie thought.

"Yeah, again!" Trevor and Teddy echoed simultaneously.

"They do this a lot?" Wade McCabe asked, looking both curious and amused.

"Mmmmmm...yeah." Teddy said. Trevor and Tyler exchanged glances and nodded their agreement.

"Really," Shane, the last of the McCabe clan, drawled, looking very interested too as he came up to join the group. He ran a hand through the shaggy, sun-streaked layers of his hair. "And just how long has this…kissing been going on?" Shane asked Annie's boys with a twinkle in his eyes.

The boys shrugged. Looked at one another. "Dunno," Trevor said finally, speaking for the group.

"And they—" Travis pointed at all three of his brothers and winked at Annie's sons "—don't need to know, either."

"Oh, we don't. Inquiring minds want to know," Jackson said, rubbing his jaw. He obviously wanted to know plenty. As did his other two brothers, Annie realized, sanguine. There was going to be no such thing as keeping their romance quiet—in this family anyway.

"Boys," Lilah spoke to all her sons as she approached them at the rose arbor with Greta close behind her. "Leave your brother alone. If Travis wants to go around kissing Annie, that's his business." Lilah looked at Annie kindly. "And hers, too, of course."

More than ready to move on to another subject, Annie said politely, "By the way, thank you so much for caring for the boys today."

Lilah beamed as proudly as any grandmother. "You're welcome," she said, her bright blue eyes twinkling merrily. "It did our hearts good to fill the house with 'grandchildren,' even if they aren't quite ours…yet." Lilah winked at the boys.

Travis's jaw dropped. He stared at his mother. "I can't believe you just said that," he murmured.

"Like Dad said," Wade quipped dryly, spreading his hands wide. "Three down and one to go. You're fighting a losing battle, buddy, if you think you're not getting married, too.''

Travis grimaced. ''Whether I am or not, that's up to me,'' he said sternly.

''And Annie,'' Greta, Shane's wife, said dryly. ''Speaking about weddings...what time is the rehearsal dinner Friday night?'' she asked Lilah.

Lilah smiled. ''We're meeting at the church at seven. We'll have the run-through of the ceremony and then head to the dance hall at eight. And Annie, we'd like it very much if you and the boys would come with Travis to see my husband and I renew our wedding vows.''

''We'd love to come,'' Annie said. She looked over at her crew. ''Wouldn't we, boys?''

The triplets nodded enthusiastically.

''Meanwhile, Annie,'' Greta interjected smoothly, ''would you have time to meet with me earlier that day—say, Friday morning during nursery-school hours? I've got a business proposition I'd like to run by you.''

''Sure,'' Annie shrugged. She glanced at Travis and could tell, just by the way he was looking at her, that even with everyone there, he was thinking about kissing her again. More amazingly yet, she was feeling the same.

''WE'RE S'POSED TO BRING our favorite storybook to school if we want to, for story time,'' Tyler told Annie over a breakfast of cereal, fruit and milk early the next morning. ''Miss Merryweather reads stories for twenty minutes every day. And she reads as many as she can read in twenty minutes.''

''Yeah, sometimes that's one, or sometimes it's

three or four,'' Trevor put in as he chased a straw-berry slice with his spoon, finally giving up and lifting the strawberry onto the utensil with his fingers. ''It just depends.''

''I know which story I want to take,'' Teddy said enthusiastically. Finished with his breakfast, he pushed away from the table and ran for the back of the house. ''It's my favorite one!''

''What favorite one?'' Travis asked, coming in the back door. He smiled at Annie. He looked handsome and at ease in a freshly laundered pale blue work shirt that was speckled with spots of paint, a very old, frayed pair of stonewashed jeans and boots that looked as if they too had seen better days. Taking off his hat, he hung it on the coat tree by the back door, ran a hand through the neatly combed layers of his hair.

''Are you gonna paint again today, Travis?'' Teddy asked, looking every bit as glad to see Travis as he was to see all of them.

Travis nodded and helped himself to a cup of Annie's coffee.

Annie watched Travis pull up a chair opposite her, and she wondered what it would be like to have Travis here with them every morning, sharing break-fast with her and the boys. There was no doubt he was like a ray of sunshine in their day, and the boys adored having him around, as did she.

''How come you're doing it again when you al-ready painted the wall?'' Tyler asked. He slid off his chair and found a way onto Travis's lap.

''Because the living room needs a second coat,'' Travis said as Trevor did the same.

''Here it is!'' Teddy came back in, waving a book.

He jumped up on Travis's lap, too, sitting squarely in the middle. He lifted the book in his hand to Travis so he could see the cover, too. "It's *The Daddy Book,* Travis, see?"

Annie's heart clenched. She'd bought that book when the boys were little. It was one of a set about families. There were volumes about brothers, sisters, mothers, fathers, grandparents, aunts, and uncles and cousins. Even one about pets. And the boys had adored them all.

"I want to show you what kind of daddy you are, Travis." With his brothers watching raptly, Teddy opened the book. He thumbed through the pages, past the fireman and policeman. "This is our daddy," Teddy said, pointing to a man in a suit. "He carries a briefcase like this, but we never get to see him no more."

"Reece is living in Japan now," Annie explained to Travis. "And you will get to see him when he comes back to the States," she said to Teddy.

Looking completely cozy on Travis's lap, Teddy asked, "When's that gonna be?" He wrapped his arm through Travis's.

"I'm not sure," Annie hedged, aware that Reece's promises on that score were about as valid as an out-of-date sale coupon. "Another year or two. It's so expensive to fly back here, he can't come to Texas very often. But when he does, I'm sure he'll see you." Annie would make sure of it. No way was she letting him hurt their sons that way. The little interest Reece showed in them was painful enough.

"Then our daddy won't be at our birthday party tomorrow," Tyler guessed, looking sad about that but not really surprised. Maybe because Reece had yet to make one yet.

"No, but I'm sure he'll call to talk to you boys and wish you a happy birthday," Annie said firmly. Mentally, she crossed her fingers, hoping that was true. Reece wouldn't be so cruel as to forget his sons' birthday altogether, especially now that they were getting old enough to comprehend the slight. And she had sent him that letter, reminding him, the month before. Still...

"Is he gonna send us a present?" Tyler asked.

Annie shifted uncomfortably, trying not to read the pity in Travis's eyes. "I'm sure he will. He just may not have mailed it yet—it takes a long time to mail things from Japan, so you might have to wait a long time for it to get here," Annie explained with a great deal more assurance than she felt.

To her relief, the boys seemed content with that explanation, at least for the moment, and she would eventually get a birthday present for them from their well-to-do dad even if she had to twist his arm to get it.

Oblivious to her thoughts, Teddy continued turning pages, flipping past the doctor, and grocery-store clerk, until he reached the heroic-looking figure of a cowboy on a horse. "See?" Teddy told Travis, beaming. "This is the kind of daddy you are!"

"I'm a cowboy all right," Travis said, looking about as much like a daddy as you could with all three of her boys seated comfortably on his lap. "But I'm not a daddy—not yet anyway."

Blushing, Annie got up and went to retrieve the boys' shoes. They really had to get to nursery school before this talk somehow segued into a birds-and-bees discussion. As it well might.

"How come you're not a daddy?" Annie heard Trevor ask. She tried not to let her imagination veer off into fantasies of sharing her life and her sons with Travis, of having cozy mornings like this, and even nicer evenings, of sharing his bed, and maybe even making a baby or two of their own.

Travis grinned as Annie came back with three pairs of sneakers. He seemed to know what she was thinking.

"Because I don't have any kids of my own," he said as Annie handed out the appropriate colored shoes to each boy.

Tyler twisted around on Travis's lap and wreathed an arm around his neck. He looked up at Travis with so much adoration it practically broke Annie's heart. "Don't you want any kids?" Tyler asked.

Travis's eyes darkened. "I do want children. Very much."

Trevor frowned as he slid off Travis's lap and plopped down on the floor to put on his shoes. "Then how come you don't got any?" he asked.

Travis glanced over at Annie for a heart-stopping moment. Something in the look he gave her made her think he had already made up his mind on that score, too—made her think he knew exactly what he wanted, and was just waiting for the right moment to come along.

"Because the right woman hasn't come along," Travis said, still holding her eyes. "Until now," he added in a soft sexy voice that sent shivers up and down Annie's spine and brought to mind all the passionate kisses and caresses they had shared the day before.

"Well, then, can you be our daddy?" Teddy asked as he struggled to put on his shoes.

"Yeah," Trevor added. "Since we never get to see our other daddy?"

Listening to her boys, seeing the need on their up-turned faces, Annie's heart broke all over again.

Travis smiled down gently at the Triple Threat. All the love Reece should have felt for them was in Travis's golden-brown eyes. "I can be your friend," he said kindly. "And I can do all the things with you that daddies do."

But he couldn't father them, Annie thought sadly. Reece had already done that. This was just one of those times when life was so unfair.

But the boys, much to her relief, were not thinking about what Reece wasn't doing for them. They were thinking about all the things Travis could—and would—do.

"Things like..." Teddy paused, thinking hard about all the things daddies did, then, "Take us places, and read us stories, and take care of us when we're sick 'cause we ate too many green apples that we wasn't s'posed to eat."

"I can do all those things," Travis said gravely, ruffling Teddy's hair.

"Will you kiss our knees if we fall down and hurt 'em?" Trevor pressed.

Travis ruffled his hair, too. "I can do that, too," he said, smiling.

"What about tucking us into bed?" Tyler asked. Shoes on, he jumped to his feet and climbed back on Travis's lap. "We liked that, you know," he said,

putting his arm around Travis's neck once again.
"When you readed us stories 'cause Mommy was
busy taking her bubble bath."

"I enjoyed that, too," Travis said. He hugged each
of the boys in turn.

Reluctantly, Annie consulted her watch. "Okay,
guys, time to brush your teeth. I don't want you to
be late for school."

"Okay, Momma."

When they dashed off, Travis rose. "I can drive
them to school for you."

Annie shook her head. "I need to stop by the of-
fice-supply place, the bakery and grocery anyway."
She wanted to give them both time to absorb what
had happened the previous day, and make sure it was
what they really wanted, before they let it happen
again. Not that he appeared to need time. He seemed
to know exactly what he wanted. When and why. But
then, he had a thriving business. She had a fledgling
one. He was single, without a personal commitment
in the world to anyone, save himself. She was divorced, with three kids. It wasn't that simple for her,
no matter how much he seemed to think it was. Her
kids had already weathered one divorce. She didn't
want them weathering a botched relationship, too, especially when it came to someone they looked up to
as much as Travis.

His slow smile threw her senses into a riot. Letting
her know in an instant that dodging him—dodging
time alone together—would not change what he
wanted, either. "I'll be here painting then," he said
with a shrug.

For the first time in her life, Annie knew what it
was like to be pursued—really pursued—by a man

with love on his mind. A man who wouldn't take no
for an answer. "Travis—"

"I want to do this for you, Annie," he told her
softly. He gave her a steady look that set her pulse
points to pounding. "I'm going to do it." And there
was nothing she could say, nothing she could do, to
dissuade him.

That quickly, the subject was closed.

FOR TRAVIS, it was the slowest-moving morning on
record. Without Annie and the boys there, the Triple
Diamond ranch house was oddly quiet, and very
lonely. That surprised the heck out of him. Up until
now, he had always thrived on being alone. Not any
longer. Annie and the boys were constantly in his
thoughts. He missed them whenever they weren't
around. Maybe more than he should have, Travis decided as he rolled on a second coat of the sunshine-
yellow paint Annie had selected for her living-room
walls. They'd just been involved a couple of days and
already he was feeling more like a husband to her and
a father to her boys than he could ever have imagined.
He had a history of helping women. He didn't have
a history of becoming this emotionally involved, or
falling head over heels in love with a woman on the
spur of the moment, but that was what he had done.
He wanted Annie to be his for all time—starting now.

Convincing her that was wise was another story.

Maybe because of her experience with Reece, she
was skittish. Wanting to be close to him one minute.
Wanting to run the opposite direction the next.

He was going to have to make her see that the two
of them were a good thing, period.

He was going to have to convince her that this

wasn't a chance she should be afraid to take, that running was no longer an option. What they had found came along once in a lifetime, if then. They'd be fools to let it go.

Just as he'd been a fool to ever promise Joe that he would work behind the scenes to protect Annie and the boys. Because now a lie of omission stood between them. And Travis saw no way to get rid of it without breaking his promise to her dad.

Travis was still frowning and wondering what to do about that when Annie's sedan rumbled up the driveway. He wiped his hands on a cloth and went out to greet her. Despite all the running around she had done—evident by the number of packages he saw stashed in the car—she looked fresh and pretty as she stepped from the car. "Get everything you needed?" he asked, noting, as usual, that several wavy strands of red-gold hair had escaped the confines of the butterfly clip on the back of her head, and were framing her forehead, the nape of her neck, her cheeks.

Annie nodded as she smoothed the cuffed hem of her walking shorts back into place. "And then some," she said.

Forgoing, for now, the desire to take her in his arms and kiss her thoroughly, Travis stepped forward to help her carry in her purchases. "More barbecue sauce?" He nodded at the bushel of vine-ripened tomatoes and sweet onions.

Annie nodded. Her chest rose as she drew in a deep breath. "Now that I've perfected my recipe, I need to get a bunch of it made. Plus, I've got to come up with a better name and packaging idea." As she bent down to start pulling packages out of the front seat, her shorts hitched up slightly in the back. Travis caught a glimpse of smooth, slender thigh before he let his gaze drop to her sexy, dimpled knee, curvaceous calf and trim ankles.

"And I got all the stuff—napkins, cups, punch, ice cream, hot dogs and buns, fruit and chips for the kids' birthday party." Annie filled his arms, then her own, and led the way into the house.

"Isabel, Lacey's mom, is making the cake at her bakery," Annie continued as Travis walked behind her, his glance falling to the sexy saunter of her heart-shaped hips.

"And she'll have it ready for me tomorrow when I pick up the boys from nursery school," Annie continued. She stopped abruptly as they walked through the living room. "You've almost finished the second coat," Annie said admiringly.

Travis shrugged and leaned down, so his face was next to hers, her lips close enough to kiss. "It goes a lot faster when all the prep work has been done and there are no beautiful women around to distract you."

Annie blushed, as if remembering the passionate lovemaking that had distracted them the day before. Her breath suddenly coming a lot more erratically, she stepped back. He searched her eyes, sensing a threshhold had been crossed, and then the phone rang.

It was all Travis could do not to swear at the interruption. He wanted time alone with Annie. Time for courting and romance. Thus far, this morning anyway, he was batting zero.

Annie, however, was still acting on the cautious side, and didn't seem to mind. She shrugged her shoulders, stepped back and said lightly, "Saved by the bell."

"For now," Travis murmured as he followed her into the kitchen.

Annie reached the phone on the third ring, picked up the receiver and said hello.

"Annie Pierce—super woman in action," she said, tongue in cheek. As she listened to the person on the other end of the line, her expression fell. The merry glimmer left her hazel eyes. "Of course, yes, I'll be right there," she said seriously as Travis took the ice cream from her and put it in the freezer.

"Travis, too?" Annie bit her lip. "Well—if you— all right. Twenty minutes, tops. I promise."

"What's up?" Travis said as soon as Annie hung up the phone.

"Miss Merryweather wouldn't exactly say. Just that we need to have an emergency parent-teacher conference, and that you and I need to get there right away."

TEDDY, TYLER AND TREVOR were sitting on the "time-out bench" in the director's office when Annie and Travis arrived at the nursery school. To Annie's relief, they looked glum and bored but no worse for wear. While the director went off to take over their class, Miss Merryweather came back to the office to join them. Annie didn't need a crystal ball to tell her that her sons were in big-time trouble.

"It must have been bad, whatever they did," Travis joked, to cut the tension.

Tyler, who had cheered up the moment he saw Travis there with Annie, lifted his hands, palm up. "Naw, we was just kissing some girls the way you been kissing Mommy, Travis."

Knocked for a loop by what her three sons had

done this time, Annie became furious. This once she wished they would beat around the bush rather than blurt out whatever was on their mind.

"Not to mention," Miss Merryweather said, taking up where Tyler had left off, "that they refused to stop when asked."

And to make matters worse, Annie realized with ever-escalating pique and humiliation, Trevor refused to apologize. "We wanna be just like Travis, and that's what Travis does," he explained to all the adults in the room.

"And anyway," Teddy put in, defending himself and his brothers hotly, "the girls liked it."

If her boys had even half of their new role model's skill in the romance department, Annie thought wryly, she didn't doubt that for a moment. "Nevertheless," Annie said solemnly, doing her best to suppress a moan of utter dismay, "you are not allowed to kiss girls at school, guys."

"How come?" Teddy wanted to know. He sat on the edge of the time-out bench, swinging his legs. He lifted his eyebrows in perfect child-logic. "Travis does it all the time."

This time it was Miss Merryweather's turn to lift an eyebrow.

"I—wouldn't say all the time," Annie sputtered, feeling as if she was going to die of embarrassment here and now.

All three boys opened their mouths at once, ready to correct her.

Fortunately, Travis cut them off by hunkering down in front of them. "You can't keep kissing the girls, because you're not old enough," Travis said before they could voice the arguments that were likely welling up inside them. "You need to be at least sixteen before you go around kissing girls, guys."

Way to go, Annie thought, silently applauding Travis's answer. Now, why hadn't she thought of that?

"How come we got to be sixteen?" Teddy persisted.

Travis leaned conspiratorially close. He spread his hands across all three boys' knees, calming them simultaneously with the gentleness of words and touch. "Because it's good to make them wait," Travis said, poker-faced. "They like it more when you do."

Ignoring the amused smirks of Annie and Miss Merryweather, Travis straightened. "'Course, that's a cowboy secret," he said, still looking at the boys. "So not everyone knows it." He paused significantly as his words sunk in. "I'm trusting you three buckaroos to keep it for me, and of course, do what cowboys do when it comes to girls."

"Which is...?" Annie asked warily, almost afraid to hear what manner of manly advice was going to come next.

"Treat them like the ladies they are," Travis said solemnly. He raised a lecturing finger their way. "And that means no kissing the girls until they're sixteen, too."

The three boys nodded.

Miss Merryweather breathed a sigh of relief.

She seemed to realize, as did Annie, that thanks to Travis, smooching was no longer going to be a problem in the five-year-old class. Miss Merryweather stood. She looked anxious to bring the parent-teacher conference to a close. "I'm glad we got that cleared up," she said, dusting off her hands.

"Me, too." Annie said. Meaning it. She turned to the boys and gave them a stern look. "Now, boys, I think you owe Miss Merryweather and everyone else in your class an apology."

"We're sorry," the Triple Threat said in unison.

"You're forgiven." Miss Merryweather smiled in a way that let them know she meant it from the bottom of her heart.

"Does this mean our time-out is over?" Teddy asked.

"Yes." Miss Merryweather consulted her watch. "We've just got time to go back for friendship circle." She beamed a hearty invitation at Travis and Annie. "As long as you're here, would you like to join us?"

"DID YOU CONVINCE HER to let you buy her ranch yet?" Wade asked later that afternoon when Travis met his brothers in town for a little midweek R&R and birthday-party strategy session.

"We haven't really discussed it." Travis took his beer over to a table at the far side of the bar, as far from the door as possible.

Wade looked at Travis in surprise as he sat down opposite him. A consummate businessman and multimillionaire himself, he knew how important it was for Travis to expand his ranch and double the amount of acreage he owned. The only way to do that was through the property Annie owned.

"Not that I could buy it now anyway," Travis continued as his other two brothers pulled up chairs and joined them at the sturdy oak table. "Annie's not speaking to me at the moment."

"Two guesses why." Shane grinned, taking a

handful of unshelled peanuts from the stainless-steel bucket in the center of the table.

Jackson, who was on call and unable to drink as a consequence, nodded as he sipped his tea. ''Because everyone in town knows you've been taking bubble baths with her?''

Travis drank his beer and glared at all three of his newly married brothers. ''I never took a bubble bath with Annie!'' he leaned across the table and insisted.

Wade shrugged and lifted his hands. ''According to Josie, who got it from Laccy, who got it from Meg Lockhart, who heard it when she was helping out at the nursery school, that's the story the boys are telling everyone.''

Shane nodded and gestured vaguely as he continued updating Travis. ''Something about you being in the bathroom with her, and candles, and music, and wine...''

Travis thought about the way Annie had looked in the candlelight, the bubbles streaming off her luscious creamy breasts as she bolted upright in the tub. Damn, but she was one pretty woman, wet or dry. Travis swallowed, aware he had gotten hard, just thinking about making love to her again. ''Annie was drinking tea,'' he informed his brothers with a scowl. ''And the music and candlelight were for her!'' He only wished they had been for him.

''So you *were* in the bathroom with her!'' Shane crowed gleefully.

Travis blew out an aggravated breath, wondering how ticked off Annie was going to be at him when she found out that story was making the rounds, too. As if she hadn't been embarrassed enough at the nursery school at noon. "I stopped by," he corrected grimly.

"Obviously." Wade waggled his eyebrows in true Marx Brothers fashion.

"I thought there was an emergency," Travis continued. If Annie was ever going to stop being mad at him, the true story had to get out. Using his brothers and their new wives and friends as a conduit was a pretty quick way to do it.

Guffaws abounded all around. "What kind of emergency?" Jackson teased, bringing his usual medical expertise—and jokes—to the group. "The kind that requires mouth-to-mouth?"

Travis downed the rest of his beer in a single gulp. "I didn't kiss her when she was in the tub!" But he had seen her breasts, and the sight of them—so pale and round and lovely—not to mention the sight of the rest of her as they'd made love—would haunt his dreams for the rest of his life.

Wade tossed a peanut into his mouth. "Then what did you do?"

Travis shrugged innocently and replied in all truthfulness, "I read bedtime stories to her boys so she could finish her bubble bath."

More laughter followed, as well as a few salacious winks. "And then you kissed her," Jackson guessed.

"Then I went home," Travis corrected sternly, aware there wasn't anything he wouldn't do to protect Annie and her reputation.

"Travis, Travis, I'm disappointed in you." Shane shook his head in silent admonition. He leaned forward urgently. "If you want to make a woman yours, you've got to put the moves on her."

Travis sat back in his chair. "I know how to handle my woman."

His brothers elbowed each other. "So Annie is your woman?" Shane asked eventually.

Travis, having had enough, glared at his three brothers. "When did you three turn into matchmakers?" he demanded as he signaled the bartender for another round.

"Since we all got hitched," Jackson said easily. When the bartender showed up, he ordered a round of cheeseburgers and fries for all of them. "We want you to get hitched, too."

Travis sighed, and knowing a change of subject was in order, brought the topic to the reason he'd asked his brothers to meet him here, after work, in the first place. "Well, that's not going to happen unless we show up at the birthday party tomorrow with the right presents for the boys." With the boy's father bailing on them, even if Annie couldn't quite admit it, he wanted them to have the best birthday ever, nevertheless. A cowboy kind of birthday. The kind they would have gotten if their Grandpa Joe was alive. The kind Travis—and Annie—could still give them.

Wade rubbed his jaw and studied Travis thoughtfully. "You still want to get the kids complete Western-wear outfits?"

Travis nodded. "I want 'em looking like cowboys from head to toe."

ANNIE WAS SITTING in the porch swing in front of her house when he drove up. She was wearing a plain V-necked white T-shirt, pale blue and white plaid flannel pajama bottoms and a pair of pale blue ballet-style slippers on her feet. In lieu of the porch light, she'd lit several citronella candles, and placed them strategically around her. They not only protected her from the mosquitoes always out that time of night, they illuminated her in a soft, romantic glow.

Travis cut the engine on the Suburban and got out. He wasn't surprised that she didn't so much as look his way as he sauntered toward her.

His mood tense but hopeful, he took the porch steps two at a time and crossed beneath the overhang of the red tile roof to her side. "The Triple Threat asleep?" he asked softly.

"Yes." Annie pushed the words through set lips. To his disappointment, she did not look at him directly and made no effort to scoot over to one side so he could sit with her comfortably on the chain-hung swing.

Travis seated himself on the low stucco wall that surrounded the stone-floored porch and stretched his long legs out in front of him. He was close enough to her to see the damp hair on the nape of her neck and smell the intoxicating fragrance of her perfume, and he knew she had just taken another of her long bubble baths.

"Still mad at me?" he asked softly. And unnecessarily, as he already knew the answer to that.

"Yes," Annie murmured noncommittally. The color in her fair, freckled cheeks deepened.

Seeing the depth of her humiliation, Travis felt the first stirrings of panic. He was irritated with Annie for not being able to shrug off the gossip about the two of them that was now circulating in Laramie, thanks to her very talkative three sons. He had expected the two of them might even have a fight about it, with him urging her to blow it off and her refusing to let it be that simple. He hadn't expected her to put him in the deep freeze, and leave him there indefinitely. Which was, Travis realized, studying the mutinous line of her lips and the chill in her attitude, exactly what she was planning to do. "For kissing you?" he asked, his tone clipped.

Annie's mouth pursed. "And making the two of us the brunt of gossip."

Travis studied her, wishing he didn't recall quite so accurately how sweet that bare mouth of hers tasted or just how well she could kiss. "There are worse things."

Annie lifted an eyebrow and shot him a pointed look. "Like what?"

Travis was quiet. He knew he deserved that. He had moved way too fast, put too much pressure on her. But damm it, what was he supposed to do? They'd taken their relationship a giant step forward, making love the way they had. Now she acted as if she wanted to forget all about it, pretend it had never happened, and make darn sure it would never happen again. And he wasn't sure he could do that. He wasn't sure he wanted to do that. He also knew that, unless he coaxed her into forgiving him, he'd never be back in her bed again, or vice versa.

He shrugged in answer to her question about what could be worse, and searched for a few close-to-home examples. "Like getting caught in front of your mother's whole bridge club—like Greta and Shane did—or lured out of a bachelor party and lassoed but good by Lacey—the way Jackson did—or finding out the tomboy you're trying hard to turn into a lady isn't who you think she is, the way Wade did."

Annie studied him, silently assessing, deciding, Travis figured, if she could trust him again. He wanted her to feel she could. He figured she had to know, deep down, he had never wanted this to happen. And in fact would have moved heaven and earth to make sure it didn't. He just hadn't foreseen it. And neither had she.

Annie sighed deeply. "You McCabe boys sure have a way of getting yourself into trouble," she said finally, shaking her head.

Travis grinned. She was weakening, he could see it. He moved from the wall that edged the porch to the swing. "And out of it, too."

She scooted over just enough to make room for him. "I like having you around," she said stoically. "Knowing I can count on you."

Travis slipped an arm around her shoulders. "I like being here, too."

Annie settled into the curve of his shoulder as they continued to swing. "But I've never had the boys in nursery school before," she said, her low voice taking on a practical edge.

Travis grinned. "I've never had any in nursery school, either," he teased.

Annie shook her head and rolled her eyes. She plucked at the thin fabric of her pajama pants covering her thigh. "I wasn't prepared for the way they'd be spilling out the most intimate details of my life to everyone."

Travis watched as some of the color left her cheeks. Then, rubbing his fingers along the curve of her shoulder, he commiserated gently, "Never mind the way it spread like wildfire, with every kid in their class running home to tell their friends and their moms what had happened in school with the kissing incident—''

''And let's not forget why that happened, Travis.''

Ouch, Travis thought. He held up both hands in a posture of surrender, knowing he was to blame for that. He never should have kissed her when the triplets—or anyone else—was around. No matter how much she needed to be held and kissed, or how much he needed to hold and kiss her. ''You got me there,'' he said, wishing he could take back the foolish risks, so the two of them would not be in this position of having to decide whether to continue or put an immediate end to their affair.

''Word of mouth is a powerful thing,'' Annie lamented sternly. She edged away from him, to the other end of the swing.

Travis nodded, having no choice but to agree with her. ''You're right.''

''And now that I know it's going to be that way—'' Annie vaulted from the swing and began to pace the length of the front porch.

Travis watched her stride back and forth, long legs flashing, breasts jiggling softly. ''You don't think you can kiss me again?'' he guessed.

Annie nodded, looking every bit as disappointed as he felt at her assertion. She propped her hands on her hips, the indignant action jiggling her breasts even more. ''Do you know there's even a story about me drinking whiskey in my pajamas in the morning, with you coming in to stop me and save the day?''

Travis struggled to contain both a groan and the rising heat in his groin. ''That is sort of the way it happened,'' he allowed.

Annie blew out an impatient breath. Stomped

closer. "You know I was just trying to taste the liquor to see if it was still good," she reminded him emotionally, the color in her cheeks heightening once again.

Travis stopped the swing and stayed where he was, hoping she would join him again. "Until I stopped you by tasting it for you," he continued drolly, still seeing a little humor in that. He didn't know what it was about Annie, but when he was around her, he was constantly overreacting.

Annie spread her hands wide on either side of her. "Can you imagine what people are thinking?" she demanded incredulously.

Travis grimaced as he recalled the conversation he'd had with his brothers. Ten to one, before too long, his parents would want to put their two cents' in, as well. "I have an idea," he said, determined someway—somehow—they would handle this without sacrificing the passion they'd found.

Annie stomped even closer, not stopping until they were once again toe-to-toe. "You're not all that upset," she accused, glaring at him.

"Maybe," Travis said, grabbing her hand and guiding her back down to sit beside him, where she belonged, "because I've figured out a way to stop it."

# Chapter Eight

"Married!" Annie exclaimed, turning to face him, a look of amazement on her face. Her knee touching his thigh, she rested one arm along the back of the wooden porch swing, again looking ready to bolt at any second.

"It would certainly stop the gossip," he said calmly, resisting the urge to pull her into his arms and kiss her again only because he was afraid she would take any move at that point the wrong way.

Annie's lips pressed together stubbornly and her hazel-green eyes glinted with temper. "The only reason I am marrying again is for love."

The only reason Travis had ever wanted to marry was for love. He just hadn't loved well enough, or genuinely enough, when he'd been engaged to Rayanne.

Sensing now was not the time to blurt out how he was beginning to feel about her, for fear Annie would think his feelings now weren't genuine either, Travis kept quiet. He would tell her he was falling in love with her—irrevocably in love—but only when the time was right. When they weren't arguing about the wisdom of their hasty, but oh so right, sexual involvement.

"Why'd you get married the first time?" he asked softly.

A troubled look came into her eyes. "Infatuation."

He wished he could keep his mouth shut, but he was curious about Annie and her life since she had left home when she was eighteen. Not to go to college, as everyone else her age had been doing, but to see the world. "You didn't know the difference?" he prodded gently as they began to swing once again.

Annie braced her elbow on the back of the swing and rested her head on her upturned palm. "I didn't spend enough time with Reece to discern the difference," she told him quietly, reaching over to remove a speck of lint from Travis's shoulder.

Travis sensed there was more.

Eventually, Annie released a long sigh and told him the rest. "I was still working as a flight attendant then," she said quietly. "I met him on the New York to London Gatwick run. Reece was consulting on several jobs in Europe at the time, so he traveled as much as I did and didn't mind my crazy schedule and frequent absences at all." Annie made a face. "Most men did. Anyway, he was twenty-seven, too, and like me, beginning to wonder if he would ever find The One. All our friends were getting married. It just seemed like a good time to settle down. And back then, we always had such a good time when we were together," Annie reminisced sadly.

Travis recalled her phone calls home to Joe. She certainly had seemed very much in love from what he'd heard from her father. "I remember you eloped."

Annie shrugged. "Without a mother there to plan the wedding, it was just easier. Less painful for me, you know? Looking back, I probably knew if I stopped to think about it much, I wouldn't go through with it."

Because Reece had not been The One for her after all, Travis thought. "You weren't married very long."

Annie shook her head and released a quavering breath. "I guess not. Although," she said, "two years can seem like an awfully long time if you're married to someone you've discovered you don't love, and vice versa."

Travis knew what she meant about that. His engagement to Rayanne had dragged on interminably for much the same reasons—because they didn't love each other the way they should have. "When did you know it was over?" Travis asked, covering her hand with his own.

Pain clouded Annie's eyes. She dropped her gaze from his and stared down at the place where her bent knee met his thigh. "I had an inkling when I got pregnant unexpectedly and he acted like it was a damn inconvenience instead of the best news in the world." Annie shook her head sadly, remembering. "I just kept thinking he was shocked, that he would adjust to the idea, just as I was, and that once the boys were born, he would love them, just as I did."

"But that didn't happen," Travis guessed, wishing he could erase that part of her life, without erasing the boys, who darn well were the best thing that had ever happened to Annie and now to Travis, as well.

"No, it didn't," Annie replied even more sadly. She lifted her head and looked Travis straight in the eye. ''Reece never did manage to work up any enthusiasm for the birth of our children. Instead, he picked up his travel schedule even more and spent even less time with me than before we were married, even though by then, because of my medical condition, I was no longer working.''

''I remember how rough your pregnancy was for you.''

''Oh, yeah.'' Annie sighed deeply and rolled her eyes. ''Multiple births are tough, no matter how you cut it. The time I spent in the hospital the last couple of months didn't help the strain in our marriage. Not to mention the fact that he managed not to be there for the triplets' birth.''

Travis tightened his hand on Annie's protectively, recollecting, ''Your dad was so ticked off about that, even though he was glad to be asked to be your labor coach and be there to witness the big event.'' Back then, Annie had made it sound as if she'd asked him because she was being practical, because Reece had to travel so much, but Joe—and Travis, too—had sensed otherwise.

Annie's soft lips curved ruefully. ''I probably knew then I should divorce Reece, but I kept thinking about the boys.'' She frowned, upset. ''Even though I suspected what the outcome would be, I couldn't give up without trying a little harder and a little longer.''

Travis remembered that, too. He knew it was foolish of him, but he wanted to beat the living daylights out of Reece for putting Annie and the boys through such heartache. Then and now.

Annie sighed. ''Then when my father got sick...'' She struggled to find the right words to explain. ''Reece just—he didn't understand what I was going

through. And he didn't really want to understand."
Gratitude abruptly filled her eyes. "By contrast, I remember how you were there for my dad, keeping an
eye on him, making sure he got to his treatments at
the oncology center."

Knowing she needed to be held now, even if she
was too proud and independent to ever let on to that
fact, Travis shifted Annie onto his lap and wrapped
both his arms around her. "It was the least I could
do for your dad after all he'd done for me." He
stroked his hands gently over the silky strands of her
upswept hair.

Annie paused, bit her lip, even as she cuddled
against him. "I really appreciated it. I don't know that
I ever said that."

Travis smiled. "You did."

Annie wreathed her arms around his neck, her fingers like silk against his skin. "Well, I'm saying it
again," she said softly, searching his eyes. "Thank
you, Travis. You were like a son to my dad in so
many ways." Her voice caught emotionally. Suddenly, tears glimmered in her hazel eyes, the loss of
her father remaining, deep in her heart, an ever-
present ache, as well as an ever-present memory of
love. "I know he cared about you very much," she
said, her lower lip trembling.

Abruptly, Travis felt the loss all over again, just as
deeply. "I cared about him, too," he said thickly.

Silence fell between them, fraught with emotion,
and tenderness. Travis drew her close and hugged her
tenderly.

Annie laid her head on his shoulder, even as she
clung to him. "I wish I'd been able to talk to you
like this then."

"Me, too." Travis waited until she drew back to look into his face. "But we were still pretty awkward with each other."

Annie blushed and abruptly looked about as ashamed as Travis had ever seen her. "I think I was jealous," she admitted reluctantly, wiping the tears from her cheek with the back of her hand. Earnestly, she searched his face. Clearly wanting him to understand the source of her feelings, she continued with difficulty. "My father seemed to need you more than he needed me," she confided, embarrassed. "Especially at the end. I remember he kept kicking me out of his hospital room so he could talk with you instead. He even wanted you there when he talked to his lawyers, and not me. And I, well, I just didn't know how to handle that."

Neither had Travis.

In retrospect, he realized he should have been straight with Annie from the first. But looking back on it, he really didn't see how he could have been, not when she'd regarded him so resentfully at the time. No, it was better to let sleeping dogs lie. Besides, what had happened then was over. It wasn't as if the legal papers he and Joe had drawn up and signed could be undone, even if he did tell her. What was important here was that he had promised Joe he would always watch over Annie and the boys, make sure they were financially taken care of, and he could do that without actually buying the Triple Diamond Ranch from Annie, as Joe had originally wanted.

Realizing Annie still wanted—needed—to hear some explanation about all those private hospital talks with her dad, Travis pushed his guilt away and said, "He needed to get some things off his chest. You know, man-to-man stuff.'' Travis paused, hurting all over again, for himself and for Annie, and their mutual loss. Swallowing around the hard knot of emotion in his throat, Travis pushed on. ''Your dad knew how tough it was for you to be losing the last of your family, and he wanted to be strong for you, to the very end.''

Annie shook her head sadly, closed her eyes. Her lower lip began to tremble. ''And all I wanted was to be close to him,'' she whispered, wrapped up in her own agony of regret.

Travis couldn't bear for Annie to think she had let her dad down, in any way, because she just hadn't. He tightened one arm around her. With his other hand, he lifted her face to his and forced her to face him, face the truth as she looked deep into his eyes and he looked into hers. ''You were close to him and he to you, Annie—as close as a father and daughter could be,'' Travis told her, believing it with all his heart and soul. He stroked the curve of her cheek with the pad of his thumb as Annie's lower lip trembled once again. ''You have to know you were the sun and the moon and the stars to him, just the way your boys are to you.''

Fresh tears spilled down her cheeks.

''Oh, Travis, I still miss him so much,'' Annie sobbed. ''It breaks my heart that my boys will never know my dad the way I did.''

Knowing this was a storm that had been brewing for a long time, Travis murmured soft words of assurance and held her close, glad he could finally be there for her when she needed him, in the way that she needed him. As the minutes drew out, Annie cried all the tears she'd been holding back, all the tears she hadn't cried during the long months of her father's illness and at his funeral. They swung together like that for a long time.

*"I'LL PROTECT YOU, Annie. I'll always be here for you, and I'll always protect you."*

Travis's last words to her the evening before, whispered poignantly as he'd hugged her and said goodnight, stayed in Annie's mind the next morning as she got the boys ready for nursery school. She couldn't believe she, who had never before cried on any man's shoulder, had broken down like that in front of him. But she had. And miraculously, felt all the better for it. Maybe this leaning on someone, just a little bit, wasn't such a bad thing, Annie thought. Certainly it was what her father would have wanted. Her dad had always been encouraging her to get closer to Travis, especially in the months before he died. Wouldn't he be surprised now, Annie mused, as she herded the boys into the sedan, to discover that his daughter was falling head over heels in love with his friend, fellow rancher and former protegé, Travis McCabe?

"How come Travis didn't come and see us at breakfast today?" Tyler asked as Annie drove them to nursery school early the next morning.

Annie smiled, thinking how quickly her boys had warmed to their new neighbor. Not to mention that Travis was an excellent male influence in their young lives. "I imagine he had things to do on his ranch," Annie said casually as she turned the car onto the highway that led into Laramie and quickly accelerated to the posted speed of fifty-five miles an hour. "He hasn't been spending a lot of time there this week, you know."

"Yeah, but it's okay if he wants to come visit us 'cause he's got cowboys to work on his ranch," Teddy reasoned with perfect four—going on five— year-old logic.

"And one cowgirl, now that Kelsey Lockhart is working for him," Annie added, thinking once again how nice it was of Travis to give Kelsey a chance to learn ranching from the ground up. But then that was Travis for you, she thought, always helping some- one…

"I want Travis to be with us, not the other cowboys and one cowgirl," Trevor said stubbornly.

"Me, too," Teddy said.

"Me three," Tyler added vehemently.

*And me four,* Annie thought wistfully, even though realistically she knew it wasn't fair of them to expect Travis to give up his own life or shirk his own re- sponsibilities just to spend time with her and the boys. Not that he seemed to mind. The only thing Travis didn't like, from what Annie could tell, was being away from them. "Not to worry, guys." She smiled at them in the rearview mirror. "Travis and all the other McCabes will be at your birthday party this af- ternoon."

An enthusiastic cheer erupted from the back seat. Annie smiled and cheered in anticipation, too. They *were* going to have fun this afternoon. She was sure of it. And speaking of what was going to happen that afternoon, she had a few instructions to give the Tri- ple Threat. "My friend Meg Lockhart is going to pick you up after nursery school. You're going to have lunch at Meg's house, with her and her little boy, Jeremy, and then she'll bring you over before the party starts."

"How come?" Teddy asked as Annie parked the car.

Annie cut the engine and removed the keys from the ignition as she explained calmly, "Because I have a lot to do to get ready for the birthday party and Meg offered to watch you guys." Annie released the catch on her safety belt, and turned around to face them. "You three promise me you'll be good for Meg?"

To her relief, they nodded seriously.

"Good," Annie said, helping them out of the car and kissing each one of them in turn. "'Cause I'm counting on you."

THE CONTRACTOR Annie had hired to convert the new barn to a commercial kitchen was there when Annie got back to the ranch. They were still talking about the proposed construction schedule and the order in which everything should be done when Travis's Suburban pulled into the driveway twenty minutes later. Annie introduced the two men. They talked briefly, before the contractor left again, promising to return first thing the following Monday morning.

"I didn't expect to see you this morning," Annie said as she opened the trunk and took out the charcoal and new barbecue grill she had picked up at the store on the way home. But she was very glad she had.

"I thought you might need some help getting ready for the birthday party," Travis said.

"You thought right," Annie said, trying hard not to let on what his low, sexy voice did to her as he carried both the grill and charcoal to the house.

"Much more of this and I'm going to think you're indispensable," Annie teased. *Just like my boys already do.*

"That's the plan." Looking handsome as could be in a plain white work shirt and jeans, Travis set down the bag of charcoal and grill box on the front porch and winked at her. "Don't want you and the boys to think you can get along without me." He sauntered closer, in a drift of intoxicating cologne, and looked down at her as if she were the most beautiful woman on earth. "If you've got a screwdriver," he offered huskily, "I'll put the grill together for you."

Annie smiled, wishing her mind weren't filled with wistful thoughts of making love to him again, when they both knew they hadn't a moment to spare if she wanted to ensure the triplets' party was a success. "That'd be nice, thanks." She pushed the words out around the tightness in her throat, then led the way into the kitchen. Travis looked down at the sketch pad on the table.

"That the new name for your barbecue sauce?" He pointed to the boldly lettered Annie's Blue Ribbon Barbecue Sauce, and underneath it, the scripted slogan, Homemade At Its Best!

Annie nodded proudly. "I have an appointment with the art teacher at the high school next week. I thought I could get her to help me design the labels. I had in mind an old-fashioned blue ribbon on the label—the kind they give out at county fairs—alongside the name." She paused, really wanting his reaction, which thus far seemed to be very positive. "What do you think?"

Travis studied the sketch with a businessman's sharp eye. Finally, he smiled, nodded, and said in all seriousness, "I think you have a real talent for this."

Annie grinned, both cheered and buoyed by his stalwart enthusiasm. "I hope the buying public thinks so, too." She rummaged around her dad's old toolbox for the screwdriver, then, thinking he might need the wrench and pliers, too, got those out for good measure.

Travis folded his arms in front of him and lounged against the counter. "Nervous?"

Annie handed him the tools, her palm brushing his larger stronger one. "A little, yeah," she admitted, glad to be able to confide in someone. "I woke up this morning in a cold sweat, thinking about the meeting with the contractor, afraid I'd bitten off more than I could chew." Annie paused. "I've put everything on the line, financially, to make this dream a reality, Travis."

"I know what that's like. I did the same thing when I started my ranch." He paused, searched her face, seemed to want to do more than comfort her. He seemed to want to help. "There is a way it wouldn't have to be so much of a risk," he said finally, pausing to put aside the tools she had just handed him.

"And that is—?" Annie prodded, already worrying she was beginning to depend a little too much on him.

Travis shrugged and braced a hand on the counter on either side of him. His eyes connected with hers and held for a breath-stealing moment. "Keep the ranch house, the barn, the ten or twenty acres around the house and sell the rest of your land to me," he suggested in a soft, self-confident voice. He leaned toward her earnestly, his entire attention focused on her. "I'll expand my ranch the way I've wanted to for years. Financially, you and the boys would be set for life. You'd have time and the means to make this dream of yours a reality, even if it didn't happen as quickly as you'd like."

He was offering her the easy way out. Annie didn't know whether to be irked—that he was asking her again because he still thought she needed the easy way out—or grateful to him for trying to supply it, in yet another way. She only knew that at the moment it still wasn't an option. No matter how much he wanted her land. Or how much it would help them both. She paused, sighed, stepped back away from him and the mesmerizing quality of his golden-brown eyes.

"I can't do that, Travis," she explained, feeling exasperated. "I can't sell off the culmination of my father's dream, which was to build this ranch, to make my own dream come true. Besides—" Annie shrugged "—I want the boys to have my dad's ranch when they grow up, so they can be ranchers if they want, and if I sell it now, that won't be possible."

Travis looked at her as if he hadn't thought about that. But then, neither had Annie's dad when he had urged her to sell after his death, if and when managing the ranch ever got to be too much for her.

"Then you're just going to have to make this product a success, aren't you?" he said finally.

Annie nodded seriously as she took his hand, gathered up the tools and led him back to the as-yet-unassembled barbecue grill. "But let's not talk about that today. It's the triplets' birthday," she said, smiling as they got started on their first chore. "And I want it to be the best darn birthday party they've ever had."

"YIPPEE-YEA, yippee-yi, yippee-yaw-hoo!" The triplets whooped it up in unison as Shane, Jackson and Wade rode the boys around the pasture. Wearing in their brand-new Western clothes, boots and hats, the triplets were each nestled in front of a grown McCabe while Travis videotaped the event as proudly as any real father. And when he was finished, each triplet took a turn in the saddle with Travis, too. After that, Travis's ranch hands—Kelsey Lockhart included—made sure that every kid at the party who wanted to ride was given the opportunity to have a turn in the saddle.

"Travis couldn't be prouder of those boys if they were his own," Lilah McCabe told Annie as the evening wore on.

"I know." Annie smiled at Travis's mother, who—along with many of the other ladies in the Laramie Bridge Club, was the closest thing she had to a mom these days. "They feel the same way about him," Annie confided happily.

John McCabe admired Travis's relationship with Annie's sons, too, although he also had a few reservations about the degree to which her sons had attached themselves to Travis. "Hope their real daddy doesn't mind a little competition," John told Annie, concerned.

Their real daddy hadn't even sent the triplets a present, Annie thought as she rushed to assure Travis's dad that Reece was not likely to mind the competition for the boys' affections, never mind bother to object to the triplets' growing attachment to John and Lilah McCabe's oldest son.

"How come our daddy didn't call?" Trevor asked sleepily as Annie tucked the boys into their beds.

Annie had been dreading this. She had hoped the hoopla of the evening would distract them from their father's oversight. "Yeah, I thought you said he was gonna 'member," Teddy complained wearily.

"I'm sure he did." Annie's smile was plastered on her face, hiding the misery she felt inside. "But it's a different time of day in Japan and maybe he's sleeping right now."

"Oh." All three boys mulled that over. "Then he'll call when he wakes up?" Tyler asked hopefully. Which just went to show, Annie thought, that all boys needed and wanted a daddy in their lives. Even a not-so-great one.

"I'm sure he will," Annie fibbed, telling herself she would call Reece and wake him up as soon as the triplets were asleep, no matter what time it was. There was no reason on earth he should be allowed to hurt them this way. She didn't care what the excuse. "And if he doesn't call, he'll send a birthday card," she said.

The boys furrowed their brows, even as they rubbed their eyes. Pushing on to another subject, Annie asked, "Did you have a fun birthday?"

Teddy, Trevor and Tyler nodded. "We like parties, Momma."

"Yeah. Especially when it's our birthday."

"Get some sleep now." Annie tucked them in, and kissed them good-night.

"Is Travis still here?" Tyler asked as Annie reached the bedroom door.

Annie nodded as she switched off the light, so that only the night-light illuminated the room they shared. "He and his brothers and their wives are helping clean up outside."

Trevor yawned again and rolled onto his side.

"Will he be here tomorrow when we wake up?" he asked plaintively.

"No, honey, he won't," Annie said gently.

"I wish he would." Teddy clutched his teddy bear to his chest.

"Me, too," Tyler chimed in.

"Me three," Trevor said.

*And me four,* Annie thought wistfully again. She couldn't help thinking how much nicer her boys' lives would be if Travis McCabe were their father, instead of Reece. But you couldn't change biology.

"'Night boys," Annie said with a smile. She blew them a kiss.

They each blew one back, chorusing sleepily, "'Night, Momma."

The three were so tuckered out, they were sound asleep before Annie had finished picking up the paper cups and plates scattered around the living room. When she walked back outside, to her surprise, Travis was the only person left. She looked around, seeing only his Suburban and her small sedan in the driveway. "What happened to everyone?" she asked.

"I told them they'd done enough and sent 'em home." Travis shrugged and smiled. "My brothers, being the nosy, suspicious sort they are, figured I wanted to be alone with you."

Annie's spirits rose at his low, teasing tone. His flirtatiousness giving rise to her own, she sauntered closer, stopping just short of him. "And do you— want to be alone with me?" She batted her eyelashes at him in her best Scarlett O'Hara imitation.

"You got that right." Travis tugged her against him and kissed her soundly, then danced her backward toward the house, until they were standing next to the back door, in the overhang of the roof. "I didn't get my quota of kisses today," he said as he fit the length of him against the length of her. His mouth came down on hers, touched briefly again, then moved to the nape of her neck where it traced sensual patterns of his own design. A moan swept through her, as fiercely as the sensual waves created by his touch. "Travis—" Annie drew in a quick breath, her pulse already dancing erratically.

"I'm not talking about anything but kissing here, Annie." His tongue dipped into the neckline of her blouse, tracing the U of her collarbone before moving back to her ear. Annie's head dropped back. She knew she was perilously close to losing all reserve.

"This isn't fair," she whispered as she felt the traitorous weakening of her knees. She stared into his handsome face, aware that her heart was beating double time. Lower, there was a telltale fluttery feeling.

With the warmth of his palms, Travis urged her closer still. "Not fair—" he whispered softly, looking deep into her eyes "—depriving me of my quota of kisses." His gaze ardently traced her face, lingering on each feature in turn. Then he lowered his mouth to hers. Giving her no chance to protest further, he kissed her long and hard and deep, drew her closer, and pressed his arousal more firmly against her. Her capitulation complete, his tongue stroked her lazily, again and again, until her middle burned with a fire only he could put out.

Knowing it was stop now—as he'd promised—or continue to the end, Travis drew back breathlessly. "I'm doing this for the kids, you know," he whispered. "Because it wouldn't do for them to find us—"

"Together."

"Exactly."

Silence fell between them. They clung together, still catching their breath. Eventually, Travis grinned. "Damn, but it's hard being a gentleman sometimes," he drawled.

"Tell me about it," Annie complained in the same teasing tone.

His profile was bathed in silvery moonlight, making him look all the more handsome. Annie splayed her hands across the hardness of his chest. She loved the warmth and strength of him. Loved the gentleness of his touch and the inherent sexiness of his kisses. So much, she didn't know how she was ever going to let him go. "The boys wanted to know if you'd be here in the morning when they woke up," she confided softly, wanting him to know.

Travis held her close and studied her upturned face. "What'd you tell them?"

"No, of course." Annie let out a soft, ragged sigh of regret. "It wouldn't look right." But she had wanted to be able to make it happen, and she knew that he knew it, as surely as if she'd said it out loud. "Besides," Annie sighed again, even more regretfully, "we wouldn't want it spread all over the nursery school."

His eyes still holding hers, Travis inclined his head slightly to the side. "Not to mention the town."

Wasn't that the truth, Annie thought. She pushed away from Travis and headed back out into the yard. Seeing the fire in the barbecue had about died down, she put the lid back on the brand-new grill.

Travis grinned as he carried over the last of the plastic trash bags and set them next to the garage before returning to her side. "Chatty little fellas, aren't they?"

Annie nodded as she gathered up the balloons she'd tied to the swing set and prepared to take them inside. "They couldn't keep a secret if their life depended on it. Never mind be quiet about anything they find exciting."

Travis caught her by the waist and swung her around to face him. "They find me exciting?"

Annie jerked in a deep breath, aware that she wanted to go to bed with him again, so much. "Oh, yes," she whispered.

"What about you, Annie?" Travis tunneled his hands through her upswept hair. "Do you find me exciting?"

"Sometimes," Annie allowed as a potent sensual shiver coasted down her spine.

"Like now?" He removed the butterfly clip and several pins, and let her wavy red-gold hair tumble free to her shoulders.

"Travis," Annie warned as a new wellspring of desire engulfed her from head to toe. She didn't know how much longer she could resist. Would even *want* to resist.

"Just ten more minutes, Annie," Travis whispered, dancing her backward to the picnic table. He sank onto a bench and pulled her onto his lap. "Ten more minutes of kissing. That's all I'm asking." He opened the first button on her blouse.

Annie caught his fingers before they could go farther. "Ten more minutes of kissing and I'm not going to be able to stop," she laughed shakily, her hair falling around her face.

Travis rained kisses over her face, her throat, her

lips. "Our kisses are that potent, hmm?" he murmured against her mouth.

Annie sighed, regretting they couldn't just forget caution and go straight to bed and stay there all night. "You know they are," she said, kissing him, too.

Travis drew back slightly, looking every bit as dazed and lovestruck as she felt. His heart was pounding in his chest. "A rain check then," he decided finally.

Annie hitched in a breath. "Collectible when?" she demanded.

"The first time we're alone," Travis said.

Annie sighed again, disappointed. "No telling when that'll be."

Travis's arms tightened around her. "We'll find time, Annie." He kissed her throat, her lips, with daunting tenderness. "I promise."

"THE BOYS SAID they had your permission to speed-dial me this time," Travis said early the next morning.

Annie grinned at the familiar sound of his voice over the telephone lines. She cradled the phone closer to her ear. She was beginning to wonder how she had ever managed without him. "I'm having a wardrobe crisis," she confided. And, oddly enough, she wanted his advice.

"That sounds…intriguing. What exactly is a wardrobe crisis anyway?" Travis asked in a puzzled tone of voice. "Did your closet break loose and run away?"

Annie sighed, rolled her eyes. "You have led a sheltered cowboy life, haven't you?"

"Yes, ma'am, I have," Travis replied, his sexy all-

American-cowboy tone of voice sending a new current of warmth through her.

"Guess that's what happens when you don't have any sisters," Annie teased.

"There are definite drawbacks to being raised with three brothers," Travis conceded in mock seriousness. "Not that I could imagine you looking anything but fetching in whatever you might choose to wear, you understand."

Annie grinned, pleased by the compliment.

"But I'd be glad to help in any way I can," Travis continued.

"Good. 'Cause I need help this morning," Annie said as she continued rifling through her closet. She paused and bit her lip, all too aware of the three little boys seated on her bed. They were staring at her curiously, probably because they had never known her to be in a quandary about what to wear. "I don't know what to wear to this business meeting with Greta," Annie told Travis. "Is she going to expect me to wear a business suit? Because I don't have one. And I've been so busy, I didn't even think about not having one till I went to get dressed this morning." Distressed, Annie raked a hand through her hair. "What do you think she's going to be wearing?"

Travis was silent a moment, thinking. "Probably a denim skirt and blouse or something. Maybe a vest. Definitely her cowgirl boots. I almost never see her without those, except when she and Shane are over swimming in Mom and Dad's pool. Then she usually doesn't wear them. Probably because they'd look a little strange with her bathing suit."

"Do you think a denim jumper is okay? Or is that too momish? I could wear this flowered dress I have, but it's a little frilly for a business meeting. I mean it's got the lace on the collar.''

''Relax. Take three deep breaths. Close your eyes. And I'll be over in five minutes to take a look.''

Before Annie could protest, the connection was cut. The next thing she knew, Travis was on her doorstep, looking as handsome as usual. As well as very, very glad to see her.

''You didn't have to come over, you know,'' Annie said, a little embarrassed about her quandary now that he was here.

Travis merely smiled, stepped into her newly painted living room, grabbed her around the waist and promptly and thoroughly delivered a good-morning kiss that was interrupted only by the sound of giggling times three from the kitchen. Annie was blushing as he lifted his lips from hers. ''Feeling calmer yet?'' Travis asked.

*Excited was the word I think you're looking for. And yes, she was.* ''Peeved,'' Annie said. What had happened to their decision not to kiss in front of her ever-so-chatty boys?

''Uh-oh,'' Tyler said, stepping forward to tug on Travis's sleeve. He craned his head back to look up at Travis. ''You won't like it if Mommy gets peeved, Travis.''

''I won't, huh?'' Travis let go of Annie and knelt down to eye level to greet the boys.

All three boys shook their head in unison. ''Peeved is bad,'' Tyler said very seriously.

''Real bad,'' Trevor and Teddy chorused, agreeing completely.

Annie rolled her eyes.

Travis rubbed his jaw and tried not to look too

mischievous. "All right. Then I guess I'm going to have to behave myself," he allowed, after a long heart-stopping moment during which Annie was sure he was thinking about "rain checks" and more kisses and more "rain checks."

As Travis straightened, Annie scowled at him sternly. She was determined to get some control over the situation, even if she had sort of started it with her urgent, flirtatious phone call to him. "You know that kiss is going to be all over the you-know-what before midmorning," she scolded.

"Nursery school," Trevor said as if supplying Annie with a word she couldn't quite think of.

Teddy held up a hand. "It's okay. Mommies are supposed to kiss daddies," Teddy said. He went back to the kitchen and sat down to finish his breakfast. Annie and Travis followed.

"Yeah, we talked," Tyler said, sitting down and spooning up his cereal, too. "We decided we need a new daddy. Our old one isn't very good." He blew out a disappointed breath. "He never 'members us or nothing."

"Yeah," Trevor said eagerly. "We want a cowboy kind of daddy."

Teddy agreed. He looked at Annie. "We talked about it, Momma, while you was getting showered this mornin'. And we decided. We want Travis to be our daddy."

FOR A MOMENT, Annie was so shocked she could barely draw a breath. Travis looked equally stunned—and touched. And beyond that, concerned. Giving Annie a look that asked if he could be allowed to handle this very delicate situation, he pulled up two chairs—

one for himself and one for Annie—and sat down at the kitchen table, along with the three boys.

"I'd give anything if you three boys were my sons," he said softly and seriously. "Because I think you three fellas are about the best little boys any daddy could have. And I promise you this, on my word of honor—and a cowboy never breaks his word of honor—whenever you need me, however you need me, as long as you need me, I will be there for you."

"But you can't be our daddy," Tyler guessed as all three of their little faces fell in heartbreaking disappointment.

"Right," Travis nodded seriously. "Because I wasn't married to your mommy then. And I didn't help make you three guys." He held up a hand, staving off interruption. "But that's okay," he continued reassuringly.

Trevor blinked. "It is?"

"Sure," Travis said easily, smiling confidently. "And you know why?"

The boys shook their head. "No," they said in unison.

"Because cowboys—even ones as little as you buckaroos—can never have too many people loving them and taking care of them," Travis explained gently, looking each one of them directly in the eye for a long, confidence-inspiring moment. "And as long as you live, I will always love you and help take care of you."

The boys stared at Travis as if he were Santa Claus and a superhero all in one. "You really love us?" Trevor said slowly, speaking for the group.

"Yep." Travis nodded. He stood and held out his arms, encouraging them all to come forward for a hug. "From the bottom of my cowboy heart," he said.

Annie watched, delighted and touched, as the boys gave and received the kind of love she had always wanted them to have from their father. If only, she thought wistfully, he were their daddy, how much simpler—and sweeter—their life would be.

Travis straightened. He gave Annie a glance that let her know they'd discuss this later, in private, then looked at the clock. "If you don't want to be late for your nine-thirty meeting with Greta, you better get a move on. Meanwhile, I know three buckaroos who are just about ready to go to nursery school. Want me to take 'em for you this morning?"

The boys looked at Annie—who was still wearing her bathrobe—hopefully. Travis was right, Annie thought. She didn't have much time. "Would you?" Annie asked.

"No problem." Travis smiled.

"Boys, run and brush your teeth and find your shoes," Annie said.

"We want to wear our cowboy boots," Teddy said.

"That's fine." Annie smiled her permission. "Just get ready to go."

They dashed off.

Travis met her eyes. "I know," he said, easily guessing at what she was about to say. "A weighty subject for so early in the morning."

One Annie hadn't expected.

Or known how to deal with, either. Then or now. "We need to talk—" Annie dropped her voice to a whisper. "At a time when the boys aren't present." She needed and wanted to tell him about her phone call with Reece last night, after Travis had left.

"I agree," Travis said solemnly. "After your meeting with Greta?"

Annie bit her lip. "I don't know if I'll have time before I have to get the boys from nursery school." She had no idea how long the meeting was going to last.

"Not a problem." Before she could protest, Travis reached for the phone and dialed. "Wade. Glad I caught you and Josie," he said as he looked at Annie and smiled. "Annie and I need a big favor."

# Chapter Nine

"Travis, are you and Momma having a date?" Teddy asked shortly after noon that day.

"I wouldn't exactly call it that," Annie hedged self-consciously as she hurried around the kitchen, putting the finishing touches on the lunch she was preparing for Wade, Josie and the boys.

"I would," Travis said smugly, releasing an impatient breath and jamming his hands on his waist. The action pushed back the edges of his lightweight camel sport coat, revealing the flatness of his abdomen beneath the starched light blue crispness of his oxford-cloth shirt and the faded, soft, torso-hugging jeans.

"So which is it?" Wade McCabe teased, looking as completely at home in Annie's country kitchen as he did behind the controls of the big black helicopter he used to travel from one incredibly lucrative investment to another.

"A date." Travis grabbed Annie around the waist and, ignoring her soft gasp of dismay, kissed her soundly on the mouth. "I'm staking my claim on this woman." Travis grinned at Annie, looking just as intrigued, just as filled with male satisfaction as he had the first time they'd made love.

"Way to go, brother-in-law," Josie said. She held up a hand sporting diamond wedding and engagement rings almost as expensive as the wildcat well she was currently digging, and she, Travis, Wade and the boys exchanged high-fives all around.

"Travis and I just have some things to talk about," Annie said, wishing everyone wouldn't make quite so much of this. She felt self-conscious enough as it was, without Travis telling everyone they encountered that the two of them were an item.

"How come you can't talk here, Momma?" Trevor persisted as Annie put a platter of sandwiches and tureen of soup on the table. "You talked here before."

"Because it's a date," Travis explained, giving man-to-man looks to all three boys. "And when you go on a date, you usually leave your kiddos at home with a baby-sitter. In this case, Uncle Wade and Aunt Josie are your baby-sitters."

"And besides," Annie said, even more seriously, as she took off her apron and reached for her brief-case. "I have some business papers to go over with Travis. We need peace and quiet to be able to do that." And she needed to get away from all these questions. Not to mention the endless speculation she saw on Wade's and Josie's faces—speculation she was sure would soon be replayed to the whole McCabe clan.

"No peace and quiet here!" Tyler piped up happily as Wade passed out the sandwiches and Josie dished out the soup.

"Nope," Trevor grinned impishly. "We sure don't got any of that, do we, Tyler?"

Tyler beamed. "No-sirree-bob! We sure don't!"

Noting all three of her boys seemed to be operating on high speed, Annie sent skeptical looks at Wade and Josie. "Are you sure you're going to be able to handle this?" she asked.

"Oh, yeah." Looking amused by her nervous Nellie routine, Wade grinned then continued like a teacher reciting that day's lesson plans, "We're gonna do another m-u-r-a-l on the—"

Josie clapped her hand over Wade's mouth before he could finish. The antics of the newlyweds slash baby-sitters made all three boys howl with laughter.

"Don't worry, Annie," Josie reassured firmly. "I've been around rowdy men all my life. If I can handle a crew of roughnecks at an oil site, I can surely keep these old cowpokes in line. Besides—" Josie winked at Annie, woman to woman "—I've got a secret weapon."

"And that is?" Annie queried as Travis took her hand and led her toward the door.

"My cooking," Josie teased, making a comical, woe-is-me face. "It's plumb awful."

Wade rolled his eyes dramatically. "I can attest to that," he said.

The remark earned him a playful punch in the arm from his new bride.

"If they don't behave, I'll just cook something and feed it to them," Josie teased.

Wade put both hands around his neck and made a choking sound that quickly had the boys giggling. He winked at the triplets. "We don't want that now, do we, boys?" he said.

The triplets giggled all the harder and shook their heads.

"Then I guess we'll just have to play board games here in the kitchen," Josie sighed, pretending to be disappointed.

"We won't be gone all that long," Annie said, consulting the clock on the wall as Travis continued dragging her toward the door. "I'll be back by three."

"Make that four," Travis said, guiding her gently but firmly through the portal.

"But we've got the rehearsal dinner for your folks tonight," Annie protested. "And I've got to get the boys ready."

Travis shook his head. "It won't take that long, will it, guys?" He looked back at the triplets for confirmation. "'Cause I'm gonna help."

They readily gave it to him with enthusiastic nods.

Josie and Wade waved goodbye. Before Annie knew it, she was standing next to Travis's Suburban, and he was helping her in. "You really think you have all the answers, don't you?" she said dryly, climbing into the passenger seat. She smoothed her skirt around her.

Travis winked as he bent over to help her with her seat belt. "That's 'cause I do."

"THIS WASN'T EXACTLY what I had in mind when I said I wanted a date," Travis drawled an hour later as he helped Annie dice up tomatoes and onions for a big batch of her soon-to-be-famous barbecue sauce.

"Ditto." Annie shook her head, aware she'd never felt as pressured as she did at that very moment. Maybe because she'd never had quite this many irons in the fire at one moment before. She looked around at Travis's large wood-floored kitchen. Like everything else on his ranch, his was twice the size of hers. But there his bragging rights ended. Annie shook her head. "I've never seen such a woefully equipped kitchen."

Travis shrugged as he fixed them both some iced tea. "I've got frying pans. Pots. Silverware. Dishes."

"But no food processor," Annie sighed, watching him slice up a lemon with swift efficient strokes and slip two slices—just the way she liked it—into her glass. "Good thing I thought to send you back for mine and everything else I needed."

"Isn't it, though." Travis rolled his eyes as he handed her her glass. "Wade is still probably laughing his head off," he complained.

Annie looked at Travis's scowl. Knowing the four McCabe brothers the way she did, she could imagine the loss of face Travis was now suffering. Not so unlike her own when the stories about them kissing and so on had spread all over town. "Wade figured we'd be doing something much more romantic," she guessed. And they probably would have, if she hadn't decided on the spur of the moment, that very morning, to honor John and Lilah McCabe's personal request for more of Annie's barbecue sauce.

Travis shrugged his broad shoulders indifferently. "I don't know about him. I sure did. I had a picnic lunch planned."

Annie calmed him down with a wave of her hand. "We'll get to that—" and maybe a few other things as well, she added silently, "as soon as we get the sauce simmering for your mom and dad."

Travis helped with the onions. "So how did your business meeting with Greta go?" he asked as Annie dumped the last of the tomatoes into the big stew pot on the back of the stove.

Annie wiped her hands on a towel and went to get the contract she'd brought along with her. Travis added the onions to the sauce. When Annie returned, she handed him the papers to peruse and went back to adding spices. "Greta wants me to supply my sauce for her restaurant, but she wants it done exclusively for The Lone Star Dinner and Dance Hall. She doesn't want any other restaurant to have it."

Travis frowned as he contemplated the pros and cons of that particular arrangement. He studied her face. "How do you feel about that?"

"On the one hand, I'm happy to have any outlet for my sauce," Annie allowed as she added apple-cider vinegar and fresh pureed jalapeños to the sauce. "Greta's is fast becoming very popular. On the other hand, I don't want to limit myself to just getting business from her, 'cause I think I'm sitting on top of a gold mine here. Especially after I get my commercial kitchen built and have the ability to produce the sauce in much larger quantities than I can now." Annie pushed garlic cloves through the press.

"So what'd you tell her?" Travis took over the stirring when Annie went to wash the garlic juice from her hands.

"I struck a deal. I told her I'd let my sauce be sold only at her place for the next year if she allowed me to sell small bottles of it to customers at her dance hall. If Annie's Blue Ribbon Barbecue Sauce takes off the way I think and hope it will, I could probably get it sold in other specialty shops as well. At cooking stores in the mall and so on."

"And hit the gourmet market," Travis guessed, looking supremely happy for her, too.

"Exactly." Annie nodded, pleased to discover that Travis shared both her enthusiasm and vision for her business. "And if that goes well, maybe I can even develop a few other Texas-style sauces—salad dressings and meat marinades and so on—and start up a mail-order business from my ranch."

Travis grinned his approval. "What did Greta say to your proposition?"

"She went for it." Annie added paprika, chili powder, salt and pepper. "She's got to talk to her attorney. And I've got to talk to mine. But as soon as we do, my sauce will be available in her restaurant all the time. In the meantime, your father asked Greta if there was any way he could get some of my sauce served at the rehearsal dinner tonight. Plus, your mom wanted to give some away as party favors, which is why we're here cooking now. I just learned about their request this morning, and didn't have enough already made to do all of that."

Travis rolled his eyes again, clearly irritated by the source and the reason behind the interruption of their first official date. "I'm sure my mom and dad never meant for you to be slaving away all afternoon on this," he said reasonably.

"I don't mind." Annie turned the fire down to simmer, and began cleaning up the mess she had made in Travis's kitchen. "Besides, it's more free publicity and good word of mouth for my sauce. I like cooking up something special for people." Annie dropped her voice a persuasive notch. "And I like the idea of easing into the specialty-food business a little more gradually than I had initially planned. It won't be the instant success I had first hoped for, but it'll be the kind of success I can handle right now." Annie went into his arms, more than ever loving the warmth and strength and tenderness he offered. "I want more time with you and the boys. And this way I'll have it," she said sensibly.

Travis threaded his hands through her hair. "I want more time with you, too." He kissed her sweetly, tenderly.

"And speaking of that," Annie said, her heart pounding as she studied his reaction gravely, "is your offer still good to buy my ranch?"

Travis frowned, perplexed. His golden-brown gaze held hers. "I thought you wanted it for the boys."

She had. And she'd been wrong. "I've been thinking." Annie swallowed and splayed her hands across his chest. Gathering her courage, she plunged on. "My dad built the ranch up to be a cattle ranch and it's a damn good one. But if I don't use the pastures and keep it up the way a ranch should be kept up, all his hard work will go down the drain," Annie concluded sadly, guilt over her own shortsightedness flooding her anew. "Twenty years from now, if and when the boys were ready to ranch, they'd practically have to start from scratch anyway. On the other hand, if I sell the majority of the acreage to you, we both know it'll remain in good working order, just as my dad would've wanted. I can still keep the house and the twenty acres or so the house is situated on, just the way you suggested to me the other day. That way the boys will always have a home. Invested properly, the money from the sale of the land will give me the capital I need to start up my business slowly and provide for the boys' college educations and anything else that we might need along the way.'' What Travis had suggested had made good business—and financial—sense. Initially, Annie had just been too emotional to see that when it came to the ranch where she had grown up. But now that she'd had time to think about it, she knew Travis had been right to suggest what he had.

Travis studied her silently as his hands warmly curved over her shoulders. ''You're sure this is what you want?'' he asked, looking reluctant to take advantage of her, even a little bit.

Annie nodded, more sure than ever now that she had voiced her thoughts to Travis. ''The boys' dreams should be their own,'' she told him calmly. ''Maybe one day they will be ranchers, like their grandpa and like you. If so—'' Annie's lips tilted into a smile ''—I expect you'll teach them everything they want to know and more, just like my dad taught you.''

Travis nodded. ''You bet I will,'' he said hoarsely, his affection for her boys evident, as always.

Annie lifted a shoulder in a delicate shrug. ''If they decide otherwise, they'll be able to go to law or medical school or even go work as a wildcatter. The bottom line is, their dreams should be *their* dreams. Not something that's been pushed on them by someone else or by virtue of their birthright,'' she said firmly.

Silence strung out between them. ''You don't look as happy as I thought you'd look,'' Annie observed.

Travis felt so stunned and guilty, he hardly knew where to begin. He had offered to buy her ranch, never expecting her to take him up on the offer. He had just wanted to put the idea on the table so she would know the possibility was there if she was ever strapped for cash in the future. And he had made the offer because he felt, given the papers he had signed with her dad, that he owed Joe that much. Joe hadn't wanted to see his ranch go to anyone else but Annie or Travis, ever. And no matter what the future held, Travis intended to see that still remained the case.

"You caught me off guard," Travis told Annie finally. He sat down on the edge of the table and guided her between his spread legs. "I didn't know that was what you wanted to talk about this afternoon. I thought it was going to be about what the boys said to me this morning."

Annie braced her hips against the inside of his thigh, and turned to face him. She sighed as she traced a mindless pattern on the buttons of his shirt. "You handled that very well. I don't imagine it's every day you get asked to be three five-year-olds' daddy."

Knowing what great kids they were, Travis wished he could be their daddy. "Did your ex ever call?" he asked.

"No," Annie related sadly as she turned her eyes to Travis's once again. "Not a word. So I called him, late last night, after you left."

"And?" Travis asked, admiring her guts.

Annie's lower lip trembled with a hurt Travis sensed was more for her boys than herself. "Reece refused to telephone the boys to wish them happy birthday." Annie shook her head with a weariness that seemed to cut straight to her soul. "He said it would be a waste of time because he had no idea what to say to three five-year-olds, and he couldn't imagine they would have anything all that interesting to say to him, either."

Travis swore, summing up in one succinct word what he thought of Reece.

Annie nodded grimly, agreeing. "Ain't that the truth," she said bitterly. Drawing a deep breath, she moved away from Travis once again, pacing over to the windows in the sunny breakfast nook and back again. "Anyway, I did get Reece to agree to send them each a present as soon as possible."

Travis admired the way Annie had resisted the urge to downgrade their daddy to the boys. They were hurt enough without her turning the situation into World War Three or making them feel even worse. He watched her pace to the stove and back again, looking ever more restless and discontent with every second that passed. "How do you feel about all of this?" he asked gently.

Annie lifted her hands and gestured indifferently. "I want to kick myself for ever marrying him." Annie shook her head in silent regret. "I never should have let myself get swept away like that, so quickly and so completely."

And now, Travis thought, she had gone and gotten herself involved in another unexpected, whirlwind romance. "Which is the real reason we're making barbecue sauce this afternoon, isn't it?" Travis guessed heavily.

Bright color flooded Annie's cheeks. She tossed her head in haughty indignation. "I don't know what you're talking about."

Travis looked at her measuringly. He was not about to play games with something this serious or potentially damaging to their relationship, even if it meant she could save face. "Annie, I saw the jars in your refrigerator," he said, his voice husky but firm. "You had enough barbecue sauce on hand for the rehearsal dinner tonight. You just wanted to make sure we were doing something that would keep us too busy to do anything else. Like make love again."

Twin spots of color flushed Annie's fair, freckled cheeks. "So what if I did?" she retorted, wiping her hands on her apron self-consciously.

His heart going out to her, Travis went over, put his hands on her shoulders. He knew how it felt to be afraid the passion was too good, too true, too wonderful to last. He felt that way now.

The difference was, he wasn't going to let his own uncertainty get in the way of what they had found, of what they could have, if only they were both brave enough to stay the course. "You admit it then?" he asked, holding her in front of him gently: "That you're stalling?"

Annie shrugged and held his eyes with difficulty. The air between them was charged with all the things they'd left unsaid the day before. "We jumped into bed awfully fast," she said.

And that, Annie thought, was something she had promised herself she would never do again. And yet, here she was... Already physically, romantically, emotionally involved with someone she was just now—today—having a first, very casual date with! Her involvement with Travis put even her whirlwind romance and reckless marriage to Reece to shame.

But Travis apparently didn't think so, Annie noted as she watched Travis's eyes darken to a deep brown.

"Come on, Annie," Travis chided, his sensually chiseled lips taking on a speculative curl. "We've known each other for years."

Annie's chin lifted stubbornly. "Not that way we haven't!" she exclaimed, refusing to let him downplay any of her concerns in deference to their physical passion. "And not on an emotional level either," she pointed out sternly.

"That was true," Travis agreed readily as he regarded her with a measure of satisfaction that set Annie's pulse to racing, "prior to this week. But now you do know me, Annie, in the most intimate, satisfying way it's possible to know another person, and I know you."

He took her into his arms and an ache rocked through Annie, reminding her how much she had wanted him the day before, how much she wanted him still. She knew what he wanted. He wanted her to fight him off so he would have an excuse to tussle with her, but she wasn't going to give it to him, just as she wasn't going to admit he was the love of her life this soon, even if he was. She just wished he didn't look so darn good. She wished she wasn't so familiar with the brisk, masculine fragrance of his aftershave, or the slightly rougher, very male texture of his skin.

"For instance," Travis continued to provoke her as his mouth slowly lowered to hers, caressed hers gently. Letting her know in a heartbeat his determination to make her face the truth was every bit as potent as her desire to run from it.

"I know you like it when I kiss you like this—" Still holding her gently, he pressed his lips to hers, molding them tenderly in a soft, tentative, undemanding way. Until she found herself swaying toward him, wanting more.

"And you also like it when I kiss you like this—" He ran his tongue along the seam of her lips, until her lips parted helplessly in surrender, until her whole body was quivering with urgent sensations unlike any she had ever felt. Her heart was thumping so hard she could feel it pulsing in her ears as he kissed her over and over again, until she was trembling and swaying against him, lifting her arms to wreathe around his neck and hold him close.

"Travis," Annie moaned, aware of the need deep inside her that seemed to grow even as it was met. Her abdomen felt liquid and weightless, her knees weak. And where he pressed against her so intimately, hardness to softness, there was a tingling ache. Unable to help herself, she clasped his head, lowered it to hers and kissed him with a fervor that surprised them both. Despite her desire not to make the same mistake again, she couldn't get close enough to him. Couldn't let the steamy embrace end just yet.

He kissed her, just as passionately, dipping his tongue into her mouth with practiced strokes, until her lips began to burn and crave even more of his plundering kisses, until the rest of her wanted completion, too.

She stepped back, suddenly aware she wasn't the only one shuddering with pent-up need. So, she thought with distinctly feminine, if somewhat irrational satisfaction, Travis was having trouble dealing with his feelings, too. The passion—the overwhelming need—was out of his control, too. "Why are you doing this to me—to us?" she murmured, knowing one more kiss, one more touch of his hand, and she would be his. Not just for the afternoon, but for all time.

"Because we belong together," he whispered huskily, without one iota of remorse. He searched her eyes. "You know it. And so do I." Taking her in his arms once again, he kissed her deeply, provocatively, leaving no question about the depth of his own need for her. Gently, he pushed the hair from her cheek, looked lovingly down into her face. "You promised me a rain check, Annie," he reminded her hoarsely. "I'm taking it."

That swiftly, he slipped a strong arm beneath her knees, lifted her and carried her up the stairs to his bedroom. Like the rest of his house, it was sparsely furnished and strictly a bachelor's domain. The furniture was sturdy and made of oak, the cotton spread and sheets done in a masculine geometric print.

He whipped back the covers, then set her down on the bed and went back and kissed her in a way that let her know there would be no more holding back, for either of them. Valiantly, Annie tried to keep her emotions out of the kiss. And found, just as she had predicted, that she couldn't win. It didn't matter that these lusty feelings were quite unlike her. When she was in Travis's arms, all she could think about, all she could do, was surrender. Surrender and make the absolute most of the moment given her. And as he wrapped her in his arms and made love to her mouth with slow, thrusting probes of his tongue, she moaned, her lips molding to his, her body curving into his.

Between long, leisurely kisses, he took off her apron, her jumper, her shirt. She took off his shirt, unzipped his jeans. Tugged them down his legs, pushed them aside. At a deceptively leisurely pace, they continued kissing and undressing until they lay naked on the bed. His hands slipped between her legs as once again his mouth found her mouth. Hot and urgent, his arousal pressed against her thigh. Annie offered no resistance as his hands cupped her breasts.

It was everything she could do to try to hold herself and her soaring feelings in check. But when he brushed her hardening nipples with his fingertips, then bent to kiss the taut, aching crowns, desire swept through her in powerful waves. "Let me," she said, wanting to love all of him in the same slow, thorough way he was loving her. She wanted to feel connected to him, not just physically, but heart and soul.

Uttering a soft, male groan of contentment, he blocked her hand. "Not yet." He was hard as a rock against her. Demanding. Coaxing response after response from her with his deep, captivating kisses. Taking her wrists in his hands, he pinned them over her head and flattened them against the bed, making no bones about who was in charge. Shuddering with anticipation, Annie sucked in a breath, saw his eyes darken with pleasure as he took her breasts greedily with his mouth.

"We're just getting started." His voice was rough against her flesh, filled not with the need to control her, but simply with longing for more.

"I know," Annie murmured back as yet another thrill swept through her. Her mouth was swollen from his. She could feel it even as she longed for his kiss again. She wanted him this way, all fire and passion, nothing standing between them. Not her kids, or the gossip in town, or even the fact this was all happening way too soon....

His golden-brown eyes darkening with pleasure, he kissed his way down her body to the silky indentation of her navel. He left a trail of burning kisses across her tummy. She gasped as he moved lower still, bringing both her hands down to her sides, his warm hard-muscled chest abrading the soft skin of her thighs. Ever so gently, ever so determinedly, he kissed his way past the nest of red-gold curls, the paleness of her spread thighs. She sighed as he regained his hold on her wrists and used both their hands to bend her knees until her feet were flat on the bed, then—letting her know he was as wild for her as she was for him—probed the delicate folds with lips and tongue. Sensations ran riot through her, thrilling, enticing. Her body went soft and hot, even as she strained against the restricting grip on her wrists. Groaning victoriously at the way she was trembling with ever-escalating need, he began kissing the tops of her knees. Slowly, he made his way up the insides of her thighs, licking, stroking, nibbling with care. Pleasure swept through her until she could barely breathe. Perspiration beaded her body. Lower still, moisture bathed the insides of her thighs. "I can't take this," she murmured, marveling at the depth of her need for him, a need only he could ease.

"Yes," he whispered back, smiling and at last letting go of her wrists, "you can." And then his hands were there, too, parting her, stroking. Moving in, up, deeper. She gasped, letting him do what he wanted because at that point nothing on this earth could have gotten her to stop. As his fingers continued to stroke inside her, his lips found the top of the delicate folds. Circling, caressing. He suckled the silky nub gently, fluttering his tongue. The whisper of sensation soon turned into a flood. Her commitment to him given, she arched against him, grasping his head in her hands. She surrendered herself, her heart, her soul, as an insistent throb swelled inside her. She matched his movements until each wave of blissful sensation seemed to go on forever. And in return he consumed, he learned, he loved, he protected her with the same wonder-filled intensity and tenderness.

Annie moaned as he moved above her, love filling his eyes. Needing him the way she'd never needed any man, she wrapped her arms around his back, her legs around his waist. Murmuring her name, he entered her with a long, slow stroke. She thrust her hips upward and cloaked him in tight, honeyed warmth. Trembling with a need they no longer wanted to deny, they moved together, slowly at first, wonderingly, then more and more urgently. Heart swelling, spirits soaring, Annie rose up to meet him. She arched. He plunged. Passion and love, want and need, swirled through them until their lovemaking was so strong and right and total it didn't feel quite real. But it was, Annie knew, as his hands swept down her body once again and he kissed her hard. And it would always be. Today. Tomorrow. Forever.

AFTERWARD, Annie nestled against him, remarkably content, and yet hungry for him all over again. She shook her head ruefully, astonished at her lack of control when it came to him. She closed her eyes, enjoying the warm, silky intertwining of their bodies, letting the aftershocks shudder through her. Her breath caught in her throat as his lips traveled down her neck, dropping kisses light as butterfly wings.

"I promised myself this morning I wasn't going to do this this afternoon," she confessed wistfully. She trembled as he shifted her more fully against him. "I wasn't going to let myself be swept away by you again. We were just going to spend time together, period." Her lips curved ruefully. "Platonic time."

"Is that what you think I've done?" he asked, his

voice low and amused as he shifted onto his side and lowered his mouth gently to hers, catching her lower lip in a soft, tantalizing caress. "Swept you away?"

And then some, Annie thought, the solid feel of him sending another rush of excitement up her spine. And yet she knew this was something they had to talk about. "My life is so hectic right now. I've got so much going on. I didn't want to be involved with anyone right now—and certainly not seriously. And yet here I am," Annie deadpanned as she blew out a lusty sigh. "In bed. With you. Again, Mr. McCabe." Whether she had time for it or not, Annie was beginning to see there was something between them that was destined. Inevitable.

Travis framed her face lovingly with his hands. "Well, you've blown that, then," he teased her gently, knowing full well she was his for the taking and had been from the moment they'd intimately crossed paths again, "because what we are doing here today is very serious."

Annie shifted, so she was lying on her side, too. "There's no getting around it then," Annie murmured. She traced lazy patterns on his chest with her finger. Studied the handsome lines of his face. "This wasn't a one- or two- or three-time occurance, was it?" She drew in a deep, bolstering breath, knowing as long as she lived she would never get tired of spending time with him. In or out of bed. "We're having an affair, aren't we?"

"Worse," Travis said, his lips curving in distinctly male satisfaction as he lifted her hand to his lips and kissed the back of it. "We're in love."

His words sent a thrilling warmth through Annie. Even as she believed him, the hurt she'd suffered in the past made her cautious. "How do you know we're in love?" she asked as her heart took on a slow, heavy beat.

"Because you don't jump into bed with someone unless you're in love," Travis said huskily, his gaze lovingly roving her face. "And neither do I." He sifted his hands through her hair, watching as it fell around her shoulders in tousled red-gold waves. His heated glance drifted lower and he stroked her shoulders tenderly.

His gaze traced the tip of her tongue as she moistened her lips. She was sure she would never breathe normally again. "Because I don't play father to little boys who desperately need a daddy in their lives if I know I'm not going to be there for them in the future." He tucked a hand under her chin and lifted her lips to his. He kissed her as if he couldn't get enough of her and never would. He kissed her until everything receded but the two of them, that moment, and the possibility of making love again. He rolled onto his back, taking her with him, so she was lying across his chest. "What we've found with each other is very, very special, Annie."

Annie looked down into his face. Into his ruggedly handsome face and adoring golden-brown eyes. She knew Travis was right—he was the love of her life. "I just wish it all hadn't happened so fast," she murmured, bending to kiss him again. Tenderly. Sweetly.

Travis's hands swept down her body, then moved back up, to cup her breasts. "And I'm sorry it took so long," he said in a voice that was incredibly deep and incredibly masculine. "Because now that I've found you, Annie, I'm not ever letting you go."

"I DON'T SEE why we should wait," Travis said as Annie stepped out of the shower and began to towel-dry.

Annie blushed at the unabashed way he was admiring her slender body from head to toe. "How about because we've just had one date?" she asked as he toweled himself off, too.

One minute he'd been telling her he loved her, the next he'd been suggesting they marry as soon as possible.

Travis grinned, opened the tucked edges of the towel around her middle and stepped inside. "Who cares how many official or unofficial dates we've had?" he teased. "When we've made love four times," he said huskily.

"Exactly my point." Blushing all the more, Annie slipped out of his arms, and went to find her clothes. "We've already jumped the gun—" She struggled into bra and panties.

Travis found his shorts. "I agree, according to ordinary rules of courtship, we've done everything all wrong," he said as he slipped them on.

Annie let her gaze drift over the heart-stopping sexy length of him. "You can say that again." She had never seen a more chiseled chest or abs, even on a hunk-of-the-month calendar or movie screen.

"But ordinary rules of courtship do not apply to what we feel for each other, Annie," Travis reminded as he tugged on his shirt. Buttoning as he went, he crossed to her side. "And you know why they don't?" he asked as he caught up with her and wrapped his arms around her waist.

Annie let out a soft little sigh, already able to feel herself weakening, and he'd barely started his why-we-should-do-this pitch. "No, but I have a feeling you're going to tell me." She smiled.

Travis caressed her cheek with the pad of his thumb and looked deep into her eyes. "Because we're not kids anymore," he told her softly, seriously. "We've lived enough to know what we're feeling happens once in a lifetime. If you're lucky. Sure—" he inclined his head casually "—we could go through the motions of dating for six more months, even a year or two years, and then get engaged and plan a big wedding. And that would be fine, except for the difficulties posed in the meantime." His eyes darkened and he frowned as he confessed, "I'm tired of spending my nights alone, Annie. I want to be with you, and not just every now and then, but every day and every night." He paused, letting his words sink in.

When she'd caught her breath, he continued in a voice that melted Annie's resistance and appealed to her heart all the more, "I want to combine our ranches and our lives and be the daddy your boys need and deserve to have in their lives even if I won't ever have the official title. I want to love you and protect you and make you mine for the rest of our lives. Say yes, Annie. Say you'll marry me, and say it today."

"HOW COME we have to wear our jackets and ties?" Tyler asked as Annie took him out of the tub and toweled him dry.

"Because everyone is going to be dressed up tonight." Annie helped Teddy and Trevor from the tub, too.

"Even you and Travis?" Trevor asked as Annie toweled him dry.

"Yes." Working as quickly but as gently as possible, Annie turned to help Teddy.

"You're not dressed up now," Tyler pointed out, nodding at her old shorts and T-shirt. Which were, coincidentally, the ones she wore when she cleaned house.

"That's because I need to get you guys ready first," Annie said, aware she had never felt as frazzled and unprepared for an evening out on the town as she did at that moment. Annie hung up the wet towels as the boys struggled into their cartoon-character underwear and socks.

Teddy asked, "Momma, when's Travis coming over?"

"Any minute now." Annie led the way into her bedroom, where the rest of the boys' clothes were already laid out, ready to be put on.

"Good." Tyler put on his yellow Oxford-cloth shirt.

Teddy grabbed his light blue shirt. "Yeah, we like Travis."

"We like Travis *a lot*." Trevor shoved his arms through his sand-colored shirt.

Now that we're on the subject, Annie thought... "How would you feel if Travis and I were to decide to get married?" Annie asked as all three boys struggled into their khaki dress pants, trying not to show the apprehension she felt.

"Where would we live?" Teddy asked, his hazel eyes widening with amazement.

That was easy, Annie thought. "Either at his ranch or here on this one," Annie said.

All three boys beamed as they mulled over that idea. "I like his ranch," Trevor said as he struggled into his socks. "He's got horses."

"And cowboys," Tyler noted happily as Annie helped him button his shirt and put on his clip-on tie.

"And Travis likes us, too," Teddy said giddily as he hunted around for his shiny new cowboy boots.

"Yeah, he likes us a lot," Trevor enthused as he found his boots, too.

"He's a very good man," Annie told her boys sincerely. The best, in fact, she had ever met.

Tyler grinned. "Yeah, Momma, he is."

"Well?" Her heart pounding, Annie waited for their decision.

The three boys exchanged looks. It was quickly clear they were all of the same opinion. "We think you should marry him, Momma," Tyler spoke for the group. "Real soon."

"I HEAR I'VE GOT a cheering section," Travis drawled that evening after they had returned home from one of the loveliest rehearsal dinners Annie had ever attended, and tucked Annie's three very exhausted little boys into bed.

Annie blushed as Travis took off his sport coat and loosened the knot of his tie. She sat down on the sofa and watched him get comfortable right beside her. "What do you mean?" she asked shyly as his golden-brown eyes roved her upturned face, then dropped lower, to linger at the open V-neck of her long and pretty floral dress.

Travis fingered the delicate lace on her lapel-style collar. "The boys want us to get married."

As Annie cuddled against Travis, she recalled with

disturbing clarity how it had felt to stretch out next to him in his bed and wantonly string kisses from throat to navel to thigh. And knew, with even more clarity, how much she wished she could do so again. Not just once or twice. But every day the rest of her life. She wanted to sleep with him and wake with him and love him every minute of every day and night the rest of her life. "They told you."

Travis smiled at her. "As you probably knew they would."

Annie's pulse points pounded at the heat she heard in his low voice. "I wanted to see how they felt about it."

Travis ran a hand through the silk of her hair and looked deep into her hazel-green eyes. "The question is," he posed softly, romantically, "how do you feel about it, Annie?"

Annie held herself perfectly still. She had promised herself she would go slow, she would wait. But even as she reminded herself of her decision, she knew it was futile. Nothing was going to change in a week or a month or a year. Her feelings were what they were, and she sensed his were, too.

*What are you waiting for?* she prodded herself silently. *You know you want to be with him, too. You know you've never felt about anyone the way you feel about Travis. He makes you feel safe, loved, wanted. He supports you personally and professionally. He adores the boys. They adore him.* There was every reason in the world to marry him. And no reason not to marry him.

Annie wreathed her arms around his neck, happier at that moment than she had ever been in her life. "The answer," she said, kissing him sweetly, lingeringly, "is yes."

## Chapter Ten

"Is it true? Is my son pressuring you to elope with him as soon as John and I renew our wedding vows?" Lilah McCabe asked early the next morning.

Annie had gone over to the McCabe ranch at Lilah's request, to help Lilah prepare the birdseed bags for the wedding guests. Birdseed, in lieu of rice, would be thrown as the bride and groom dashed from the church to the limo that would take them to the reception.

"How'd you hear that?" Annie asked as she cut off the top of the birdseed bag and poured it into a four-quart mixing bowl. For someone who was getting married all over again today, Lilah was awfully calm.

"His brothers and my husband," Lilah reported happily as she handed Annie a stack of white mesh squares and kept another for herself. "Apparently he asked Shane if he'd be available to oversee his ranch, and Jackson and Wade and their wives to care for the boys for a couple days, if you said yes. Then he asked his dad if he knew any places where you two could get married quickly that were nicer than the bait-and-tackle shop where Shane married Greta."

Annie shook her head as she scooped up a quarter cup of seed and put it in the center of a mesh square. She should have known they would not be able to keep a secret from the lively McCabes. "Travis likes to plan ahead," she said dryly, watching as Lilah did the same.

"Plus, the triplets told John at the rehearsal dinner last night that you might 'lope with Travis and they wanted you to 'lope with Travis 'cause they love Travis and Travis loves all of you, only they didn't know what 'lope meant."

Annie fought a blush as she gathered the mesh together tightly and tied a thin ribbon around the top. Shaking her head, she said, "I can't keep a secret around them, that's for sure." She and Travis had been sure all three of her sons had been wrapped up in looking for cows and horsies when they were ever so carefully and cryptically discussing eloping during the drive to the church the previous night.

"So is it true?" Lilah leaned forward intently, bright blue eyes sparkling. "*Is* my son pressuring you to forgo a wedding with your family and friends in lieu of doing something quick and easy?"

Unsure how to answer that without getting Travis in hot water with his mother, Annie watched Lilah snip off slender satin ribbon in precise six-inch lengths. "We're both awfully busy—"

Lilah cut her off with a decisive shake of the head. "That's no excuse, Annie," she said sternly. "When you and Travis get married, it should be with all your loved ones and friends present." Giving her heartfelt words a moment to sink in, Lilah paused, then continued softly, persuasively, "You know that's what your own parents would have wanted. And it is *definitely* what John and I want for our son Travis.''

Annie could see that.

Lilah studied Annie's uncertain expression, then continued as generously as usual, ''If you're worried about planning the wedding all by yourself, or not having someone to walk you down the aisle, you needn't be. I'll help you plan. And as for the other, John would be happy to do it. Or you could even have your three boys give you away.''

Annie couldn't deny that she would like to do this right. But there was more to consider than what she wanted here. She bit her lip. ''Travis seems dead set against a big wedding, Lilah.'' And that being the case...

''Because of what happened to him before,'' Lilah guessed unhappily, reminding them both that Travis's previous fiancée, Rayanne, had died en route to her wedding to him. And there were some who said Travis still wasn't quite over the tragedy yet.

Annie sighed and continued making up birdseed bags. ''He didn't say so directly—''

''But he was obviously thinking it,'' Lilah guessed with a frown. She put down her scissors with a thud. ''You can't let him run away from this, Annie. I know you love him with all your heart—''

''It's that obvious?'' Annie interrupted, not sure whether to be annoyed or pleased about that. She thought she did a better job keeping her feelings to herself, at least where everyone but Travis was concerned.

Lilah nodded, confirming it was so. ''Every time the two of you look at each other, we can all see how much in love you are. There's just no hiding it, dear.

And Travis adores your boys as deeply as they adore
him. John and I think—as does everyone else who
knows you—that the five of you were really meant to
be a family. But when you do that, when you take
that leap of faith, you've got to do it right. And you
can't be running from any ghosts in the process,'' she
said sternly.

Annie finished filling another bag and looped a ribbon around the top. ''Is that what you think Travis is
doing in wanting us to elope?'' she asked.

Lilah paused as if not sure how to answer. Finally,
she said, ''After Rayanne died, Travis was so hurt, he
felt so responsible, well, we didn't think that Travis
would ever get seriously involved with a woman
again.''

Annie shot Lilah a bewildered look. What was Lilah talking about? she wondered, stunned. ''Travis
wasn't even with Rayanne when the accident oc-
curred.'' Annie paused. ''Why would *he* feel responsible?''

Lilah's hands stilled abruptly. ''He hasn't talked to
you about this at all?'' Clearly, she thought as close
as Annie and Travis had become—close enough to
want to get married right away—that Travis would
have.

''No,'' Annie said quietly, beginning to feel a little
upset as well as confused. ''Travis's relationship with
Rayanne never came up.'' *I never brought it up.* Just
as with Reece, she hadn't delved too deeply into anything she thought might give her second thoughts
about becoming so intimately involved with him.

Annie took a deep breath to steady herself. She
knew Lilah. Lilah didn't interfere unless she thought
it was necessary. She studied her mother-in-law-to-

be. "You think what happened with the two of them is still affecting him, don't you?" she asked Lilah. Telling herself she wasn't making the same mistake here she had with Reece.

Lilah let out her breath slowly. She seemed to be struggling with her need to protect her son and her desire to see that Annie and Travis didn't fall into the same pitfalls he'd fallen in years before with Rayanne.

"Of all my sons, Travis has always been the most responsible," Lilah said carefully. "Even when he wasn't responsible for something, he felt responsible. He can't seem to help it. And he was that way long before his dad and I ever asked him to watch out for his younger brothers because he was the oldest. It's in his personality. Plus, he's so tender and loving— deep down, he can't help but feel badly about the way things ended with Rayanne," Lilah concluded sadly.

"Then the stories are true?" Annie asked, feeling her own apprehension grow. The night before at the rehearsal dinner, though outwardly genial, Travis had seemed distant and distracted several times as he watched the minister explain who stood where and when and helped John and Lilah rehearse their vows. She'd just assumed he had a lot on his mind—her, the boys, his folks' wedding, his ranch. Now she wondered if he hadn't been brooding over the past, too. Harboring his own regrets. "The two of them had a fight the night before the wedding?" Annie—who hadn't been living in Laramie at the time—conjured up what she could recall of the gossip from years ago.

Lilah nodded. "His father and I saw the tension between Travis and Rayanne during the rehearsal dinner. To this day, I still don't know what their disagreement was about. Just that the morning of the wedding, Travis wasn't even sure the ceremony was going to take place.'' Lilah sighed as if it hurt her deeply, recalling it all. She got up to get her and Annie both some more coffee.

Coming back to the table, carafe in hand, she refilled their cups. ''Rayanne had run off after their fight—no one knew where, not even her parents,'' Lilah continued, shaking her head and uttering a sad sigh. ''John and I told Travis it was only a case of prewedding jitters and that of course Rayanne would come to her senses and show up at the church in time. They'd been in love with each other forever, dating only each other from the time they were sixteen and all through college, and then engaged for almost five years after that.''

Annie remembered seeing them together in high school. Rayanne's dad had been a rancher too, and a schoolteacher by profession. Sweet and down-to-earth, she would have been the perfect rancher's wife. ''How many years were they together in all?'' Annie asked curiously.

Lilah had to think about that. ''Eleven or so, I guess,'' she said finally.

That was quite a history with one woman, Annie thought.

And now Travis wanted to marry *her* after just a week.

Why? What was the rush? Annie was pretty sure it wasn't only the gossip potential or the inconvenience of trying to manage a love affair. Travis was a man who could be very patient when it came to getting what he wanted—he'd had to work years building up his ranch. Yet he wanted her and the boys and a life together right away.

Realizing abruptly how much she was suddenly doubting Travis and his love for her, when up until now she'd had absolutely no reason to, Annie sighed, and pushed her doubts away. "Well, whatever it was, Rayanne must have forgiven Travis, because she would have married him that night if she hadn't had a car accident on the way to the church."

Lilah nodded firmly. "You're right. She would have. Because she had her wedding dress and everything she needed with her in the car."

Annie fell silent as she sipped her coffee. She knew Lilah. Lilah wouldn't be telling her all this, reminding her, if the woman didn't think Annie should follow through and investigate Travis's motives for eloping and his feelings about weddings in general on her own. And as much as Annie was loath to, she had to do this, for herself, for Travis, for her children. "But he still blames himself for her death," Annie guessed unhappily.

Lilah nodded as her blue eyes took on a worried, maternal gleam. "I'm only telling you because I think Travis needs to talk about this, Annie, and I think he needs to talk to *you*."

"GET ALL THE BIRDSEED BAGS ready?" Travis asked Annie shortly after lunch later that day.

Annie nodded. Her boys, exhausted from the previous day, had fallen asleep in their sleeping bags on the living-room floor within five minutes of starting their favorite video. She took Travis by the hand and led him out onto the front porch, where they could talk without fear of waking the boys, who desperately needed a long nap if they were to make it through John and Lilah's wedding that evening.

"Yes. But that's not really why your mother asked me to come over there," Annie said, figuring she might as well get this over with, and the sooner the better.

Travis quirked his eyebrow curiously.

"She thinks your wanting us to elope has something to do with your botched wedding to Rayanne," Annie continued.

Travis scowled, letting Annie know in a heartbeat that as far as he was concerned, that subject was completely off limits. "She had no right bringing that up," he said tersely.

Annie drew in a jagged breath as she settled on the porch swing, aware her pulse rate had picked up marginally. If only she had talked about potentially problematic things like this before she had agreed to marry Travis, she wouldn't be in such a fix now. She waited for him to settle beside her on the swing. "She also thinks we owe it to ourselves to have a church wedding with all our loved ones in attendance."

Travis's eyes gleamed with a mixture of displeasure and disappointment. He took her hand in his. "I explained to you why I didn't want to wait."

"I don't want to wait either, Travis. I'd like us to get married today, if possible. But I also think your mother is right. That if we're going to do this, we should do it right. Unless there's some reason you think history might repeat itself here?"

"Why would you think that?" he asked sharply, vaulting to his feet. His gaze took on an accusing quality.

"Suppose you tell me," Annie said, aware she had

stumbled onto something here. Something she might not have seen had it not been for Lilah. "What really happened between you and Rayanne the night of the rehearsal dinner?"

Travis blew out an uneasy breath, looking less willing than ever to confide in her. But to his credit, he lifted his eyes to hers, and said evenly, "We had a fight."

Annie tilted her head to the side and drew another, deeper breath. "About...?"

Travis shrugged, slid his hands into his pockets and sat down on the low stone-and-stucco wall that enclosed the porch and edged the front of the ranch house. Lips pressed together grimly, he replied, "It was about me not loving her the way I should."

Annie blinked, amazed. "How could she say that?" Annie said emotionally. Rising, she crossed to Travis's side and sat down next to him on the wall. "The two of you had been together for eleven years."

Travis pivoted slightly to face her. His voice was low, sad, introspective. "Actually, it was closer to twelve."

Annie studied him, knowing no matter how difficult it was for her, these things needed to be said, and said now. "Why would she have doubted you then?"

"Because," Travis said heavily, his guilt apparent, "I didn't love her. Not the way I should."

Annie stared at him, stunned, as all the old feelings, all the self-doubt, came rushing back. Travis sighed heavily, and not waiting for any more questions, continued sadly, "Rayanne saw it in my eyes, she said, at the rehearsal. Or rather, it was what she didn't see," Travis amended even more self-deprecatingly.

"Which was...?" Annie asked, not so sure she wanted to hear the answer now.

"Overwhelming passion. Adoration. Crazy-in-love lust." Travis sighed heavily, ran a hand through the short, neat layers of his hair. "She said I was marrying her out of friendship and duty and responsibility and habit and convenience." He recited the words as if the litany of complaint had haunted him a very long time.

Annie's heart went out to him. "And were you?" she asked cautiously, needing more than ever to understand what had gone on with Travis and Rayanne so the two of them wouldn't make the same mistake.

Travis pressed his lips together and looked even more unhappy with himself, for what had happened, and with Annie, for bringing it up. "Rayanne and I'd dated a long time," he said finally. "Got serious physically maybe before we should have. And once that happened—" he shrugged in his Mr. Responsibility way "—I couldn't leave her. And then time passed, and I did care about her the way I should have. We were great friends. We wanted the same thing, a life here in Laramie, a big family with four or five kids, a ranch to call our own. I added all that up together and thought all that was love."

Annie studied the hurt simmering in his eyes, just below the regret. "When did you realize it wasn't?" she asked gently, knowing firsthand what it was like to discover that an involvement with your "chosen mate" was a mistake.

"During the engagement..." Travis blew out a deeply aggravated breath. He looked angry and upset with himself again. "The closer we got to the wedding, the less I wanted to actually go through with it.'' He paused, shook his head. "Rayanne must have sensed it, even before I did.''

"And called you on it,'' Annie guessed, able to imagine how unpleasant and traumatic that must have been.

"The day of the rehearsal dinner,'' Travis confirmed as he got up to pace the length of the front porch once again. Through the living-room windows, Annie could see all three boys, still sleeping soundly on the floor, in front of the TV. Assured all was well for the moment, she turned her gaze back to Travis.

He continued, "She accused me of not really loving her. I said of course I did, but as we went through the rehearsal at the church, I—well, there's no other way to say it—I wanted to be anywhere but there. She knew it. Said she wasn't marrying for anything less than love, threw her ring at me and took off.''

Which had probably made Travis feel even more guilty and more of a heel, Annie thought. She studied the tortured expression on his face. "Did you then realize you loved her after all?''

"No.'' Travis looked at Annie steadily, man enough to admit, "I knew that I really didn't love her, because what I felt then was relief.''

"And yet you didn't call off the wedding yourself,'' Annie said.

Travis spread his hands on either side of her. He looked at her beseechingly as he explained, "I couldn't humiliate her in front of all her family and friends.''

"So you would have married her if she'd come back, and stayed with her,'' Annie guessed, not sure how she felt about that.

Again, Travis shrugged, as if his duty to Rayanne—the ill-thought-out commitment he had made to her—had ultimately been far more important than what had been in his heart. "I owed her that much," he explained as if it were the most rational thing in the world. "I'd promised her I'd always be there for her. I'd given my word. I couldn't have gone back on that, Annie," he said stubbornly. "And to this day, I still wouldn't."

"Is that why you don't want a big wedding?" Annie asked after a moment, still mulling over what he had told her. "Because you're afraid if we wait, something will jinx it or you'll change your mind about marrying me?" She hated to think their love was that tenuous.

"No." Travis grinned. "I don't want a big wedding because I don't want to have to wait to be with you. However… " Travis took Annie in his arms and said with a half smile, "I am prepared to compromise on this wedding dilemma."

Annie caught the teasing glint in his eyes and couldn't help but grin. "Compromise how?" she asked, loving the way he felt against her, so warm and tall and strong.

"By doing both." Travis traced the upswept strands of her hair. "Elope now," he suggested firmly, "in the next day or so—so we can start living in the same house together—and then have a second formal ceremony after the fact for all our loved ones when my folks get back from their second honeymoon. That way, we both get what we want. You and I get to be together—now. The boys will have an on-the-premises daddy to love them and help take care of them. Everyone's happy. It's the perfect solution."

Annie shook her head, wondering how she had ever

said no to him, even for one second. "You're really determined to do this, aren't you?" she remarked playfully.

"Yes, Annie, I am." Travis bent his head and kissed her tenderly. "I want us to blend our lives, and the sooner the better."

Annie wanted that, too. So much so that she knew she was going to give in to him, even against her better judgment, which was still telling her simply to wait, be patient just a little longer, and do it right— once—and only once.

"Before we can get a license, we're going to need a few things," he said.

"Such as?"

"Your birth certificate and proof of your divorce."

Annie groaned.

"Don't have it?" Travis guessed.

"It's probably with my papers, which I dumped in with my dad's papers, which are all in the cedar chest in the bottom of the hall closet."

"How long do you think it will take you to find it?"

Annie rolled her eyes, said drolly, "If I'm lucky? Since I never have gotten around to creating a filing system for any of my important documents—a couple hours."

THE TRIPLETS WERE STILL SLEEPING blissfully and Travis was down to the ice in his glass of lemonade when Annie finally came back out onto the porch, manila envelope in her hand, with her father's hand-writing on the front. She looked pale, upset. Why, Travis couldn't fathom, unless she had been unable to locate everything they needed to get married.

"Find what you were looking for?" he asked curiously, unable to mistake the boiling resentment and fury in her hazel-green eyes.

"And more," she announced flatly, opening the envelope and shoving the contents into his hand. Travis looked down at the legal agreement that dealt with the eventual sale of Annie's Triple Diamond Ranch. Like lightning, the guilt that had been weighing on Travis since Annie's dad had talked him into making the deal behind Annie's back came back to haunt him. He felt he couldn't breathe. Like he'd never be the same again. It had been hell, keeping this from Annie all this time. Trying to make her see reason about it now was going to be even harder.

Knowing nothing would be gained from either of them becoming emotional, however, Travis took Annie's wrist in his and pulled her down beside him on the swing. The situation was bad, he reassured himself firmly, but not unsalvageable, and it wouldn't be unless he lost his head.

"I'm sorry you found out about my contract with your dad this way," he said gently. "But, before you make any snap judgements," he warned, "I can explain—"

Annie tore her wrist from his hand and vaulted from the swing. "I'll just bet you can." She glared at him.

Travis sighed. "Annie—"

She stalked into the front yard, making sure they were out of earshot of the house, when she spun around to face him. "You made a deal with my father to buy this ranch before he died and you never told me?" she demanded incredulously.

Travis took her elbow and steered her out of the

hot Texas sun and into the shade of the nearest tree. "Your father didn't want you to know." Sensing Annie was going to bolt again, Travis guided her back against the tree trunk. "He thought you'd be upset if you knew he was taking care of the financial aspects of your inheritance from him before he died."

"You bet I'm upset!" Annie sent him a withering glance, making no effort at all to contain her hurt over the deception. "My father told me he was leaving this ranch to me!"

"And he did leave it to you," Travis explained patiently. "He just didn't expect you to want to live here with the boys after he was gone. And since you wouldn't even discuss selling the ranch with Joe before he died—"

"Of course I wouldn't!" Annie said, tears filling her eyes. "This ranch was his whole life. How could I sell it out from under him, knowing how little time he had left on this earth with us?"

"He understood it was an emotional issue for you," Travis said heavily.

"An emotional issue!" Annie repeated, incensed.

"But he couldn't rest until he had worked things out to his own satisfaction."

"With you!" Annie said, looking even more upset. "Behind my back!"

Travis sighed. He could see Annie was ready to call it quits with him right now. But throwing everything away for something that could never be changed, no matter how much they wished it could, was crazy.

"Your dad wanted to make sure the land would be taken care of, Annie," Travis continued to explain.

"He knew I wanted his land if and when he ever decided to sell."

Annie tried to step past. Travis braced a hand on either side of her and blocked her way. "So we agreed. After Joe was gone, when you were ready, I would buy the ranch from you and pay you fair market price at the time of the sale. Your dad figured the money from the sale would leave you and the boys set for life. And it would give me the larger ranch I had always wanted. So we worked out the conditions with our lawyers—"

"That's what all the meetings with the lawyers were about," Annie said, looking even more angry.

Travis nodded, confirming this was so. "And we signed the deal."

Annie shook her head, determined, it seemed, to think the worst of him. "Was marrying me part of the deal, too?" she demanded with an icy hauteur that would have sent a lesser man running for the hills.

"No." Travis stared at her in frustration.

Annie sent him another withering glance. "But you did promise him something, didn't you?"

"Yes." Travis stepped closer and took her rigid body in his arms. "I promised him I'd always look after you and the boys."

Annie's chin lifted. She speared him with a censuring, holier-than-thou gaze. "To the point you were willing to be a daddy to my boys and marry me, obviously," she concluded in a low voice dripping with sarcasm.

"My marrying you had nothing to do with my promise to your father," Travis said archly, his own temper beginning to flare. "As for the kids, I love them, pure and simple, the same way I love you, and would have no matter what.''

"Don't kid yourself, Travis.'' Annie shoved away from him. She whirled on him, eyes glittering furiously. "You're a responsible guy who takes his promises to others very seriously.'' As she spoke, her face grew pale, her shoulders even stiffer. "And this ties everything up very neatly, doesn't it?'' She advanced on him, not stopping until they were nose to nose. She stabbed a finger at his chest. "By romancing me, you got the sons you always wanted, my land, and fulfilled your promise to my father all in one fell swoop. And whaddaya know—'' she threw up her arms and stepped back "—you had a little sex thrown in, just for fun. What more could a lonesome cowboy want?''

Travis grasped her arms and held her in front of him. "How about a woman who knows he loves her, no matter how things look?''

"That's the trouble with me, Travis.'' Annie stood still and lifeless as a statue in his arms. "I pay attention to what's right in front of my eyes. I own up to my mistakes. I call a *halt* before it's too late.''

Stung by the look in her eyes, as much as her words, Travis let go of her and stepped back. With a growing sense of helplessness, he ran both his hands through his hair and asked, "What are you saying?''

"The engagement's off.'' Annie glared at him, then continued in a choked voice, "And so is our romance!''

"I don't want the ranch, Annie,'' Travis retorted, wishing there were some way to make her believe that. "You can have it.''

Annie shrugged and continued in a cold, calm

voice Travis found much more terrifying than her anger. "Texas is a community-property state. You marry me, you'll get it anyway."

He advanced on her slowly, his eyes holding hers. "So we'll have the lawyers draw up a prenup," he suggested, not caring how they resolved this as long as they *resolved* it.

"Don't you get it?" Annie told him heatedly, the hurt of his betrayal glimmering like tears in her eyes. "I can't trust you to tell me the truth, the whole truth, and nothing but the truth! And if I can't do that," she cried sadly, "we have nothing, Travis. Nothing."

## Chapter Eleven

The phone was ringing as Travis let himself in the door. He was tempted to just let it ring, but given that his parents were renewing their wedding vows in a few hours, and he was still Annie's closest neighbor, and she and her sons had at least one emergency, if not more, a day, he couldn't exactly do that.

Muttering cantankerously to himself, he stomped to the phone and snatched it off the wall. "Rocking M Cattle Ranch," he snarled. "Travis McCabe speaking."

Static and heavy breathing followed. "Travis, Momma's crying," Tyler reported anxiously.

If truth be known, now that Annie had kicked him out of her life, her home, and her heart, Travis felt like crying, too.

"Yeah, and she's locked herself in the bathroom again," Teddy added over his brother's voice, just as worriedly. "Only this time she knows we're awake!"

Tyler sighed loudly. "She says she needs a bubble bath. Momma never takes bubble baths in the afternoon, especially after we waked up from a nap."

Travis shut his eyes and rubbed the tense muscles in his neck. The last thing he needed was to picture

Annie in the tub again. Seeing her that way—all luscious and beautiful and neck-deep in mounds of frothy bubbles—was part of what had gotten them to this place. He needed to stop thinking of her as a woman and the love of his life, and start thinking of her as just any other neighbor. Travis cleared his throat. "Maybe she needs a time-out, guys," he said gruffly.

"Why?" Tyler demanded amidst the commotion on the other end. "Did she do something bad?"

"No." Travis sighed heavily, cursing himself for ever having deceived Annie, no matter what her father had wanted. "I did."

There was a baffled silence on the other end as Annie's sons tried to absorb what he'd said. "So how come you're not in time-out?"

Knowing he'd never be able to explain this to a five-year-old, not in a million years, Travis sighed. "I am."

"Are you sitting in a chair?" he asked curiously.

Travis grimaced as he recalled the look on Annie's face as she threw him out. "It's not that kind of time-out," Travis explained.

"What kind of time-out is it?" Tyler persisted amidst all the static on the other end.

*The kind where Annie never wants to see or hear me again. The kind where I sleep and eat and live alone for the rest of my life, knowing I was this close to having the woman of my dreams forever.* "It's complicated," Travis said finally, wishing he could go to Annie and start all over again. But that wasn't going to happen. She wasn't going to forgive him. And for that, he could hardly blame her. He wouldn't have wanted to be deceived by her, either.

Loud commiserating sighs echoed on the other end of the connection. "That's what Momma said right before she started crying real hard." Tyler said. "She said her heart is smashed all to pieces."

In a low, concerned voice, Tyler reported, "She said she's never gonna love anyone the way she loves you."

Travis paused, the first glimmer of hope radiating in his chest. "She told you that?" Travis straightened.

"No. She told one of her friends—back in Dallas—before she went in to take her bubble bath," Tyler continued. "She said she's never gonna stop crying in a million years."

"Yeah, and we don't got that much Kleenex," Teddy added.

Well, here it was, Travis thought, the moment of truth. Rayanne hadn't believed he loved her when he said he did, because—bottom line—he hadn't felt about her the way he should, the way he felt about Annie.

Annie didn't believe he loved her, either.

But this time was different.

He had to make Annie see that.

And he would, doggone it. Whether she wanted to or not. "Hang in there, guys," Travis reassured Annie's sons. "I'll be right over. And one more thing. No, make that two more things," Travis decided rapidly. "Are you listening?"

"Yes." This was followed by the sound of a lot of heavy breathing over the phone. He could just see them listening real hard, struggling over the phone reciever. "Behave yourself until I get there," Travis continued sternly. He waited until he had elicited solemn promises from all three. "And don't tell her I'm coming. It'll take me about thirty minutes."

ANNIE CAME OUT of the bathroom wrapped in her favorite terry-cloth robe. Pink, frayed everywhere it was possible to be frayed and so thin from repeated washings it was practically threadbare in places—just the act of putting it on usually made her feel better. Not today.

Grabbing her tissues, she headed past the living room. And stopped dead in her tracks at what she saw. All three of her sons were lined up on the sofa, watching TV, the most innocent expressions in the world on their faces. They never sat and quietly watched TV after they'd had a nap, they were always too wound up and full of energy. Plus, they were upset that she was upset, even though they didn't seem to understand that she and Travis were through. Finished. Over.

"What's going on here, guys?" Annie asked suspiciously, knowing with a certainty as solid as gold that *something* was up.

Their little elbows went into action. Their eyebrows lifted with choirboy innocence. "Nothing," they said in perfect unison.

"Oh, I can see that," Annie drawled. Curious now at what they'd done—she didn't see any new murals on the living-room wall—Annie padded closer. "Did you guys get into something you weren't supposed to get into?" She should have known better than to take a long bubble bath while they were still awake. Even if she and the boys did have a wedding to attend that very evening.

Although how she was going to get through that

when she knew she had to see Travis there, and his entire family, including John and Lilah, the bride and groom, and his three happily married brothers and their wives. Well, it was going to be murder on her, no doubt about it. Probably him, too.

Oblivious to her thoughts, the boys remained perfectly silent. A difficult accomplishment for three five-year-olds who could never seem to stop talking— to each other and everyone and anyone else who might happen by. "You're not going to tell me?" Annie persisted, her curiosity piqued.

The boys continued to avoid her eyes with great difficulty. "We can't," Tyler said finally.

Annie frowned, hoping this wasn't the prelude to another emergency. The last thing she wanted to do was call Travis and ask him to come over and help her out again. "Did you boys break something?" Annie persisted. "Eat something?"

The doorbell rang, interrupting her.

Annie's frown deepened. Tyler, Teddy and Trevor straightened, looking not at all surprised at the interruption, and attempted to look all the more innocent. "Please tell me that's nothing involving the three of you," she muttered beneath her breath.

Annie walked over to the door, peered out. Saw Travis standing on the front porch. Dressed as he had been the last time she'd seen him, in chambray shirt and jeans, he looked loaded for bear. And as coolly determined as she had ever seen him.

Her heart thundered in her chest. Her spirits rose and crashed and rose again. Temper simmering, she tightened her threadbare pink robe around her and swung open the door with a flourish. Two could play at this self-confidence game. "Go away," she snapped, her cool haughty look giving him no alternative but to do just that.

She expected him to react angrily.

Instead, Travis grinned as happily as if she had just given him the sweetest welcome possible, and caught the door one-handed before she could slam it in his face. "Thanks. Don't mind if I do," he drawled smugly, as though she'd just invited him in.

He shouldered past her when she wouldn't step aside, a ranch-size first-aid kit in hand. But it was no ordinary first-aid kit, Annie noted. Without warning, all three boys were off the sofa and beside them.

"What did you bring?" Trevor piped up.

"I'm glad you asked." Travis swept off his hat genially and set it aside. "I have here in my hand an Emergency Feel Better Annie First-Aid Kit."

Cute, Annie thought, still glaring at Travis, and it wasn't going to work. "We don't need one of those," Annie told him stiffly.

"That's not what I heard, Miss My Heart Has Been Smashed All To Pieces."

Aware she had been ratted on, Annie gasped. As all three of her sons ducked their heads, Travis raked Annie with a glance, then sat down in a chair, caught Annie's hand and pulled her down onto his lap. "Want to see what's in it?" he asked.

"No," Annie said stiffly as she folded her arms in front of her. She was not going to let him get to her with sweet talk. And sweeter kisses. She was not!

"Okay, I'll be glad to show you," Travis said genially as he opened his kit and spread it out on her lap. "One engagement ring—still in pretty good condition despite having been thrown in my face, if you don't count the smidgen of barbecue sauce on the side. Two wedding rings to match. Kleenex—can never have enough of those, especially for happy occasions like our wedding.''

At the mention of their marriage, Annie's sons brightened. ''I am not marrying you!'' she told Travis hotly. Her sons' faces fell.

Travis gave her a look that said: *We'll see about that.* ''And one empty jar,'' Travis continued confidently as her sons gathered round and relaxed once again.

Despite herself, Annie had to know. ''What is that supposed to be?'' she scowled at the jar.

''It's all the love I have in my heart,'' Travis said softly, enough tenderness in his eyes to fill all the oceans in the world. ''I was saving it for you, Annie, but if you're not going to use it—'' he regarded her steadily ''—then it'll just have to sit on a shelf, 'cause I'm not ever gonna use it on anyone else. And last not but least,'' Travis finished, ''is a contract I signed with your dad, Annie. Because we won't be needing that. This ranch belongs to you and your sons. And it's going to stay yours until the boys are grown up. I'll keep it in good working condition. I figure I owe you that much.''

Annie felt a lump the size of a walnut gathering in her throat. ''For what?'' she croaked out, determined she was not going to cry.

''For smashing your heart in a million pieces, of course.''

Annie shot a disgruntled look at her boys. Caught having spilled all to Travis yet again, they jumped up from the sofa. ''I think I wanna go outside and swing,'' Trevor said urgently.

''Me, too,'' Tyler added swiftly.

"Me three," Teddy agreed.

Without waiting for permission—or denial—they raced out the door.

Unwilling to admit how good it felt to be sitting on his lap again, Annie sighed and looked at Travis. It was all she could do not to throw her arms around his neck and forgive him all that very second. "They called you again, didn't they?" she guessed wearily.

Travis nodded as he put the Emergency Feel Better Annie First-Aid Kit aside and wrapped his arms around her affectionately. "You bet they did. They said it was an emergency." He lifted the hair away from her neck and nuzzled kisses along her chin. "And you gave them permission to do so, but only in an emergency."

Stubbornly, Annie ignored the tingles of desire he was creating. "I was fine," she told him haughtily.

Travis snorted in derision. He took one of her hands and lifted it to his lips. He kissed the underside of her wrist. Then, for good measure, the back of it, too. "You were crying your heart out. They were very worried."

"They're not anymore." Annie glanced out the window and saw them climbing merrily on their swing set.

"That's because they know I'm here." Travis cupped her face in his hands and looked deep into her eyes. "And as long as I'm here with you, and you're with me, everything's going to be all right."

He made it sound so simple. Annie knew it wasn't. "I shouldn't forgive you," Annie said stubbornly.

"But you're going to," Travis retorted just as stubbornly. "And you know why?"

Her heart took on a staccato beat. "No. But I suppose you're going to tell me."

"Because you love me, Annie," he said. And then he kissed her with a thoroughness that left her trembling and weak and made all her doubts about him seem inconsequential. "As much as I love you. And that kind of love is too precious and too wonderful to waste, no matter what problems come along," Travis whispered, looking as if he might be blinking back tears of happiness, too.

The tears she'd been holding back spilled down Annie's face.

Travis reached over and retrieved the packet of tissues. "See," he teased as she cried all the harder, "I knew these would come in handy."

Annie gave him a punch to the chest. She should have known she would never be able to stay angry at him. "Were you really going to leave your heart on a shelf?" She wiped her eyes and smiled through her tears.

Travis nodded soberly, his happiness underscored only by his need. "You're the only woman for me, Annie," he said huskily. "It took us a long time to really get to know each other, but in this past week I realize we were meant for each other, and I'm not ever going to stop loving you. And I'll wait the rest of my life for you if I have to."

It was time to fish or cut bait. "You don't have to," Annie said.

He searched her face, wanting her to be sure. "I don't?"

"I love you, too," Annie said thickly, through a brand-new wave of tears. "And for the record, I'm still selling my ranch to you."

When Travis started to protest, she put her finger to his lips. "It's the right thing to do," Annie told him gently, knowing she had never been more sure of anything in her entire life. "My dad knew it, you knew it, I even knew it before I lost my temper. That way, I'll know you're not marrying me for my ranch. And so will everyone else." Annie put her arms around his neck and kissed him soundly, wishing they could stay this way forever, but knowing that like it or not, they had obligations that had to be met. "And speaking of weddings, cowboy—"

Travis groaned. He rested his forehead on hers. "We have one to attend in a couple hours, don't we?"

Annie nodded. And with John and Lilah expecting them, they had to go. She glanced at her watch, and then at the three boys outside, who, somehow, had managed to get filthy from head to toe in the few minutes she and Travis had been kissing and cuddling inside. She sighed. "They're all gonna need a bath, aren't they?" Travis said.

Annie nodded. She looked at Travis. "Think we'll get there in time?"

"If we don't, my mother will skin us alive," he drawled, and Annie laughed.

Travis let go of her reluctantly. "You owe me another rain check, Annie."

"Deal."

He gave her a hug that let her know he was looking forward to climbing back into bed together as much as she was. "I'll get the boys ready. You just take care of yourself."

"TELL ME you're not still planning to elope," Lilah demanded of Annie and Travis as soon as she'd heard the news.

Annie and Travis exchanged looks. Unable to resist sharing their good news, they'd gone to see Lilah in the anteroom off the main chapel. "We really want to be together," Annie confessed, reluctantly letting Lilah know that those were indeed their plans.

"If we could get married tonight it wouldn't be soon enough," Travis told his mother bluntly.

Lilah, who was looking stunning in a tailored floor-length gown, pillbox hat and veil—grinned her approval at their impatience. "Wait here," she said, rushing off in a rustle of satin brocade.

She came back two minutes later, her husband, John, in tow.

"Hey," Travis said, frowning at his tuxedo-clad father, "I thought you weren't supposed to see the bride before the wedding."

"That was our first wedding. This is our second. In your second wedding you can do whatever you want," Lilah explained.

Travis, who knew better than to argue with his mother about matters of the heart, looked at his dad. "Guess you heard the news, too, then?" he said.

"That you and Annie want to get hitched, and the sooner the better, I sure did!" John grinned as big as all Texas. "Your mother and I couldn't be happier, son." John McCabe hugged Travis—and then Annie—warmly.

"Which brings us to our next suggestion," Lilah said, looking at both Annie and Travis. "We just spoke to the minister and the city clerk. We pulled some strings. They've agreed to get the paperwork in order and marry you tonight."

Travis held up a hand. "That's very nice, Mom, Dad. But this is your wedding."

"It could be yours, too," John told them.

Lilah nodded enthusiastically. "You know how much your father and I want you to get married in front of family and friends. We would love it if you two got married first tonight. Then your father and I will walk down the aisle."

"Two separate ceremonies," John added.

"Sort of the double feature of weddings. One the town will never forget."

"And we'll go to the reception together." Lilah looked at Annie, as determined as her husband that this be a real family affair. "Jenna Lockhart's got a wedding dress at her shop that would be perfect for you, and she's offered to run and get it. The florist has a bouquet. You've already got the rings." Lilah shrugged as she looked back at Travis. "Why not make this an evening none of us will forget?"

HALF AN HOUR LATER, music swelled in the packed community church. Annie walked down the aisle on John McCabe's arm. Travis and his three brothers— all groomsmen—were waiting for her. Josie, Lacey and Greta, their wives, were serving as Annie's attendants.

There wasn't a dry eye among them as Annie and Travis said their vows.

The tears of joy increased minutes later as John and Lilah recited their wedding vows and recommitted their lives to each other for the second time.

A reception Laramie, Texas, was likely never to forget followed.

As John and Lilah danced in each other's arms,

they couldn't help but look around at the other couples on the dance floor. Annie and Travis were dancing right alongside Tyler, Teddy and Trevor, who were busy cutting the rug with three girls from their preschool class. Lacey and Jackson seemed lost in a world of their own. Greta and Shane were teasing each other and laughing softly. Josie and Wade were sneaking kisses when they thought no one was looking. Lilah and John were doing the same.

"We really did it," Lilah murmured as she snuggled contentedly against John's chest. "We got all four of our sons married to the loves of their lives, and in under a month. And collected three grandchildren in the process!"

John winked at her, looking pleased as punch, too. "Sounds like we've got ourselves a new hobby, now that we're retiring."

"Matchmaking?" Lilah smiled at the thought. Nothing made her happier than seeing others fall in love.

"You bet." John looked around at their guests, zeroing in on the four Lockhart sisters—none of whom had a date for the evening's festivities. He looked back at Lilah. His smile turned contemplative. "You thinking what I'm thinking?"

Lilah nodded and snuggled closer. "As soon as we get back from our honeymoon," she promised softly and gave her husband a squeeze. "They're next."

# HARLEQUIN®

## AMERICAN ◆ ROMANCE®

*Coming in January 2000—
a very special 2-in-1 story...*

**Two sexy heroes, two determined heroines,
two full romances...one complete novel!**

Sophie's a stay-at-home mom.
Carla's a no-nonsense businesswoman.
Neither suspects that trading places for a week
will change their lives forever....

# HIS, HERS AND THEIRS (#808)
## by Debbi Rawlins
## January 2000

*Join us for twice the fun, twice the romance
when two sisters-in-law trade places and fall in
love with men they wouldn't otherwise have met!
Only from Harlequin American Romance®!*

Available at your favorite retail outlet.

# HARLEQUIN®
*Makes any time special* ™

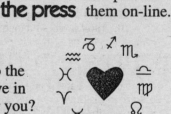

**3 Stories of Holiday Romance from three
bestselling Harlequin® authors**

# *Valentine Babies*

## by

# ANNE STUART

# TARA TAYLOR QUINN

# JULE McBRIDE

**Goddess in Waiting** by Anne Stuart
Edward walks into Marika's funky maternity shop to pick
up some things for his sister. He doesn't expect to assist
in the delivery of a baby and fall for outrageous Marika.

**Gabe's Special Delivery** by Tara Taylor Quinn
On February 14, Gabe Stone finds a living, breathing
valentine on his doorstep—his daughter. Her mother
has given Gabe four hours to adjust to fatherhood,
resolve custody and win back his ex-wife?

**My Man Valentine** by Jule McBride
Everyone knows Eloise Hunter and C. D. Valentine
are in love. Except Eloise and C. D. Then, one of
Eloise's baby-sitting clients leaves her with a baby to
mind, and C. D. swings into protector mode.

## VALENTINE BABIES

**On sale January 2000 at your favorite retail outlet.**

**HARLEQUIN®**
*Makes any time special* ™

Visit us at www.romance.net

PHVALB

*This holiday season, dash to
the delivery room with*

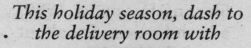

**The McIntyre brothers of Bison City, Wyoming,
have no idea they're about to become daddies—
until a little stork tells them to hustle down to
the delivery room!**

*Don't miss this exciting new series from three of
your favorite American Romance® authors!*

**October 1999
BABY BY MIDNIGHT?**
by Karen Toller Whittenburg (#794)

**November 1999
COUNTDOWN TO BABY**
by Muriel Jensen (#798)

**December 1999
BABY 2000**
by Judy Christenberry (#802)

*Available wherever Harlequin books are sold.*

# Starting December 1999,
## a brand-new series about
## fatherhood from

Three charming stories
about dads and kids...
and the women who
make their families
complete!

Available December 1999
**FAMILY TO BE (#805)**
by Linda Cajio

Available January 2000
**A PREGNANCY AND A PROPOSAL (#809)**
by Mindy Neff

Available February 2000
**FOUR REASONS FOR FATHERHOOD (#813)**
by Muriel Jensen

*Available at your favorite retail outlet.*

# HEART OF THE WEST

# Every Man Has His Price!

Lost Springs Ranch was famous for turning young mavericks into good men. So word that the ranch was in financial trouble sent a herd of loyal bachelors stampeding back to Wyoming to put themselves on the auction block!

HARLEQUIN®
*Makes any time special*™

Visit us at www.romance.net

PHHOWGEN